FATHER
FORGIVE

Breaking the Chains

JERRY THOMAS

ISBN 979-8-89428-690-7 (paperback)
ISBN 979-8-89428-691-4 (digital)

Christian Faith Publishing
832 Park Avenue
Meadville, PA 16335
www.christianfaithpublishing.com

Cover design: Jerry Thomas
Poem: Jerry Thomas

Christian Faith
PUBLISHING

Printed in the United States of America

CONTENTS

ACKNOWLEDGEMENTS

I KNOW MORE PEOPLE WHO DESERVE my thanks than I would have room here to name. Pastors in my past and present have played an enormous role in shaping my life so that I might be able to write Christian novels like this one and others. Many close brothers and sisters in Christ who have, without even knowing it, aided in this writing, especially the ending of this publication. I must acknowledge a lifetime of positive and negative experiences that are invaluable for the outcome of *Father Forgive*.

I will give two names, however, that are above the rest for my gratitude. The first is my wife, Marilyn, who is my confidant, my faithful companion, my encourager, my soulmate, and my best friend.

The second name I will mention is the name above all names. I give thanks and glory to God, who, through His only Son Jesus, saved my soul for eternity, and for the guidance of His Holy Spirt in the writing of every chapter of this novel.

CHAPTER 1

If...?

"THERE IS NO END TO the number of stories that I could tell you," the story master announced as he took the stage. He had been introduced to his listeners only as "the Narrator." It had always been his desire to not have his name mentioned, and he did not provide a reason, except that he just enjoyed the anonymity. "I have stories," he went on to say, "that involve one man or one woman, or a married couple, or children. I know stories about people from every walk of life. Old or young, rich or poor, who believe that they have been wounded emotionally beyond repair. There are thousands of people who live, work, and share our church pews with us, whose wounds have penetrated every square inch of their reasoning so that there is little to no room left for real love or lasting peace. And yes, I mean Christians also. Wounded men and women, some of whom have committed the most appalling of sins, because of someone else's appalling sins that were committed to them. Men and women who end up believing that they have no chance to be forgiven for all they have done, or if they do believe, they continue to do their daily 'I'm still struggling' act. Some also think that they cannot possibly forgive the one or ones who did 'this horrible thing' to them. They simply live their lives out daily, *thinking* that there is no help at all for them. That there is no amount of teaching, *they think*, or counseling or compassion or patience or love that can possibly take away the killing pain that has been imparted into them, sometimes from birth...*and*...has lasted for decades. They are destined to die, *they think*, either a young horrible unloved death, or end up bitter beyond comparison for the lack of being able to be set free from their pain." The Narrator took a step closer to the front edge of the stage and just looked out and across all the people who came to listen to this *in-demand* story master tell one of his tales.

"Well," he told them, "this is a unique opportunity for you all. I am going to give you the chance to choose which of my stories you would like me to talk about. Maybe the one about a man who learned *how* to live only days before he was about to die. Or the story of a couple who got married for all the wrong reasons, culminating in an adulterous affair less than a year after the 'I Dos' grew impatiently cold. How about a narrative of one man's daughter who grew up unable to tell the truth? How she hated her father, who tried everything in his power to gain her acceptance but never got it. Or an almost unbelievable accounting of a single mother, who through no fault of her own, could not provide all the outlandish wants her two selfish daughters demanded of her. How, in the end, she was expected to raise each of their unwanted illegitimate children. I could open the diary of a man who was diagnosed with cancer at a young age, whose wife was having an open affair with another man, and how she could not wait for her husband to die. Or I could tell you about the lifelong pain of a daughter who lived firsthand the rejection her mother levied on her and never knowing why. How she lived with her mother's contempt while seeing her siblings being lavished with the love she never received. How about the tragedy of a man who attempted murder of his estranged wife to prevent her from changing the beneficiary on her life insurance policy after their divorce?"

The story master stood in silence waiting for anyone to choose. He looked around for a moment, but he only achieved silence in return. "Believe it or not," he went on to say, "all those stories that I could tell you have some interesting, in depth, and very similar attributes." He waited again for a lengthy time, but no one seemed to be willing to choose. "So," he finally said, "I will choose one of my other stories to tell you, and this saga involves several hurting people. It begins with a poem though that I have written specifically for this one story alone. I entitled the poem 'Just One Life'." He paused briefly, took a breath to calm himself, and began to recite:

In a backstreet bar, on the low side of life
A drunken man turned, and he pulled out his knife
He thought he sensed someone, though no one was near
But he noticed his own self, framed in a mirror
He quickly turned away for the image he cast
But then turned back around as he lifted his glass
He wondered again what he was ever meant for
As he toasted himself all the way to the floor
"Welcome home," he thought, "I've been here before"

"Get up and get out and go home," they all groaned
And then insults were thrown like spit from old crones
One stepped on his hand as they gathered and cursed
The cruelest obscenities, with malice and worse
They grabbed both his feet and dragged him outside
Where the alley filth smelled like something had died
He tried to get up, and he tried to complain
But could move not a finger, or even explain
"Why?" he kept thinking, but his thoughts were in vain

Out back in that alley on the low side of life
Back there in the midst of the sewage, lay strife
A could-have-been man with no reason to live
Who, with his last thoughts, had nothing to give
No lie was there left, and no pretense to show
Why he should be spared, this broken John Doe
So as tears and filth shared the face of this wretch
This unwanted man gave into the stench
Unloved, with a thirst that he never had quenched

Why is it some men end up broken and lost?
Perceiving their worth is less than their cost
What happens to some who just lie down and die?
For earning all zeros and not knowing why
How can it be fair while most learn to cope?
There is always that one who can never find hope

Where loser has branded his brow for all time
And no one he knows would lend him a dime
What happens to that one who cannot make the climb?

After he finished his poem, he fell silent for a moment and then said, "That wretched man in my poem had lost all his capacity to be forgiven, partly for lack of being able to forgive. That man ended having *no chance*...seeing *no escape*...and believing that he had *no hope at all*," and the Narrator hesitated again before continuing, "or could he have had hope?" he said very slowly. "Or could I?" He paused for a moment. "Or how about...you?"

Well, if you or someone you know is one of those thousands, maybe millions of wounded souls, listen carefully. You *most assuredly* do have hope. No matter where you have walked or fallen. No matter how long you have been doing whatever or how long ago or what you have done or what has been done to you, *you positively* do have *hope*, and no small measure of it. Additionally, you *most certainly* can overcome. *You will also succeed* at being forgiven as well as forgiving the worst of all your enemies.

Now to say that that will be easy is not correct, but to say that it will be *too* difficult would be a lie. Your success at overcoming depends on only one thing, and if you do that one thing...correctly, honestly from your heart...it is almost guaranteed." He paused again to capture the attention of his listeners, then *slowly* he told them, "There is an '*IF*' in there though."

The story master stopped talking but maintained a concerned gaze on his audience for a moment. Then he turned and sat on the chair that had been provided for him on the stage. He asked for a drink of water, took a sip, and smiled again at his now spellbound audience. After he got himself comfortable and adjusted his microphone, he leaned back, looking up as if deep in thought before continuing his very comprehensive tale. He brought his eyes back down to face his inquisitive viewers and began to speak.

"Picture an extremely cold and bleak January morning before dawn..."

CHAPTER 2

Just Go Away

A BOY BABY CRIED OUT with his first breath, announcing his arrival. He was a miracle issued into existence to one of the most dysfunctional families known. Like so many self-centered home environments, no one knew just how sorry the life of this newborn was to become. Some people who suspected though were told to respect the parents' right to live the way they wanted, and to raise and treat their children the way they wanted. Those then who could have done something about the abuses that took place, were issued warnings that changed their minds if they were so inclined to do so. So like all of us, life began with a hard-core slap on the butt for one Jeremy Townsend. Unlike the rest of us, though, that scar never healed, because from birth going forward, a new slap of one kind or another was added every day of his life. Not only physical slaps either but also serious emotional and psychological gut punches that would eventually be the proof needed for this young soul to believe beyond all doubt that he really was worthless. Proofs that additionally would build walls around him, that would become barriers to prevent healing in his future.

The boy sat frozen to the edge of his chair, unable to speak or move or even think for the fear that consumed him entirely. His father, sitting imperially just a few feet away, was again enraged at the boy for something young Jeremy Townsend had no idea what it was that he had done. Jeremy had just turned thirteen years old that day and could not, and in fact never could, say or do anything correctly to satisfy his father. So here he was again waiting for the end to come.

How many times had he found himself not really knowing if his father was going to reach over and just smack him right to the floor?

"Stand up, boy," he yelled at his son. *"Stand up while I'm talking to you. How many times have I told you that you got to show me respect."* His rampage continued for several minutes, raking the boy over a set of coals that had nothing to do with whatever it was that brought him into his father's anger in the first place. The only thing the boy could do was desperately try to figure out what he had done this time because he knew that his father was going to demand that he confess, and he honestly, like so many other times before, had no idea what it was that ticked his father off.

"You listening to me, boy? Are you paying attention to me, or you just drifting off like you usually do with your 'I didn't do nothing wrong' attitude again?" He stood up to face off with his son, which was never a good sign. *"You know what you did, now confess!"* Those last words came out of his father's face with such angered velocity that it pushed Jeremy back a step, and that angered his father even more. *"What, you afraid of me, boy? Well, that makes sense. You are a coward along with everything else. You are just a no-count coward."* One might wonder how this man's rage could possibly reach another level, but it did. He swung his arm back, looking like he was going to hit the child, and stopped but kept his arm at the ready. *"Well,"* he commanded in an even louder voice, *"speak to me, boy."* And there was a short pause, and his father reached over and roughly pushed the boy to his seat. *"Oh, just shut up and sit down you worthless excuse for a child. You are no son of mine."* His father slammed a fist on his desk as he sat down again. He turned his head away, making it obvious that he was ashamed of his son and just seemed to be seething in his uncontrolled anger. Then, suddenly, he snapped around again, staring directly at the boy, pushed a fist up in front of the child's face and yelled again, *"CONFESS! or I'll knock you all the way into next Tuesday."* Then he noticed that the boy had wet himself, and that really set the man off. *"You are a coward, aren't you? Now confess, or you will sit there all day."* He waited for the boy to speak and saw that young Jeremy was trying but could not get the words out. Jeremy was trembling

and stuttering, but finally he mouthed just above a whisper, "I did it."

"Yeah, I know you did, and you know what?" his father announced arrogantly to his son as he leaned back in his desk chair, *"you could have saved both of us a lot a trouble if you would have come to me about all this before I found out. Now go to your room, and I do not want to see you any more tonight."*

Jeremy Townsend still had no idea what it was that he just confessed to doing. He got up shaking from the fear but was also relieved that it was all over. He slowly walked from his father's courtroom, holding back his tears. He did not want his father to see him cry. He had been so excited just a few hours earlier at the thought that he had finally became a teenager, but now he slipped quietly into his room, gently closed the door, laid down on his bed, pulled a pillow over his head so as not to be heard, and bawled like a baby. There would be no birthday cake this year and no present either. Not even a card wishing him well.

To say that Jeremy would remember his thirteenth birthday is not the most accurate statement to make here. Rather, the more truthful evaluation would be that Jeremy would *never* forget his thirteenth birthday. Most people can remember a change in their lives when they became a teenager, but Jeremy's life of dark days that led him to want to die began on his thirteenth birthday. His life did change but not the way most will remember their change. His change became almost instantly apparent because there were not many times that anyone saw a smile on his face again.

Prior to that day, Jeremy lived in a constant state of fear. His father was on his, ah, butt, so to speak, literally every day for something. *"Why can't you do what I want, when I want, the way I want,"* was his father's irate demand every time Jeremy did not respond in a manner equal to what his father expected. And that was nearly all the time. He was *never* content with Jeremy.

Now the result of that was that Jeremy would internalize his father's demanding, insulting, humiliating, tyrannical hatred toward him as, *"I know it is me. I am guilty again."* Alongside Jeremy's fear was his acceptance that his father was simply a righteous man, and that it was he himself, who, if he could only try harder to please his father, it would all work out. Jeremy believed that he really was stupid, and there was nothing he could do about it. Up to that day, that is. Until that day, Jeremy blamed himself for all his father's discontent with him. He lived in a perpetual state of pain and fear, but his real *bottom line* was, *"I just want to make him love me."* Interestingly, though, despite all that occurred in his life thus far, Jeremy possessed an oversized compassion to love and, if it would have been nurtured, would have been a marvelous attribute. But on that day that Jeremy turned thirteen, his *bottom line* just dropped out of existence altogether. A new bottom line instantly appeared, amplifying his desire for not needing to live at all, let alone to please his father.

He had been living in a state of what the professionals may label as a "love/hate" relationship with his father. However, on this momentous day, his "love/hate" syndrome was permanently altered to a "hate/hate" life evaluation.

If it was his father's goal to kill his son's spirit, he succeeded completely. Jeremy still was truly convinced that he was the worthless cowardly child his father had always told him he was, but now he carried a new attitude. He walked through a door marked, "I don't care anymore," and "I will just get even. He can beat me up all he wants," he concluded. Jeremy turned into the "no-count" that his father had always told him he was. He became argumentative, deliberately divisive, defiant, and full of hatred. He became passive-aggressive, looking for ways to bait his father's anger. He lied about everything just to cause his father pain. That cost him on numerous occasions after that, but he did not care. "What's the difference?" he reasoned from then on. He dropped out of high school at sixteen and ran away from home at seventeen with his father yelling at him as he left the house for the last time. *"Don't let the door hit you where the sun doesn't shine!"*

Jeremy had no life skills to offer, but like most young men, he did not think about that. He just wanted to be free from this monster of a man that he was unfortunate enough to be born to. Jeremy was never taught how to do anything, correctly or incorrectly. So Jeremy Townsend stepped out on his own with nothing. He learned to steal his food and to con his way into getting the shelter he needed to survive. He was rejected for being lazy, although the few times he was given a chance to work, he proved to be a good worker. But he could not get a real job. He had no skills and no education and no way to earn any of those things. He also lacked the knowledge on how to use any social services. In fact, he did not even know that there were any social services to draw from. That did not matter though because he decided that he would rather die than go back home, and he meant it. He was labeled just another one of those "rotten, no-count drop-outs who bleed the system." When he heard people accuse him of bleeding the system, he would fire back at them. *"What system? I am just trying to find a place to live."* But he had earned the label "no-count," and it was just not going to go away. And "just go away," were three other words he heard most often during the next three plus years of him trying to survive.

Let me tell you what so often happens to a man who from his first recollection was trained to believe that he would "never amount to anything…ever." In a nutshell, what most likely will happen is that he will end up not amounting to anything ever. Maybe worse.

CHAPTER 3

Bada Boom Bada Bing and Gone

"THE SURVIVAL GAME," JEREMY NAMED it, took on a whole new meaning for him as he lived out his next three years. He had become somewhat skilled at that game using the only tool he had—his imaginative wit. But he discovered that survival meant getting by on so much less of everything than he would have guessed it meant when he started out on this self-imposed journey. So…it did not take long before Jeremy was hit with the temptation to give up and go back home. He had traded all that pain, humiliation, discontent, anger, hatred, dysfunction, and misery for a "going nowhere, having nothing, and attaining no prospects…ever" lifestyle. But he had made up his mind that he would rather die than to go back to where he came from…and he meant it. Plus, he knew in his heart that his father would never let him come back anyway.

The only upside to his lacking of normal creature comforts was that he was not alone. He met so many men and women living on the edge the same way he was and some for the same reasons. They simply lacked the wherewithal to live any other way, never learning how to cope normally in society. Many just slipped through the cracks somewhere along the line and were stuck. Some, he learned, had a real heart-wrenching, unbelievable medical situation, or other things in their lives that literally prevented them from any advanced lifestyle at all. But then, several of the ones he met were flat out lazy, and they just refused to follow any form of a functional society. Selfishness and rebelliousness were the honest reasons for their continued decline.

Jeremy learned much about the reality of life during those three years, and he did try to better himself but just could not find a way to get that job done. He simply existed daily in that perpetual survival mode. He really did not know a better way to keep himself from possibly ending up dead under some bridge somewhere. He eventually did end up with a small one-room apartment, if you can call it that, to live in. His bathroom was "down the hall," and he had no conveniences other than a bed, a sink, a hotplate, and dinky old refrigerator to give him the impression that "this is home." In order to pay his rent and buy some food, he was able to work for money under the table doing anything or, on occasions, would work day jobs for some agency. He had no real skills, though, to offer even them. Unfortunately, all that he was able to do did not provide enough for him to live on, even the way he was living. So…often, he would "*do whatever it took*," he would tell himself to survive, short of committing a felony. To his credit, Jeremy was not the kind to knowingly hurt anyone. Overall, his character had some pros, but to Jeremy at this time in his life, his happiness hinged on finding a warm bed and a sandwich to eat every day.

Jeremy's "luck," if you will, took a dramatic turn for the good one day while sitting in a Starbucks drinking a cup of coffee. Starbucks was his "reward" once a week that he treated himself to, even though it was more costly than he would have wanted for the use of some of his limited funds. He would sit there and pretend that he was normal like everyone else. Starbucks was packed on this one Saturday morning, and only a few seats remained for someone to sit in. He did not pay much attention to his surroundings until… "Mind if I sit here?" came the sweetest voice he had ever heard.

"Sure," he said, looking up, and there looking down at him was Patricia, "his one true love," he afterward named her. After they began to talk, Jeremy quickly realized that for the first time in his life, he had met someone that he had no trouble talking with. She brought out his belief that he might have something to offer after all, and after only a few minutes, he was more at ease with his own life. He let all his guards down and became the real Jeremy. He really had a very charming side, although no one ever saw that in him. No one knows why one someone is attracted to another someone, but he certainly was attracted to Pat. It was not her good looks either, it was something else that he could not put his finger on, but he sure did like spending this time with her.

Meeting someone was the last thing on Pat's mind when she walked into Starbucks that morning. All she wanted was a good seat to sit in to enjoy her coffee. There were only four seats to choose from. Two were unoccupied at a table where two women seemed to be locked in a very deep conversation, and Pat was not interested. Another empty seat was at a four-top where three men were doing some kind of business, and the fourth was at a two-top where Jeremy was sitting and gazing out a window. Pat had always been shy. She never liked meeting anyone on the fly, but, *Well, I'll just take my chances,* she thought, as she approached his table. No one knows why one someone is attracted to another someone, but Pat, after maybe ten minutes, certainly was attracted to Jeremy. She could not help but notice that he was not so well off financially, but that did not matter to her. She had not had a boyfriend since high school, and she just was not the "I'm looking for a boyfriend" type anyway. Truth was that she did not have men lined up who seemed interested enough to ask her out. Jeremy had something, however, that really sparked her interest. He listened to her go on and on about anything she wanted to talk about. Being shy like she was, she marveled at two things. First at herself, for talking so much, and secondly at him for wanting to listen. She had never experienced that in any man ever. That one trait alone was what made this a special moment for her as well. They just sat and talked for a couple of hours when they both agreed that this happenchance meeting was a once in a lifetime experience for each of them.

"Have you ever heard the phrase 'Bada boom bada bing?' Jeremy asked her.

Pat looked down feeling embarrassed because she kind of knew where he was going with that. "Yeah," she finally said sheepishly through her wall of shy.

"Well, Pat, you are my very first 'bada boom bada bing' moment."

Shy as she normally was, she looked up and smiled at him. "Ah, me too," she said. Yeah, me too." She could not wipe the grin off her face.

"Tell you what," he told her, "let's just name this our Starbucks bada boom bada bing moment. What do you think?"

She smiled again and nodded her agreement, and that, as they say, was that.

They got married about six months later, just after Jeremy turned twenty-one. It was in the courthouse, and when asked why he did not have any of his family there, he returned their question with a question, "Is that a requirement?" Jeremy's mother was gone, and he was surely not going to invite his father. He did have a half sister, though he was not remotely close to her. She and her husband and Jeremy could not even remember his name, seemed to be ultrareligious, and except for a couple of times a year, he did not see them. So other than the two of them, and Patricia's mother, that was all who were there. Oh, and the justice of the peace, of course, and two strangers who agreed to be witnesses.

They had one son, Randy, who was born to them just about a year after they got married. Patricia had insisted that they name their boy after Jeremy's father. She had not had a relationship with her own father or grandfather, and she was not convinced that things were as bad as Jeremy made them out to be about his father. She thought that by naming their son after the boy's grandfather, it would help bring them all together like a family should be. Jeremy would not allow that, though, and he was just as insistent as she was, so they settled on Randy for the boy's name.

The marriage lasted just few months over two years when Pat took their baby boy and moved back with her mother. She really did love Jeremy, but she was nonstop afraid of him. He had an explosive temper. She feared for herself and Randy as well. He never once hit either Pat or Randy, but Jeremy had this temper at times that he himself could not understand. She never knew if he would finally go off the deep end and do something to her or their son. It started almost immediately after they were married, but unlike his father,

Jeremy always showed genuine remorse for his outbursts. He was sincere when he would tell her he was sorry, but it was not very long, and it would happen again. His temper could be triggered by almost anything. She would often think back to why she married him in the first place and recalled seeing a side of him that showed her more love than she had ever known. But his uncontrollable tantrums were off the charts scary, so finally she felt she needed to protect herself and their child. She obtained a restraining order against Jeremy the day she moved out and filed for divorce. She was shocked at his response when the restraining order was delivered, as well as later when the divorce papers were delivered to him. He did not object, find fault with her, or try to fight the issue. "I do love you, Pat," he said calmly, one time he was allowed to visit their son, "and I totally understand." He made it clear that he would move from their house, and that her and Randy could move back in. It was mostly her money, along with her mother's aid, that bought their house in the first place. It was also her income that paid most of the bills.

In the settlement side of the divorce, he signed everything, what little there was, over to Pat. "It's the right thing to do," he told her, and just then, when he did that, she saw that side of him that she loved.

During the next several years, Jeremy bounced in and out of Pat's life. Sometimes, Randy looked like he was glad to see him but often appeared to be guarded in case Jeremy lost his temper again. His son ended up being almost as afraid of him as Jeremy had been of his father. Jeremy could see that Pat and Randy were always set in a protective mode whenever he did visit. He really did love them, but most of the time, their relationship was a shipwreck. It finally left Randy not wanting to see his father. Jeremy tried desperately to control his outbursts and did most of the time. Occasionally, however, something would trigger a serious heartbreak, and he would snap, and when he snapped, he really did lose it. In addition, Jeremy lived in a constant state of self-condemnation. He knew that he was the cause of Pat's fear, and he also understood why Randy was becoming more and more afraid of him. That added to Jeremy's concern that he would soon become totally rejected, so he just phased out his visits thinking he was not wanted anyway. He did not blame them at all, but once again, to Jeremy, this was just one more proof that he really was the no-count worthless piece of flesh his father always told him he was.

Jeremy had been abused by his own father so completely that confusion was just one of his major setbacks for his success. Run and hide was protection for him from facing life in general, and his tumultuous outbursts were a form of protection also.

After their divorce, he continued to flounder, finding different places to live/survive. Although it finally became apparent to Pat that he really was never going to be physically violent with her or Randy, she still could not convince Randy of that. She had learned that his outbursts were always directed at himself or at his father. Nevertheless, he still was scary, and Randy could just not believe that his father was not going to hurt him.

After more and more of his nomadic lifestyle and wondering what he could do, Jeremy decided that he wanted to get closer to his half sister Rebecca. He found that he was welcome there, "whenever," Rebecca would tell him, for a great meal. "You do not need an invite either," she told him. In time, he learned to trust her and her husband Samuel. He ended up visiting them a couple of times a month, and sometimes, just for grins, not only for a free meal. He often talked about his marriage and had no problem admitting his blame for his divorce. He did reject any advice Samuel would try to give him about reconciliation with Pat or Randy. "I don't want to put them through all that again." Although that was true enough, the biggest reason he had no interest in listening to his brother-in-law's guidance was because Samuel always wanted to use the Bible to prove his point. Eventually, he felt he had to tell Samuel, "Look, religion is just a crutch, and I do not need that." Jeremy had made up his mind that he was never going to be what they wanted him to be.

Samuel and Rebecca had not yet met Pat or Randy but often would ask if they could make contact. Jeremy vehemently asked them not to. "She's my ex, and that is all my business." Of course, the reason was simple. He was ashamed of himself and felt that if they contacted her, his time with them would be over. He had found a place with Rebecca and Samuel that he believed was his, and if Pat and Randy were allowed to step in, he was going to have to step out. "No way," he stated, and it was not a request.

They told Jeremy that they understood, but occasionally during the next few years, they would ask about Randy. "He is our nephew, you know Jeremy," they would remind him, "and we would love to meet him and get to know him. Is there any way that you would bring him around for us?" Rebecca pleaded with him, but that is when he confessed to them that Randy was afraid of him, and that he would not want to go anywhere with him.

Samuel and Rebecca both understood, more than Jeremy thought they did, but again they assured him that they would not try to contact Pat or Randy without Jeremy's knowledge.

It took a long while, but one day, right out of the blue, Jeremy conceded. "Okay, look, this might be the best thing for Randy, so go for it." He gave them Pat's phone number. "But you need to know that she, well, or her mother are not religious either. That is why we got married in the courthouse in the first place, but—" then he stopped talking and hung his head in what looked like shame. "Yeah," he very sadly consented, "that might be good for Randy." He got up, apparently hurt, and quietly walked out. They did not see him again for several months.

Sad and understanding as she was over Jeremy's situation, Rebecca jumped on his compliance to let them contact Pat. That same evening, in fact, was when she called to introduce herself and had a short chat with Pat. She shared with her who they were to Jeremy, and that Samuel was a pastor of a local church. Not much else was talked about for their short awkward conversation. She did suggest that they meet, but it sounded like Pat was somewhat guarded, and she did not commit to anything. She said her pleasant goodbye, and that was about it.

Pat knew nothing about Jeremy's half sister or her pastor husband other than the very few bits of information Jeremy had offered. She and her mother were believers in God but hardly ever went to church, and having a pastor for her son's uncle was not that appealing to her. It was a few months later, however, when she took the initiative to call Rebecca back.

"I am so sorry," she began, "that I have not taken the time to get together with you and Pastor Samuel before now, and I know that I should have, but—"

"It's all right," Rebecca assured her, "no problem. What would you like to do?"

"Well, it is Randy's sixth birthday, and I was wondering if you would like to come to his birthday party?"

"Without a single doubt," Rebecca almost shouted her excitement. "Certainly, we would, and thank you so much for asking."

That was their first contact with Pat and Randy. They went and found that Pat and her mother were very pleasant, but Randy was not so impressed. He was quiet and could not wait to open his gifts and escape to his room.

"This was a great start," she told Samuel on their way home. "Pat said that Jeremy came by yesterday to bring a birthday present and a card for Randy but did not stay long. She said that he deliberately stayed away today for Randy's sake. You know," she said, "I would love to contact him, but remember the last time we saw Jeremy, he told us that he moved again, and he never answers his phone. We are stuck, aren't we, in a holding pattern, just waiting and hoping that he will drop by. I am so concerned for him."

"Jeremy sure is mysterious," Samuel confirmed. "I think he is afraid to let anyone get too close. I would love to help him, but he will not allow it…yet. We will not give up, though, will we?"

CHAPTER 4

A Thimble Full of Compassion

JEREMY HAD NOT SPOKEN TO his father, not even once, since he walked away from him at seventeen years old. Pat and he have been divorced, "For what, eight years now?" he said to himself. Randy was going to be nine soon, "And what about my dad?" He could not stop thinking about his father. Even though Jeremy hated his father, he nevertheless always came back to the thought that "if I had only been a better son, he would have loved me, and things would have been different, and I would have finished high school, and I would have a good job, and I would not get angry all the time, and Patricia would have stayed with me, and Randy would want to be around me more, and...and...and..." "What?" Jeremy would scream into the privacy of his bathroom mirror most mornings. "What am I supposed to do?" So finally, he decided that it was time for him to go see his father. He was hoping that, "well, maybe he has changed?" Jeremy certainly did not have much hope for that, "but it has been a bunch of years," he concluded. "Maybe?"

He was seriously apprehensive but made up his mind to go. He drove over to his father's house but could not even get out of his car. He tried the next couple of nights, but the same thing happened. Then one night, after a couple of beers, he worked up the courage to knock on his father's door. The door was opened by a woman he did not know.

"Hi," he began, "my name is Jeremy, ah, Jeremy Townsend, and I was…"

"You're Daniel's boy," she announced with contempt in her voice. "He told me all about you. What do you want?"

"I was hoping to see my dad. Can I come in?"

She paused, just staring at Jeremy for a moment, and then closed the door after saying, "Wait here, I'll go and ask."

After a few minutes, she came back to the door and said, "You know, your father is ill, but he said that you can come in."

His father was just a shadow of the man he remembered. He was thinner and looked fragile. "Hey, Dad," was all he could get out of his mouth when he recognized that same bitter, scolding look on his father's face. "I was out and thought that it was way past time that we talked."

"What's to talk about?" he shot back at Jeremy, and when he spoke, Jeremy noticed that his voice was thin also. "You left me the way your mother did. She left me about a month after you walked out on me. But then you know that, don't you? You and her became great pals, didn't you, after she left. She died sucking on a bottle of rum, didn't she?"

Jeremy just looked down at his father. He did not even offer to shake his son's hand, not that he expected him to, and he just wanted to punch his father right in the mouth. Of course, he did not. Instead, "Look, Dad," he said, "I thought maybe we could, oh, I don't know, maybe make up or something?"

"See this woman here?" he told his son. "This is Carlotta. She is a nurse, and the only person I have ever met that understands me. I told her all about you, so she has got your number too. I have cancer and they give me a year, maybe two, to live. I pay her a lot of money to take care of me and to keep me company, so, when I go, she gets everything. You get nothing, just so you know, in case the real reason you came by was for some money."

"No, Dad. The reason I came over after all these years was to try and make up with you. That is the truth."

"Yeah? Well, I told you a long time ago that you were a worthless no-count coward, and nothing has changed. You are no son of mine, and you are stupid." Those last words were loaded with hatred. That instantly took Jeremy back to his thirteenth birthday, but his father was not finished. He continued his tyrannical rampage with, "You have not made anything of yourself, either, have you? You know what that makes you? A class act loser, that's what, and that is all you will ever be. And another thing, you—"

Jeremy did not stick around to hear the rest of what this evil man wanted to say. He stormed out of his father's house, climbed into his car, and slammed the door. He cranked up his engine and peeled rubber as he left. "What on earth made me think that he might want to see me?" he cried out through his angry tears, but then he had enough sense to pull over because he could not see where he was going. "I hate him!" he screamed loud enough that he figured they might hear him in St. Louis. He turned his engine off and sat in his car for over a half hour locked in a crying jag. He was caught halfway between anger and desperation wondering if what his father had accused him of his whole life could possibly be true. "Am I a loser?" he questioned to the inside of his car. He had nowhere to go, so he decided to get drunk. He looked in his wallet and saw that he had only three dollars. He started his engine again as he looked down at the gas gauge and saw that it registered empty. He knew that he would soon run out of gas again. "Why was I even born?" he said out loud, and he turned the engine off. He just sat there in his car in the dark of the night and wondered what he was going to do next. It must have been a couple of hours when he finally decided to drive over to Patricia's house. He knew he had enough gas for that. He knocked on her door and waited. After longer than he thought it should take for her to answer the door, he started to knock again, when he heard her sweet voice, "Who is it?"

"Ah, it's me, Pat. It's me Jeremy. Can I come in?"

There was another long pause, and then he finally heard the door lock click, and the door slowly opened. He could see her through the screen door, as she flipped on her porch light. Bluntly, she told him, "No, Jeremy, you cannot come in. What do you want?" she asked, and it sounded like she was very unhappy that he was standing on her porch.

Jeremy sighed heavily before speaking. "I don't know what I want," he said softly. "I guess I am just in need of a friend. I need help, but I do not even know what help I need. I guess I just want to talk. Please, can't I come in?"

Pat saw that he was very troubled. "Jeremy, honey," she said with compassion, "wow, Jeremy, listen…Randy is asleep, and Mom is spending the night. This is not a good time for you to be here."

"I get that," Jeremy conceded. "She does not like me either, does she? I don't blame her at all." He held up his hands in resignation of his position. He began to sob lightly, and as he backed up, he said, "I'm sorry, I'm just so sorry."

Pat was looking at what seemed to be an absolutely destroyed human being. Jeremy seemed to be drowning in an invisible pit that was way over his head. All he could do was stare at Pat as for real deal elephant-size tears just emptied down both sides of his face. Finally, he dropped down heavily into a chair that she had sitting on her porch. "I really do understand, Pat," he said, "honestly, I do. I was not there for you for all these years."

"Jeremy, it is after eleven, what is going on? What do you need?"

He did not answer for a while, but after urging him again, he spoke. "Well," he began as he tried to wipe the tears from his eyes. "Let me see, my rent is due, again, and I do not have a job, again. My car is about to run out of gas, again, and I finally went over to see Dad. Can you believe that? I actually went over there," but silence took his voice away for another long moment, "earlier this evening," he continued. "I haven't seen him in what, thirteen, fourteen years? I cannot believe I did that. But guess what? Without wasting any time at all, like 'how are you, son?' or 'what's going on'…nothing, he just confirmed that I really am the worthless no-count coward he always told me that I was, and that I am no son of his. He called me a loser and said that that is what I will always be." Jeremy buried his head in his hands again and sobbed uncontrollably for several minutes. "You know," he finally said looking up, "I never stopped loving you, Pat, but I know that you and Randy needed me to be strong, and I was not. Something is wrong with me, and I do not know what it is, except that maybe Dad was right all along. I am just flat-out worthless. What do you think? Is there anything else I need to know to destroy any hope I ever had of being any kind of man that anyone would want?"

Pat thought that Jeremy looked like there was nothing left in him to be able to find any reason to continue to live. "Pat, I have nowhere to go, and truthfully, I'm not looking for somewhere to go any more."

"Oh, Jeremy, I am so sorry. I do not know what I can do for you. Tell me."

He could not say anything at all, so she asked him again what she could do for him.

"Nothing, Pat. I do not know what you could do. It does help that you listened to me. Thanks."

"Do you need some money? I could give you maybe twenty. I am not rich."

Jeremy was not in the habit of asking her for money. In fact, he probably hit her up for a few dollars only, and that only maybe half a dozen times in all the years since their divorce. Even then, he looked at those times as loans. It usually took him a lot longer than it should, but he always paid her back. He knew that she needed all her money, and since he had nothing to give for Randy's support, he did not want to burden her. But now, he was thinking strongly about her offer, and after about a minute, he nodded. "Yeah, sure. That will help, thanks, but I really did not come over here looking for a loan."

"It's not a loan, it's a gift, but use it for gas, okay?"

"You are kind, Pat, thanks," he said.

"Jeremy, it's okay, you wait here. I'll be right back."

When she came back to the door, she paused briefly reminiscing the reasons she fell in love with this brutally broken man in the first place but said nothing about that. "Have you been over to see Rebecca and Samuel?" she asked. "You know they would love to help. I have gotten to know them well in these last three years, and I know they love you, Jeremy."

"No," he told Pat, "I have not, and I do not want to see them. I know that you and Randy, even your mother, are close with them now, and I am glad for you, but that has kind of put me on their back burner, or maybe it was me who put them on my back burner. Doesn't matter, though, either way." He fell speechless for a moment, but then, "I guess all I can say is I am glad for you."

"Okay, I understand, but seriously, they do love you. Here, I have thirty dollars I can give you." She opened the screen door to give it to him. "Good luck, Jeremy."

He got up and received the money from her but could not raise his head to look at her for the shame he felt. "Thanks," he said to her again but just above a whisper. He paused, holding the cash for a moment not looking at her, and then turned and walked away. To himself, he said, "This will be the last time," but over his shoulder, to her, he said, "I promise you, I won't *ever* bother you again."

Jeremy did not lie to Pat by telling her that he would buy gas with what she gave him, but he did deceive her by letting her believe that he would. He had no intention, however, of spending this gift that way. From the moment she made her offer to give him some money, he had begun to formulate a plan for how he was going to commit suicide.

When he left, he went to the cheapest bar in the city that he knew of, Bobo's Bar and Grill, to get drunk. Truth be told, he did not have much of a plan, but he knew that getting drunk needed to be his first step to gain the courage necessary to finish the job. When he walked into Bobo's, he pulled all the money he had out and laid it on the bar. "You just keep the beers coming," he told the bartender, "until this is gone." Jeremy was not a stranger to the patrons of this low-life establishment. He was known, mostly, for how he could not shut up, after he had had enough to drink, being argumentative about most things. He really did not fit in and was considered an annoyance by everyone. Some, though, even hated that he was allowed to be there at all, and those are the ones who nicknamed him "the Loser."

Talking too much was not Jeremy's personality this night, though. He chose a place at the bar, planted himself, and was stone quiet. "Now that is a first," he heard from behind his back a couple of times. Although he tried to ignore what he heard, it did peak his paranoia. He tried to stay focused, though, on how to finish his life.

It must have been a couple of hours, but he knew it had been long enough for him to get "falling down" inebriated. He was slurring his words as he mumbled to himself and staggered a little from side to side. But then that is what he was hoping for. He had brought a knife into the bar with him, although he kept it hidden. He felt that if he got plastered enough, he would be able to slide out the back door and slit his wrists in the alley. The knife was not very sharp, though he thought it would be enough to do the job. As his head tipped back to receive a swallow from what he believed to be his last beer, he suddenly heard, or thought he heard, someone come up behind him. He swung around rapidly and pulled the knife out. No one was there, but everyone in the room was staring right at him. Across the room, however, was a large mirror, and he caught his own reflection in it. It sickened him, so he spun back around at the sight. "What was I even born for?" he asked himself, but just a moment later, he turned back around and lifted his beer as if to toast the man who was looking back at him from the mirror. He stood motionless for just a moment until the beer bottle slipped from his hand and bounced loudly off the wooden floor. As he looked down at the noise, he collapsed in a drunken heap. He heard people milling around, and one even stepped on his hand. He heard some loud curse words, he knew were meant for him, and again he wondered, *What was I ever meant for anyway?* but no words came from his mouth. They dragged him out through the back door of Bobo's and deposited his body on the concrete. As they left, one of them said, "There probably is not a soul alive who would be able to come up with any more than a thimble full of compassion for this useless man." Agreeing, another said that his epitaph might simply read, "Here lies the loser."

Jeremy heard the back door of Bobo's slam shut and the metallic sound of a bolt closing inside, finalizing his separation from the world. But then he felt himself being dragged again, and this time, when they stopped, it felt like someone was pulling at his clothing. He could not identify anything at all, but he thought he saw flashes of light and sensed that he was laying in some garbage. Suddenly, though, it felt like he had been kicked and kicked very hard, and maybe several times. He did not feel a great deal of pain, thanks to the alcohol he had consumed. It created a kind of anesthesia effect for him. He managed to roll his body over just a couple of inches to tilt his head up in the darkness. He began to cry in his hopelessness and then collapsed. The last thing he saw was a dim flicker of a pulsating light bulb, hanging from a single cord over another huge steel door. The thought that he may die right here on this spot came to mind, but he smiled because he really did not want to do any more life anyway. "Thanks for the memories," he sang silently to himself in his mind, and he remembered no more.

CHAPTER 5

Inner-City Mission Trip

AT FIRST, THE SOFT ALMOST inaudible buzzing sound was not recognizable, so Samuel raised his head slightly off his pillow to get a better grip on what he was hearing. He quickly identified it as a cell phone silently vibrating on the bedside nightstand. It was pleading for attention, wiggling for its life on her side of the bed. He could have just reached across her and answered the call, but he instantly knew that that would have woken her just as completely as if he put a well-placed foot in the small of her back and gently nudged her into awareness, so...

"Whaaaaaa," was her first response, but then she too heard her phone and shot up quickly to answer it. She was too late...the caller had hung up. She looked at the clock and saw that it was eleven forty-five, as she turned on her light. Samuel too sat up wondering who was calling.

"What's up?" he said. "Who was calling you at this hour? What time is it anyway?"

"It's eleven forty-five," she announced as she was fumbling with her phone to see who it was that called.

"It has to be pretty important for someone to call at this hour," he complained.

"Yeah, it's Pat," Rebecca said flatly.

"Pat? Wow, I wonder what is wrong. Maybe Randy is sick or something. You better call her back," he said with genuine concern in his voice. But she already had her phone to her ear.

"Pat, it's Becca. You okay? What's up? We woke up to the phone ringing, well vibrating, and since it was so late, we thought something is wrong. What do you need?"

"It's Jeremy," Pat said.

"Jeremy? What in the world? Is *he* okay?"

"Well, he came by about half an hour ago wanting to talk, I think, but Mom was here. Her and I were up talking about him, ironically, so I did not think it was smart to let him in."

"No," Rebecca confirmed. "That probably would not have been a good idea. What did he want?"

"Like I said, just to talk I think." Pat just fell silent for a moment.

"Pat?" was all Rebecca said.

"Yeah, I am here. I do not know what he wanted exactly, but he needed money for gas, and I gave him some, but the reason I am calling you is because of something he said."

"What was that, Pat?" Pat went on to share the whole conversation that she had had with Jeremy. Stopping to emphasize all the years of hurt that he, "well and you too," Pat inserted, "had received from your father."

"He got it much worse than I ever did by far," Rebecca said, "but I do remember. I was younger too, by a long shot, when Dad's rampages ended in my life, but that is another story. Go on."

Pat continued to share about Jeremy's visit and what she saw that touched her so deeply. "He said that he finally went over to see your dad for the first time in all these years, and—"

"Bet that went well," Rebecca interrupted sarcastically.

"Jeremy said that his dad told him again that he was a no-count stupid useless coward just like he had been telling Jeremy all his life, and that Jeremy was no son to him."

"Oh my," Rebecca mouthed quietly. And she turned to face Samuel who had been listening to her side of the conversation. "Poor Jeremy."

"Well, I've been here with Jeremy before when he went off the deep end about his father." Pat paused for a moment before continuing, "but tonight was different."

"Keep going, Pat. Tell me everything."

"Well," she went on, "I have seen him down before, but almost always, he would carry such hate and anger for his dad. Tonight, well, was different. He felt totally shamed. Deep shame and regret, and he could not quit crying. Becca, I mean out-of-control sobbing like I do not think I have seen in anyone, ever. He seemed to really believe all those things his father had told him from the time he was born. Oh, he was angry too, no doubt, but deeply hurt."

"Yeah, I remember that emotion," Rebecca said, "trust me."

"I know you do, Becca—"

"Well, *did*, anyway," Rebecca inserted. "*Did*," she repeated emphatically. "That part of me has been healed."

"Yeah, I know," Pat replied, "you have shared some things with me before, but it was what Jeremy said this time that made me want to call you. I did not catch it at first, but after he left and I was thinking over what he had said, I became alarmed, so I thought it best to call you. He said…"

"What did he say?" Rebecca stood up in a very alerted state of mind. "Tell me."

"He took the money I had for him, but I could see that he felt totally ashamed in receiving it. But then with his eyes overflowing with tears, he turned and walked away as he said, 'I promise you I won't ever bother you again.' I was left with that word '*ever*' hanging in my head until I decided to call you. Becca, I think he wants to kill himself. What do you think?"

Rebecca silently mouthed to Samuel, who stood up as concerned as Rebecca when she stood up. She had pushed her phone into her chest to make sure Pat could not hear her. "Jeremy, maybe suicide!"

"Pat, listen," Rebecca asked her, "is there any way to get in touch with him?"

"No, he does not have a phone any more. I wanted to drive over to his apartment to check on him. I know Mom would watch Randy, but that kind of scares me. You know where he lives."

"Yes, we know where he lives, and no, certainly not, not at this time of night anyway," Rebecca confirmed. "Just call us back if you hear anything, and we will do the same. We are already praying for him. Love you, Pat."

"Thanks," was the only word that Pat said, but it was laced with sadness.

Rebecca disconnected and looked at Samuel. "Pat thinks that Jeremy is planning to take his own life. I know that for years now we have heard his ranting and raving about how awful life is for him, but tonight, apparently, Jeremy came across so differently that Pat really believes that he might do it."

"No way to call him either," Samuel asked, "is there?"

"No," Rebecca said, "and Pat is scared to death to go anywhere near his apartment, and I do not blame her. Not at night, certainly."

"I'll go," Samuel said.

"I do not want you to go either. That neighborhood he lives in carries a higher crime rate by double than anywhere else in the city. You know what Roger told us."

"I remember," Samuel said with emphasis, "and he has been on the force for what, over a dozen years? He said that even when the police get a call for aid from that part of the city, especially at night, they are extra protective-minded for themselves. They do not avoid going but are often tempted to take their time getting there just to give whatever the situation is, time to cool itself off."

"That," she said to her husband, "is why Pat doesn't want to go down there, and," she added, "that is exactly why I don't want you to go down there tonight either."

Samuel put his hand on Rebecca's shoulder and then wrapped his arm around her and pulled her close to himself. "I have to go, and you know it. He will not admit it, but I am Jeremy's pastor as well. You just be faithful and keep us up in prayer." With that, Samuel got dressed, grabbed his keys, kissed his wonderful wife on her forehead, and headed out for yet another inner-city mission trip.

Rebecca watched as her husband, soulmate, and the most dedicated man she had ever known walk out of their front door, like he had done so many times in the past.

There were two distinct roles that Pastor Samuel Kensley lived out daily. She respected both the husband hat he wore, as well as the dedicated man of God hat that he wore. She knew, however, that his heart for ministry was mostly for the down and out. Those who were homeless, and for those who leaned on, with or without their own culpability, the lower side of society. She knew that he "had" to go and try to find Jeremy tonight.

"There's nothing to do now but wait," Rebecca told herself. She prayed standing right there at the door for Samuel, and then she prayed for her half brother Jeremy also. "Lord, watch over them both tonight."

CHAPTER 6

Who, What, When, Where, and How

"IT'S THE WAITING THAT IS the hard part, isn't it?" Rebecca said out loud as she closed her mind to the what-ifs. She shuffled off to the kitchen in her bath robe and put a pot of water on for a cup of tea. She sat down at the table and prayed again for Jeremy and her husband while she waited for her water to boil. She and her mother were the only ones who truly knew exactly what Jeremy was going through. She remembered what she had said to Patricia earlier though that 'he got it much worse than I ever did by far' and he did, didn't he?" she said out loud again to herself. She got up and made her tea and shuffled back into the living room to wait for her missionary husband to come home, hopefully with Jeremy. She turned off all the lights in the room, except for one small table lamp in the corner, so that she was not in total darkness. Then she covered up with one of the warm throws she kept hanging over the back of their sofa. She spent a couple of moments just getting warm and comfortable. The tea was too hot to drink, so she held her mug up close to her mouth with both hands and gently blew across the top of it to help cool it down. She sat in silence as her thoughts wandered back to her own dysfunctional life that had begun decades earlier, and she began to recount.

Rebecca's father, Daniel Townsend, who is Jeremy's father as well, was married to Della, Rebecca's mother for nine awful years. Then suddenly, out of the blue, her father announced that he wanted a divorce. Jeremy was not even heard of yet at that time, and it would be many years before Rebecca or her mother even knew that there was a Jeremy. Della had less than little to say about anything while she was married to Daniel, let alone what was going happen to them after they were basically thrown out. Their life became best described as a modern-day act of survival. Rebecca's father was ordered by the court to pay child support, but he rarely did. Simply put, they were left to "make it on their own." Her mother had never held a job of any kind, so she was not well equipped to suddenly find a way to support them after the divorce. While they were married, it was a hard life for them, and by Rebecca's definition, it was plain hell. Those years after the divorce were hard years also to be sure, but there was one consolation. Regardless of the new and different hardships they were forced to accept, both said with great relief, "At least that part of our life, living under that tyrant's rule, was finally over."

Rebecca was going on ten when her mother started looking for any kind of employment anywhere. It was not her mother's fault, but almost overnight, Rebecca was left to her own devices, and that convinced her that she really was not wanted by anyone. She not only had a father who never cared for her and went out of his way to prove that, she now lost her mother to the workforce as well. The only work Della could get quickly was a night job at minimum wage. Rebecca could not rid her mind of all the evil things her father had said and done to her. There was one memory in particular that was so powerful that it kept her awake almost every night. She could hear his voice in her mind, "Get away from me you sniveling stupid child. You are worthless, and you are no daughter of mine. Just go away." She was bitter to the hilt and believed totally that she was not loved by anyone. She thought her mother loved her "kind of" she would say. "But she's never home," Rebecca thought often, "so why should I care what happens?"

"Whatever were you thinking by marrying him?" Rebecca remembered, asking her mother long after she had grown up.

"Actually," Rebecca said out loud to herself as she took a sip of her tea, "that wasn't so many years ago now, was it?"

"Well," her mother had told her. "It is not that unusual of a story. I was young, and I had no idea a person could be like that, and I did not find that out until after we were married. He 'seemed' to be all of what any young lady would want in those days, and I fell for it. We were not married a year when I became pregnant, and that one thing turned him against me. From then on, I could not do anything right. I had no rights, and from your birth, he found justification to treat you like you were not even his child. In fact, he accused me, clear up until the time that he threw us out, that you were not his daughter.

Rebecca had finished her cup of tea and got up to fetch a second cup. She prayed again for "my two guys," she started calling them and sat back down at the kitchen table to wait again for her teapot to boil. She made her second cup of tea and headed back to her vigil for Samuel. She got comfortable again, but her thoughts of Jeremy captured her complete attention. "Oh my," Rebecca whispered, "I do know what you are going through, Jeremy," she spoke to the empty room. She could empathize with him for wanting to end it all. "I did once myself too," she said softly, "Wow! Hold on, kiddo," she said, speaking to Jeremy as if he could hear her. "You don't know it, but you are not alone. No," she thought, "I was not alone back then either, but I was blind. Just as blind as Jeremy is now." She looked at the clock, and although it seemed longer, it had only been about twenty minutes since Samuel had left. She allowed her thoughts to return to where she left off like she was reading a book, only it was time to turn the page.

She remembered it was after her twelfth birthday when she noticed that her mother seemed to change. She had gotten a better job and was working days steadily, and that was a huge blessing to them both. She was earning a decent income and was home every night. Her mother had gotten a sitter for her when she did have to work nights, but this was so much better. There was something else, though that had taken place, and

Rebecca noticed it. It was about a year after her mother changed jobs, but she did not know how to put it into words. Her mother seemed to possess this uncharacteristic peace about almost everything. She did not demonstrate any worries or look like she lacked any sleep like she almost always noticed in her tired old mother before. She told her mother that she noticed these differences and asked her about that.

Rebecca smiled as she stopped to recall that special time with her mother and how that was the beginning of a new life for them both. She sipped her tea that was just getting cool enough and replayed the conversation she had had with her mother back then in her mind.

"What differences do you see in me, Rebecca?"

"I don't know," she said, "you just seem to be happier. Kind of like nothing bothers you like it used to. Is it because you got a good job?"

"I guess that would have something to do with it," Della told her daughter. "It is a lot better now that I can be home at nights with you. It is also nicer that we can afford a lot of the things we could not buy before. It is a lot better for you too, isn't it?"

"Yeah, you bet it is," Rebecca confessed, "but I am talking about how you act when things are not so good. You used to just slump down in your chair and cry. You do not do that anymore. And sometimes when you would think about how Dad treated us, you would yell at him like he was here and could hear you, or you might just slam a door...or something."

"I see," she said, looking at Rebecca. "I do know what you're talking about, and I'm glad you noticed because something really wonderful did happen to me."

Of course, what had happened to Della was that a friend of hers invited her to come to church. She accepted the invite and went that next Sunday, leaving Rebecca at home in bed. She heard the story of how Nicodemus came to Jesus and confessed that they knew that he, Jesus, was a teacher come from God, for no one could do these signs that He did unless God was with him. At that, the pastor put the Bible down and said, "You know, Jesus could have taken that one time in history to teach Nicodemus, and thus all of us today, to just go back and tell all the others what he had just learned. Or he could have said to Nicodemus, well, it is about time, I have been trying to tell you all along...But he did not. What he did tell Nicodemus was, "Unless a man be born again, he can't see the kingdom of God." Della remembered hearing a couple of other times in her life that "you must be born again" but did not know what that meant. But just as she was thinking that, the pastor finished the story and made it clear as ringing a bell. Later he asked if there was anyone who wanted to have that same thing happen to them to come up front after the service, and he or one of the elders would pray with them. Della went forward that first Sunday morning, and her life forever changed.

"That is what happened to me," she said, looking at her daughter. "It has completely altered the way I think about everything, even about your father. You see, I have had to learn to forgive your father and to forgive him in the same way God, the Bible calls him our Heavenly Father, has forgiven me. It was not easy, at first, and it took me almost a year, but I finally realized that for me to find true happiness and peace, I first needed to accept the truth about our Heavenly Father's only Son Jesus and then forgive others, and that had to include your father. And to forgive him in the same way that he, our Father in heaven, had forgiven me. This process started about a year ago, but it has only been a couple of months now that I was able to apply that to all areas in my life, and that is probably when you noticed the change in me."

Now, sitting here in her living room, sipping on a cup of hot tea, Rebecca remembered the last thing her mother told her then. *"Rebecca, honey, I want the same thing to happen to you."*

Rebecca lowered her head, remembering what her response was to her mother all those years ago. *"Wait, are you telling me that you think that you were as bad as Dad? That you need as much forgiveness as Dad does?"*

"It does not have anything to do with who did more wrong or less wrong," her mother told her. *"Or who is more guilty or less guilty. All it*

has to do with is that I understood that I have sinned against God and his ways, and that for him to forgive me, I need to forgive others, any others, anything they have done to me. That then, for me, included your father. Your father is not off the hook because I have forgiven him. He, in turn, will or will not understand that he needs to be forgiven for the sins he has committed against God and us. Forgiving your father and forgiving him correctly simply set me free from all the anguish, pain, and sleepless nights caused by my vindictive vengeful thoughts."

"Boy, are these memories good for me now or what?" Rebecca asked herself out loud. "It will help me to stay focused for Jeremy." She allowed her thoughts to return to the yesteryears of her life once again.

"So you want me to forgive Dad," she remembered asking her mother, "after what he did to you and to me? Do you honestly think that I would ever do that? In fact, I wonder how you could do that yourself, let alone say it. Not a chance!" Rebecca told her mother, and she ended the conversation by crossing her arms and turning sideways in her seat to look anywhere but at her mother. She just sat there seething.

Rebecca was not convinced that what her mother had shared with her was real, especially the part about forgiveness. "No way," she remembered saying, was she ever going to forgive her father, but she absolutely believed that her mother believed it. Plus, she saw such a change in her mother that she agreed to start going to church with her. Rebecca started going to the youth gatherings as well, but it was not until three years later that she gave in and did accept that same life-changing experience in her own life. She remembered asking her youth leader right after she believed the truth of who Jesus really was if things were going to change in the way "I feel about my father." He assured her that "it can," but he told her that "it really is up to you." She, too, had to come to grips with this forgiving thing the Bible teaches the same way her mother did. She certainly had some rough times with that, but in the end, she understood how important it was to forgive her father if she was ever going to feel good about herself. She discovered that forgiving her father was about honesty, truth, and fairness, and had nothing to do with feelings about how bad her father had been. She knew what she had done against God that needed forgiving in her own life, and that Jesus paid her debt. She finally understood what God was asking her to do. She knew that he was asking her to forgive her father and to do that in the same way that God had forgiven her.

Rebecca finally was set free from all the memories that hurt and haunted her. She realized that no matter how bad, mean, wrong, or rude her father had been to her, she was given the ability to forgive him. She remembered crossing that ugly bridge she named "unforgiveness of my father," by acknowledging God's gift of his Son Jesus for her. She just cried like a baby when that happened because for the first time in her life, she could see that she was going to experience peace, purpose, happiness, and joy.

"Wow, that was a bunch of years ago," she said, forcing her thoughts to return to the now, "and what about that youth leader?" She giggled like a school girl at that thought. "Well, I married him, didn't I?" She beamed a peaceful love-centered smile for her eventual life-changing conclusion to all her discontent and hatred. "I've been healed completely, haven't I, Lord?" she spoke to the walls of their living room as she got up out of her straight back chair and headed for the kitchen yet again. "Jeremy's a long way off from that, though," she said, frowning.

She looked at the clock and realized that it had only been a little over a half an hour since Samuel had left, so she was not expecting him home just yet. She deposited her mug in the sink and went back to her still warm chair in the living room. There was no way she was going to go back to bed, so she started to pray for Jeremy again. Sitting still in silence with nothing else to do, she continued her mental march back in time.

Rebecca did not find out that she even had a half brother until she was sixteen years old. She knew that her father had remarried someone a few years back, but they did not find out that he had sired another child. They obtained that information quite by accident. It was when Della had contacted Daniel to try and get help with some medical bills for Rebecca. Of course, he blew up at her, telling her that he was he not made of money, and that it was hard enough with a "stupid toddler" running around under foot all the time. She shared that with Rebecca, but no more information was forthcoming about her half brother, not even a name until several years later.

It was Jeremy who found Rebecca after he was on his own. He was struggling to even eat on a regular basis when he found out that his mother, who also wanted to "get out of Dodge," was hoping that Jeremy would save her. Of course, he could not even save himself, but the two of them kind of teamed up for mutual survival. It was hard because between the two of them, they did not have two quarters to rub together. Daniel Townsend's solid MO put both him and his mother on his "you don't exist" list. What made it impossible also for Jeremy was that his mother had learned to escape life by diving uncontrollably into alcohol. His father had decided years prior to demonstrate his hatred for her daily just as he did for Jeremy, and his mother just could not take it. Jeremy understood, but there was nothing at all that he could do to help her. She did not last a year and she died basically by spending too many nights in a row alone with her only two friends in the world…rum and coke.

However, before she died, she contributed some very interesting information for Jeremy to chew on. She told him that his father had been married before, and that he had a daughter from that marriage. She did not know much else because Daniel never spoke of them. She said that she found out about them by accidently running across some papers that Daniel left unattended in the upper drawer of their dresser. She was not snooping for anything, she just wanted to know if she could use that drawer. She saw his marriage certificate to Della, as well as Rebecca's birth corticate. When she told Daniel that she found them, he, of course, blew his stack at her, took the papers, and told her to never spy on him again. She told Jeremy that Rebecca would be over thirty years old, but that was all she knew. The excitement that he had a sister, even a half sister, was so compelling for him that he began to see if he could find her. All he had to go on were the names Della Townsend and Rebecca Townsend. He had no idea what to do, so he asked a man who he had become friends with to help. The man owned a small garage where Jeremy was allowed to work some days to earn a little money, and he told Jeremy that he had a friend who might investigate it for him. It took a couple of months, but one day, his friend gave Jeremy a piece of paper with his sister's name and address on it. He was surprised to find out that his half sister Rebecca was married and living in an addition on the north side of town. So he decided to connect. He did not have a phone, so he just took a chance one Saturday, got on a bus, and went to see his sister, Rebecca Townsend Kensley.

"I remember that day like it was yesterday," Rebecca said, standing up. She looked at the clock again and saw that it was a little after one, so she figured that it was about time for Samuel's return. She hoped that he would have good news, and that he would not only find Jeremy but also bring him back home to spend the night, "or a couple of nights," she said again to herself. Then she sighed at the thought that he might not find Jeremy. "Well, if he does not," she paused briefly, "well, then, neither of us will end up back in bed tonight. Either way, we will still need a pot of coffee." She went to the kitchen, put the coffee on, and pulled three cups from the cupboard, "just to be positive about it," she told herself and waited.

CHAPTER 7

This Is Different

THE DRIVE TO JEREMY'S APARTMENT was about thirty minutes, and the neighborhood was as much of a "down and out" ghetto as ever there was. Samuel had been there before when he brought rent money for Jeremy, but that was always in broad daylight. Jeremy lived on the third floor of a walk-up tenement building that looked like it should have been condemned and torn down ages ago. He had only one room, with a small bathroom. Well, a toilet in one corner that was supposed to be covered with a curtain. That one room was where he slept, ate, and whatever else one can do to call living. He had an old small black-and-white TV that was given to him, but most of the time, it did not work. There was only one window in his room with a not so well fitted blind hanging down half covering it. When Samuel got to the narrow hall where Jeremy's door was, he could not see much because the ceiling light's single bulb was either missing or burned out. There was just enough light coming from under one of the doors across from Jeremy's door for Samuel to be able to see without tripping. He knew which door was Jeremy's anyway, and he tapped lightly several times. He did not want to knock loudly for fear of waking any of his neighbors. He did not want to disturb them for normal reasons, but he also feared some kind of confrontation. Nevertheless, he had to be sure, so he knocked on the door a lot louder, and then with no response, he really let the door have it. That brought some response all right, but not from Jeremy's side of the door. It came from some of the other doors on his floor. Curses were thrown like shotguns going off, so Samuel figured that

40

Jeremy was either drunk and in bed, or he just was not home. As he turned to leave though, he bumped something with his hand that was attached to the door. He turned the flashlight from his phone on to see that it was one of the largest padlocks he had ever seen. It was attached to two steel plates, making it impossible for Jeremy to open his door if he wanted to. "That's it, then," Samuel said. "He is not home, and he will not be coming home either," he figured correctly. He made his quiet escape, hoping that all of Jeremy's disgruntled neighbors would just go back to whatever. He walked back down and out of the building, and decided to look for Jeremy's car. It would be easy to identify, even in the dark, because it was missing both the front *and* rear quarter panels on the passenger side. "How can he even keep that thing on the road," he thought as he started his search. He walked for a block in both directions on both sides of the street and could not find it, using his flashlight as he walked to be sure. He went back to his car, started the engine, and just prayed for Jeremy's safety, and then headed back home. He could not stop thinking of where Jeremy might be. He also remembered several other times where Jeremy just disappeared for days, "worrying all of us," Samuel said out loud, "only to show up like nothing had happened."

Rebecca thought she had Samuel's return timed pretty good when she put the coffee on. It was at least a half hour later though, before she heard his car door. She ran to the door and flung it open, waiting for Samuel to make it up the steps.

"Did you find him?" was the first thing out of Rebecca's mouth, and she was looking past him as he came in the door.

"No," Samuel said sadly. "No, and I looked up and down his street for his car too, but it was not to be found. He is not going to go back to his apartment either. His landlord padlocked the door shut. You should see the size of that thing. I have never seen a padlock that large. I think it had Fort Knox stamped on it." He chuckled. "I have been praying for him all the way home."

"So have I, and I was just reminiscing the many years of our unpredictable relationship with him. What are we supposed to do?" she asked without really looking for an answer. "I put a pot of coffee on, you interested?"

41

"Oh yeah. I am up," Samuel said as he sat down at the kitchen table. "It's what Pat told us that is plaguing my thoughts. If it were not for that, I think I could go back to sleep."

Rebecca picked up the third cup to return it to the cupboard. "This one was for Jeremy," she told Samuel. "I was hoping." She filled the other two and sat one in front of him as he continued his thought.

"It is not like we haven't been here before. Jeremy has been out all night several times. Remember how we used to stay up all night sometimes worrying about him, praying for him, only to have him resurface the next day or so like nothing had happened?"

"You bet I remember," Rebecca said sarcastically. "We just seemed to get used to it after a while though, didn't we? But," she paused for its importance as she frowned, "this is different."

"Yes, it is," Samuel said, leaning into the table with his cup of coffee. "That word 'ever' is stuck in my head, and I know that you too are thinking the same thing. I will bet Pat is not sleeping either. What exactly was it that she said he told her when he left her house?"

"I promise you I won't ever bother you again," Rebecca said instantly, not needing to check her memory. "It scared me then, and it's scary now." She fell silent as she put her cup down kind of hard and scooted her chair around close to Samuel. Her face distorted at the saddened pain she felt. "You remember what I told you early on in our marriage?'"

"Yes, I do, Becca." He reached over and patted her hand. "I didn't believe you at first, but then, of course, I finally did."

"Mom never knew, and I do not want her to ever know. It is completely behind me now anyway. But there really was a time when I was literally half on and half off that proverbial railing called suicide. The only reason I never took that jump was because of people like your father," then she smiled at Samuel, "and that good-looking young youth leader who would always be there for me."

"Good-looking, huh? You think so?" Samuel said as he wrapped his one arm around her.

"Yeah, and he is still good looking today! Thanks for all you did for me back then and for all the years since. I would marry that youth leader again in a flash."

"Really," Samuel said, mocking a surprised look, "well, Rebecca Kensley, I would marry that young and still beautiful woman again also."

They both fell silent enjoying the moment, but then Rebecca brought them back to the point at hand. "I think my memory of what I could have done to myself back then is why I am so concerned for Jeremy now. I honestly believe that he could do it, and that is why that one word '*ever*' is keeping me from being able to want to go back to bed. I truly am healed from all that myself, but I know he is not."

"I believe that he could take himself out too," Samuel agreed. "That, of course, is why we are both up drinking coffee in the middle of the night, instead of leaning on the other side of that coin. We were always worried about him before, well, ever since he started coming around after their divorce, but you hit the nail on the head when you said, '*This is different.*'"

"So what do we do now?" Rebecca asked for the second time in their short conversation. "We cannot contact him, and we have no idea where to start looking for him. Are we just supposed to sit here and pray, hoping he has enough concern for us, or Pat, to let us know what is going on?"

Samuel raised his arms like he was being robbed. "Do not have a clue at this point," he said with doubt written all over his face. As he lowered his arms, he asked, "How about another cup of coffee?"

As she got up to get their coffee, Samuel put his "thinking out loud" cap on. "Isn't it interesting?" he conjectured. "No matter what the cause of our depression, anger, hatred, or our disbelief, the key to being set free completely has always been linked to our ability to forgive…that would include ourselves. Real peace only comes when we can do that. Even in Jeremy's case, the single most important issue that is blocking him from seeing truth and finding that peace is his inability to forgive his father.

"Oh, I agree," she said, "and that is not easy, is it? To forgive and make it count anyway. What that means is that we need to release those who hurt us so deeply from any punishment we honestly believe they deserve. We need to set *them* free before we can be set free, and setting *them* free is not what we want, is it? What we want is for them to suffer, at least as much as we have suffered, but that harbors all kinds of things, doesn't it? Resentment, depression, anger, revenge, doubt, and a bunch of other equally undesirable things. It even escalates our unforgiveness into finding fault sometimes, where none initially existed. It will not end either…well, until we learn how to forgive. We could write a book, couldn't we?" she mused.

"We don't need to," he said, "one has already been written, but Jeremy sure does not want to hear anything about God or the Bible, and I have tried. I have gained a bit of ground with him though, I think, these last couple of years, just trying to be his friend. Whenever he would stop by for a meal, I always tried to encourage him and even pray with him. Remember how he finally opened up about his relationship with Pat and Randy? Remember the story he told about his thirteenth birthday? Wow, if even half that story is true." Samuel stopped talking and just froze mid-sentence with his hand gesture hanging midway between his chin and his coffee cup. He looked like he had suddenly seen a ghost.

Rebecca became instantly aware something was desperately wrong. "What!" she said loudly, and she looked around the room as if he had seen something that was not supposed to be there. She looked back at him and said with alarming intensity again. "WHAT!" she almost screamed the word.

Samuel looked at Rebecca. "You know, that was just last month when he told me that story. I heard it before, but this time I really thought that I had made a great breakthrough with him. He seemed to listen to me, and that was the first time that I can remember him even slightly appearing like he understood. I told him that I thought he had made his first ever start to overcoming his anger."

"Yeah, I remember you telling me that," Rebecca said, sliding in closer to the table. "But what are you trying to tell me now?"

"Becca, I told him that night that I thought that it might help him to confront his father. I think it was me who pushed him into that move he made tonight. I gave him some other advice about that also, and I do remember warning him strongly to *not* go alone."

"So are you blaming yourself for what Jeremy did tonight?"

"No, not blaming myself exactly. Just looking back at that time in retrospect, I wish I would not have told him that."

Rebecca looked at the clock. "It's going on two thirty," she announced, "and we are back where we started…again. What do you think we should do? I wonder if Pat is still up. You think we should call?"

"Sure, why not," he agreed. "Wow, what a mess, though." Samuel picked up his phone and speed-dialed Pat. It rang only once.

"Hi," she said, sounding so tired. "Find out anything?"

"No, we did not," he told her. "I went over there to see if I could find him, and I could not even find his car. Is there any way to get in touch with him? Any way at all?"

"Not that I know of. I think he had a phone about a year ago," Pat said, "you know one of those pay as you go types, but he did not keep it up."

"Do you know of any place that he would go at this time of night?" Samuel asked.

"No, I don't," she said, "well except for his apartment. I do not think he has any good friends that would take him in. Maybe, I guess, but I doubt it from the way he always talked about not having any friends who cared about him. It might be some bar, but they are all closed now anyway, aren't they?"

"Yeah, I think most of the bars are closed," Samuel agreed. "Is there any place that he ever mentioned that he might go?"

Patricia let out a mild chuckle. "Bozo's," she said.

"Bozo's, what is Bozo's?" Samuel asked. "Bozo's?" he asked again.

"I do not know what it is exactly, but I think it is a bar or an all-night restaurant. I am not sure if it is even called Bozo's. I heard him use that name or something like that a couple of times before. Once when he came around to visit Randy. He just mentioned Bozo's or at Bozo's or those Bozo's. I am not even sure if he used the word Bozo's, but it sounded like that. Not sure if he was not referring to the people who went there. I am sorry, but that is all I know."

"Okay, Pat," Samuel said, "you keep the faith, and we will too. We are in prayer for him," and then he added, "for you too. Try to get some sleep, and we will do the same. We will certainly call you if we hear anything. We love you, Pat." Samuel thought he heard a light sniffle from her before she hung up.

"Bozo's." What do you think that is?" he asked Rebecca, but she was already searching for it on Google.

"Bozo's. No, no Bozo's under restaurants." She went to the clubs/nightclubs/bars and again came up with nothing. "What's another name it could be if it isn't Bozo's? What, Rolo's? Dobo's? Gobo's? Hobo's? Yeah, how about Hobo's?" She went back to search and got nothing closely related to a bar or restaurant. "Kobo's? Lobo's? Mobo's? Nobo's? Pobo's? Robo's," she said again "Tobo's? Wobo's? I cannot find anything like that." She then typed in diners, coffeehouses, and all-night grills, instead of restaurant. Again, nothing came up, except one name Bobo's Bar and Grill. "Bobo's," she said, "I think it's Bobo's." She almost yelled it at Samuel. "Call Pat back and ask her if it could be Bobo's Bar and Grill? It is over on Sixth Street. Sixth Street?" Rebecca questioned out loud and with a huge frown on her face, "Boy is that on the low side of life or what?"

Samuel called Pat back to ask. "We found a Bobo's Bar and Grill, Pat. Could that—"

"That's it," Patricia interrupted. Yeah, Bobo's Bar and Grill. Do you think he is over there?"

"Don't know," Samuel said, "but I am going to find out. I will drive over there right now. I will call you back later." And he hung up.

Samuel looked at Rebecca. "Sixth Street, huh? Yeah, that really is a bad section of the city, well, so they tell me anyway." He got up to say goodbye to Rebecca, but she anticipated him leaving her alone at home again, and she stood up as well. She just stared at him for a fleeting moment with her hands on her hips like a soldier defending her commanding officer.

"You're not going without me," she said, and that came out sounding like she *was* the commanding officer. "I'll only be a minute to get ready."

Samuel knew from experience that there was going to be no debate. She was going.

When they got in the car, Rebecca entered Bobo's Bar and Grill's into her GPS, and off they went.

CHAPTER 8

Mac

S AMUEL AND REBECCA LOVED ADVENTURES. An adventure, for them, could be something planned or not planned. It could be something as simple as being out on an unscheduled drive and discovering their new most fabulous restaurant. "How about this," she told Samuel, "for an adventure? Cruising the inner city at three in the morning, looking for our misplaced Jeremy?"

"This sure is an adventure," he agreed and then fell silent. Silence, in fact, soon dominated both their thoughts as they drove. The what-ifs were so overpowering, as they were trying to anticipate a wide range of possibilities. They were uncontrollably contemplating the worst-case scenario while simultaneously hoping for the best. Finally, Samuel bridged their silence. "You know it's highly possible that Jeremy is sleeping it off somewhere, and once again, we are up wasting a good night's sleep."

"Yeah," Rebecca agreed, "and I hope that is the case. I would love to lose another night's sleep if I had to, compared to..." She paused, searching for the right words, "well, playing the pragmatic here, one day, we may find him face down in some ditch somewhere way past anyone's hope for his survival."

Samuel visibly cringed. "Good gracious, Becca, what a thought, but the truth is that I was just thinking the same thing."

Finding Sixth Street was the easy part, but their GPS did not acknowledge a park that someone thought would really enhance the neighborhood some decades ago. It split Sixth Street in half, causing anyone who did not know better to believe that Sixth Street just dead-ended into the park. They had to drive around and simply discover that the street picked up again on the other side. The park was totally run-down like the rest of that section of the city. Homeless people were sleeping there, and who knew what other activity was going on unchecked every day, let alone at night. Samuel took a moment and prayed for the people who occupied the park, knowing that many of them were left with little to no choice for lack of anywhere else to go. They did not stop, though, to ask for directions. They just drove on, eventually locating Sixth Street again. Their GPS announced that they had arrived, but they could see nothing that looked remotely like a bar. They saw no signs, so they were simply left to their ambiguous imagination as to where exactly Bobo's Bar and Grill really was.

"Slow down," Rebecca blurted out. "I think we are getting close. I cannot see, though. I just saw that one number on the corner, and we are in the right block, I think. I do not see anything that looks like a bar, though." They kept driving down the block very slowly trying to look on both sides of the street but could not identify anything. "Are all the streetlights out in this neighborhood?" she asked rhetorically. "There's a small light on up there," she said. "Wonder if that's it?"

They came to a stop where one small light was illuminating a sign for an Asian grocery store. "No, that's not it," Rebecca said disappointedly, so they went on. But finally, she sat back in her seat, resolving herself to the fact that they would not be able to see any house number or identify any bar and grill. "Samuel," she asked, "why aren't there any streetlights? We are driving down a narrow street with some cars parked on both sides in almost total darkness. What are we going to do?"

"Don't worry," he assured her, "with our headlights I can see if there is a place to park. Then we will just have to get out and use our flashlights. And yes, all the streetlights on this street seem to be out of service. What is that all about? Come on, just keep praying, and we will be all right. Anyway, I think I saw what looked like a beer commercial sign in a window back there a couple of doors down from that Asian place. It was not lit up, and it was small, but that may be Bobo's. I just caught a quick glimpse of it as our headlights flashed across it. Either way, if that is it, they certainly are closed because all their lights are off. I am not sure what we will accomplish."

"Where is Jeremy's apartment from here?" Rebecca asked.

"Not sure," Samuel said, "I am completely turned around. Look, I can get the car in over there," he said, pointing. It was almost to the end of the block, and he parked and turned the engine off, turned off his phone's mapping and was reaching for his door handle to get out when he felt a heavy tug on his sleeve.

"What?" he said as he snapped around to face Rebecca. "What is it?"

It was pitch black in the car, and although he could not be sure, he sensed that she was staring right at him. "I'm scared," she said. "I'm sorry, and I thought that I'd be braver, but how do we know there isn't some guy out there waiting for us to get out and mug us?"

Samuel reached over and touched her arm and said gently, "We do not, but we also will not know if Jeremy needs our help if we do not get out and go looking. I clearly understand your concern. I have the same concern."

"But you do not seem to show it," she told him. "Well, you never did though, did you? You know the people around here cannot see that cross on your chest like I can."

"No," he said gently again, "but God can, and that is all there is to that. I would encourage you to stay in the car. In fact, the only reason I agreed to let you come down here in the first place is that I knew you would not accept no for an answer. But since you are here, I would feel better if you did stay in the car."

"No," she said quietly. "No, he is my brother, I have to know, and I want to help if he needs me. I would never forgive myself if I did not go." And with that, she grabbed her door handle with the energy of a professional wrestler, yanked it open in one quick bravado moment, and stepped outside. An invisible and uncontrollable shiver ran up the length of her spine and back down again, though. She did not confess that to Samuel.

Samuel shined his phone flashlight up quickly against one of the house numbers to see if they were on the right side of the street. He then swung the light around them 360 degrees to capture any ill-looking characters and saw no one. Then he looked down at his watch and noticed that they had been looking for Bobo's for the better part of an hour. "One good thing," he said very quietly to Rebecca. "It's going on three twenty-five."

"And how is being three twenty-five in the morning, in the totally wrong section of the city out for a stroll, a good thing?" she asked back in an equally soft voice.

"Because I think at this hour, even the most unsavory people are probably sleeping or headed that way."

"That's a nice thought, but I do not necessarily buy that," she retorted as they slowly made their way back down the block to where Samuel thought Bobo's might be.

"Have you noticed that this block seems to be the length of two normal blocks?" she said to Samuel.

"Yes, I have. It is not, of course, but it does look longer than a normal block. It just makes our effort a little more difficult, that is all. We will be fine," he said.

"Yeah, fine," she said curtly in the quietest of whispers. They were shining their lights down to keep from tripping, and when they came to a new walk that led up to another house, they would very quickly shine a light up against the house and then back down again. They kept an eye on that one small light they first saw by the grocery store, and it looked like it was still a long way away. Finally, they came to one house that had an old sign up against the front that read, "Bobo's Bar and Grill." They could see that it was only two doors down from where they saw the Asian grocery. An old two-story brick building stood between that grocery and Bobo's.

"What? Are you kidding me?" Rebecca proclaimed. "This is just another house. I see the sign, but that is about all that could identify it as a business of any kind."

"Shush," Samuel said, half begging and half commanding, "Let's just go up and have a look see."

Just then, though, they heard what had to be the sound of a glass bottle breaking on concrete, either on the walk behind them or in the street. It could not have been more than half a block away. They instantly flipped their flashlights off, and Rebecca grabbed

Samuel like she had rarely ever done. They froze in their tracks and waited. Then it seemed like no more than half a minute later a shot rang out coming from the same general area accompanied by a string of indistinguishable curse words. They huddled down holding each other and found a large tree to hide behind.

"Isn't this a real horror movie come to life?" Rebecca whispered to Samuel. "That came from just down the block where we parked our car. What are we supposed to do now?"

"It is not a horror movie, Becca, it's an adventure," he whispered just underneath a mild giggle. "Just stay calm," Samuel soothed. "Don't panic."

They waited frozen in total silence for what seemed like an hour to Rebecca, but in real time, it was only about five minutes. When they heard no more *inner-city life* sounds, they decided to walk up to the front door of Bobo's.

Rebecca could not help herself and whispered to Samuel, "Most unsavory people are probably sleeping, huh? What do you think? That shot came from a savory person or maybe from one who was sleep walking?"

"Cute," was all Samuel said.

When they got up on the porch, they shined their lights in through a window where the shade inside had been pulled up about half way.

"It's a bar all right," she said. "Different though. There is the bar and the bar stools, and I see some tables. Not many though. I would be hard-pressed to see the grill part of Bobo's Bar and Grill."

"Okay," Samuel said, "here we are, in a kind of singing voice, so where might Jeremy be?"

"Yeah...here you are!" came a very loud and rude voice from directly behind them. They both jumped almost out of their skin. They jerked instantly around to see a very large man with a super bright light, and it was shining directly into their faces. "What do you want?" he yelled at them, and at that, they heard someone from the second-story window of a nearby house boisterously command, "Keep the noise down!"

"You shut up, or I'll put a forty-five slug through your window," said the large man. He ignored Samuel and Rebecca for a few seconds as he just listened. When no one challenged his threat, he turned his attention back to them. They saw that in that small exchange of angry words this oversized man was waving a handgun around. "Now what do you want?" he ordered again.

"Nothing," was all that came from Rebecca, and there was no mistaking the immense fear in her voice.

Samuel stepped up in front of her and raised both his hands in surrender. Then after a few seconds, he spoke very calmly, choosing his words carefully. "We are looking for someone. We are certainly not any trouble to anyone, I promise. We are here to try and find her brother who we feel might need some help."

"Everyone in this neighborhood needs help," he told them in that same rough voice. "And another thing. I have lived here all my life, and one thing I have learned is that nobody really helps anyone."

It did not escape Samuel's trained insight that this abrupt assertive huge man had lowered his weapon. He also noticed that although he kept the bright light on then, he had lowered it away from their faces. From those two things, he could discern that this man was not intent on hurting them.

"My name is Samuel, and this is my wife Rebecca," he said, as he lowered his hands, but stretched them out sideways hoping to signal acceptance and peace. He started to slowly walk toward this huge man, "and if you don't mind me saying it, you"—he took another step—"look like someone who is maybe one of those rare ones, who does help people?" Samuel made that last observation in the form of a question.

"What makes you say that?" the man barked, as he lowered his light even further. "Are you some kind of mind reader or a priest or something like that?"

"No," Samuel said as he inched his way even closer. He lowered his arms and told him, "I am a pastor of a church, and most of my ministry has been involved with helping people. I, ah, just recognize the character, that's all."

The big man just gawked at Samuel for a long moment and then, "Name's Macpherson, call me Mac, and as far as helping people," and he fell silent for another moment, "don't tell anyone," he flippantly added. "But, look, you are in the most, and let me accent that again...*the* most dangerous section of town, so what on earth brings you down here and at four in the morning?"

"Well, like I said, we are trying to find her brother. Maybe you could, ah, help?"

"What's his name!" Mac commanded out the question with that same gruff tone. "I know everyone who lives around here."

"His name is Jeremy Townsend," Rebecca broke in, having captured her courage. "We got a phone call from his wife, ah, ex-wife, last night, and she told us that he might frequent this place and that he might be thinking of, well, killing himself. We have no other place to look. Only Bobo's Bar and Grill, so here we are looking for him."

"Sorry," Mac said, "don't know any Jeremy. A lot of people do not like to use their real name down here, though. Is there another name he might go by? What's he look like?"

"He is thirty-one, maybe six feet, and thin. Never had much money, and—"

"That does not tell me anything. Nobody in this place has any money," Mac interrupted. "Anything special I would know him by?"

In the light of his flashlight, he saw that Samuel and Rebecca just looked at each other with a kind of "I don't know how else to describe him" expression on each of their faces.

Mac was as sharp as a tack and possessed as much discernment as anyone anywhere. "You do not know him that well, do you?" he said, looking directly at Rebecca.

Rebecca sheepishly looked up into the silhouetted face of this huge man and began to cry. "No, we had different mothers, and our dad was a very difficult man. I did not even know I had a brother until he was seventeen years old. In recent years, though, we"—she pointed to Samuel—"have tried desperately to get closer to him, but—"

"I get it," he told them. "Kind of determined. Like the rest of us, huh?"

At that moment, Samuel saw a little more intelligence in this Mac than he initially believed was there. "Street-smart, though," he thought, "not sure yet."

"Well," Rebecca continued, "any help you can give us to find him tonight would be greatly appreciated. We think he may have been here last night, ah tonight, and that is our only clue."

"I can't help you there," Mac announced. "I own Bobo's here, and I work twelve-hour days trying to stay afloat, but last night, I took off around seven for a one-night break. I have a friend who works for a few bucks under the table, and he was here last night, but you will not see him till next Thursday. He went to see his mom for a few days. Left just after three when I close. I live up there"—he pointed with his gun up to an adjacent building—"and I came down like I always do for one last check and found you. Is there anything else that you could tell me about your Jeremy?"

Samuel and Rebecca looked at each other again, thinking and then, "Oh, ah," Rebecca remembered, "on his birthday last year, we gave him this rather nice leather 'Steelers' jacket. He just loves it, and he wears it everywhere. It was brown leather with—"

"Steelers in large letters arched across the back," Mac interrupted. "Yeah, I saw that. So that's your Jeremy?"

"Maybe. It could be," Samuel said.

"No, that must be. I immediately recognize that jacket as being very expensive. It is a wonder no one ever took it from him. No one in this neighborhood could ever afford something like that. I even thought that he must have stolen it himself, but you know, you just do not ask. But I never knew his name, and you are right, he does frequent here. He was always just known as, ah, ah, well, we did not know his name." And with that, Mac just stood there obviously waiting for them to say something.

"Was my brother ever any trouble?" Rebecca asked. "Or did he have any friends?"

"Don't know that he had many, ah, any friends. He sure did talk a lot when he got ticked off or when he had a few too many beers. No offense, but I do not think that anyone really liked him," he concluded. "I honestly do not know what else I can tell you." Mac was done talking. He made that perfectly clear when he said, "I am pretty sure you are safe with me in this neighborhood, so I will walk you back to your car." And with that, he just started walking out toward the street. "Which way is it?" He paused at the front walk just long enough to get their direction.

"Thanks so much for your help, Mac," Samuel said as they followed him down the street.

"I told you," Mac shot back, "don't tell anyone, but then a little softer, he said, "I got a reputation to keep."

He got them to their car, and after they got in, Rebecca rolled her window down to say goodbye. "You're a nice man, Mac, and you've been found out."

"I would advise you to just leave and not come back. Good luck finding your brother," Mac said, roughly walking away.

"Wait," Samuel said, and Mac turned.

"What?" Mac loudly ordered the question out of the side of his mouth.

"I would really like to get to know you. Do you mind if…" But Mac was gone.

"What do we do now?" Rebecca questioned.

"I don't know that there is anything else we can do," Samuel commented in desperation. "Go back home, I guess, and pray for him. Need to pray for Pat as well."

"And for our new friend Mac," Rebecca added.

Samuel looked back to where he had last seen Mac, but he could not even see the trunk of his car in the darkness that enveloped them. He started his engine and slowly crept back out into the street to find their way out of this unscheduled, surely never to be forgotten adventure.

CHAPTER 9

Dead or Alive

PULLING OUT ONTO SIXTH STREET at four in the morning immersed in darkness was not the most pleasant thing to do, especially having to dodge broken glass, but they had no choice. At the end of the block, Samuel turned right onto yet another unlit street. It was one-way, and that would take them over to Seventh Street, Samuel thought. Once on Seventh Street, he was pretty sure he would know how to get home.

He had gone less than half a block, though, when… "Look," Rebecca said, "there is one streetlight that is still on. Oh, and another one up there on the corner. I guess not all the lights in this neighborhood are…WHOA… why are you stopping?" she said as she was being pushed forward in her seat.

Samuel obviously saw something that made him want to stop. He put the car in reverse and carefully started to back up slowly. He seemed to be looking intently for something on his side of the street. Finally, he stopped but then pulled forward again. "Check this out," he said as he finally came to a complete stop.

"What!" she said, "I can't see anything."

Samuel rolled his window down and just gazed at a parked car that he had stopped beside. "I couldn't see anything either, except for our headlights as we passed that," he said as he pointed. "That is Jeremy's car."

"Oh, sure it is," she replied. "Really? I can't see a thing from this angle. How can you be so sure?" she asked.

56

"Look at the front and rear quarter panels that *are not* there. How many cars do you think are on the street that look like that? That is Jeremy's car."

"I will just take your word for it. So where is Jeremy?"

"I do not know, but I think we can make the educated guess that Jeremy would have been at Bobo's last night. Why else would his car be here?" Samuel got out and, using his flashlight, looked inside the car. No Jeremy. He got back in his car and plugged Jeremy's apartment address into the GPS and discovered that it was about six blocks away. "Close enough to walk home, I guess, but why would he if he had his car?" Samuel said out loud. "Hmmm, unless he ran out of gas. I wonder, but that is not plausible to think that he would run out of gas right there where he had parked. Or he may have known he was going to, and decided to walk. Pat told us that she gave him money for gas, but I will bet he used that at Bobo's. We cannot tell anything, without asking him, can we," he concluded. "Does not matter anyway. If he did walk back to his apartment, he would have found it locked up by his landlord and would have had to go somewhere. So," he pondered out loud, "where is that somewhere?" He started to drive forward again until he could see an alley off to the right. "I'll bet that goes down in back of Bobo's." He stopped the car right at the entrance of the alley. "What do you think?"

"I'm sure it does," she confirmed. "But what makes you think that Jeremy would be somewhere down this dark," and she paused, feeling a sudden tug on the wisdom side of her brain, "oh my, that is a dark alley, isn't it? So you are thinking, what, that we should just *diddy-bop* our way back there just to see what we can see?"

"Got nothing else," he explained. "His car is right here, so I think he was at Bobo's last night. He is not in his car. He is not at home or in the bar. He is not at Pat's house, and for sure, he is not at our house. We have been told often, and we know anyway that he was mostly a loner who did not have many, if any, friends who he trusted. It is the middle of the night, so yeah, I think we should."

When he turned into the alley, he saw that it was in poor condition. Their car bounced gently up and down over some of the now loose chunks of concrete. There were some broken down garages on both sides, and they saw some old cars parked precariously, some of which looked like they had been abandoned. "And no streetlights here either," Samuel said.

"What is it about this area of the city?" Rebecca asked again. "No lights? One would think that this is one of the most needed places for lighting."

"Oh, it is," he confirmed, "but it is a possibility that the streetlights have been broken out, maybe even shot out so many times that the city just stopped trying to fix them. It is like any other depressed area anywhere in the world. People just give up, opening the door for blight to move in and just take over. Oh, and here is another thought. We know that darkness cannot hide in the light, and who do you think wants control of this area?"

"Hmmm, what a way to look at it, but I think that pretty much spells it out," she agreed with him.

They could see, looking down into the darkness, a dim light shining out from one side of the alley. As they approached that area, they saw that the uneven alley they had been trying to navigate had surrendered to several very large concrete slabs in perfect condition. It appeared that they had been poured in recent years, and it looked way out of place. Samuel stopped to investigate and saw that there was a single bulb hanging hazardously from a cord just above a heavy steel security door. It flickered on and off with what seemed to be an electrical arc as the wind would blow it left and right. He pulled off the alley and onto this "new" concrete, where his headlights instantly, identified another steel door that had "Bobo's" stenciled in faded red letters across it. "Okay," he told Rebecca, "here we are."

"Yeah, here we are," she mused. "The last time you said that, we faced off with that unbelievable larger-than-life Mac who was waving a gun around."

He turned the car to the left some to get a better look at the rest of the area. He could see the steel door with the flickering light. That had to belong to that Asian store because it had some kind of Oriental writing on it. There was a large commercial type dumpster that had been placed against one wall. "Wow," he said, "I wonder how long it has been since the city was here to pick up all that trash."

The dumpster was full to overflowing, and there were what seemed like over a hundred other bags of garbage lying around. It looked like those bags were just tossed *at* the dumpster, not even trying to put them on top after it was full. But what made it worse was that most of the bags on the ground had been ripped open, exposing their contents. The garbage was not only strewn out mostly near the dumpster, but also tossed around to cover a rather large area. There was no garbage at all directly behind Bobo's, though. It was evident that someone took great care to keep that section of the concrete cleared off.

He hesitated getting out of the car, just looking through the windshield at the mounds of garbage, but then he told Rebecca, "You know we need to go hunting through that garbage."

"Yeah, I kind of get that," she said with doubt hanging on each syllable, "but I kind of do not get that also. You want us to go shuffling through that garbage to look for Jeremy?" She did not want to agree with him, and she did not make a move to get out of the car. Then, after a long pause, she amplified her feelings again. "Do you really think he might be out there? I mean what would he be doing in the garbage? I do not really want to go out there, do you?"

"No," he assured her. "No, certainly, I do not, but…" He hesitated again and finally said, "what if he is out there, and we find that out tomorrow that we could have done something about it?"

"Okay," she said, complaining, "but I still do not buy it. Why in the world would he be out there in the garbage? It makes no sense to me at all."

"We don't have anywhere else to look," Samuel said, and he was finished with the debate. He grabbed his flashlight and got out. "AAARGH!" he exclaimed. "Wow…that garbage sure does stink!" He turned and bent down looking into the car and grinned at Rebecca. He covered his mouth and nose with his hand, and saw that Rebecca appeared to be at that gag reflex stage, leaning against the dashboard.

"That is nasty," she said.

Samuel just ignored her last statement and proceeded into the unknown. It was only a few seconds later that Rebecca mustered enough courage to follow. Both had their hands over their faces, as they began to walk up to where all the garbage was scattered. Then they began carefully to step tippy-toed through the garbage, using the light from the car's headlights and their flashlights to guide themselves.

Samuel was a dozen or so steps ahead of her and was silently concentrating, looking from side to side as he got closer to the over-filled dumpster. He discovered that in some places, the trash was piled up over a foot deep. There were not many places to step where there were not several bags of rotting garbage. Rebecca stopped because she noticed that Samuel was bending over to look at something. "Don't pick anything up, Sam," she warned, "you'll…" But she froze as she saw Samuel stooping over a hand sticking up out of the trash. She did not care any more about the garbage or the stench and ran through it, kicking bottles and cans aside until she saw Jeremy laying there in what looked like a drunken stupor. He was not buried in the garbage, but it was deep enough around him that you would not be able to see him in the dark, unless you almost stepped on him.

"Oh, Sam, is he okay? Is he…can you check his pulse?"

"I just did," Samuel said. "He is alive, but he is unconscious, call for an ambulance."

She dialed the number and waited for an answer.

"Nine-one-one dispatch, what is your emergency?" a female voice announced.

"We have an unconscious man who needs medical assistance. He is bleeding some from his mouth. We need an ambulance."

"What is your location?" she asked.

"We are at a bar, out back of it in the alley. It is called Bobo's Bar and Grill, but I do not remember the address, it is on—"

"That's Bobo's Bar and Grill on Sixth Street?" the dispatcher asked.

"Yes, that is it. You got it. Please hurry."

"I will need a little more information," the dispatcher told her. She asked about his breathing, posed a few more questions, and then told Rebecca that an ambulance and the police had already been dis-patched and for her to stay on the line until the ambulance arrived.

It was a longer wait than it should have been, they thought, but finally they heard the siren, and shortly after that, Samuel saw the lights coming up from the opposite way in the alley. "Stay with Jeremy," he said, "I need to get our car out of the way." He ran to the car and backed it up and then forward again. He drove down the alley a long enough distance to make sure there was plenty of room for the ambulance. He got out and started to walk back. "Sheesh," he said out loud. "Is this dark or what, and no moon to boot." He reached for his phone to flip his flashlight on, and it did help but not a lot. He also kept his eyes on the lights from the ambulance that had just pulled into where he had pulled out of for additional guidance.

He was doing good until something caught his peripheral stepping out from the blackest of shadows. "I'm guessing that's your Jeremy," Mac's voice boomed even in his attempt to lower its effect.

"Wow!" was all Samuel could say for a moment, as he recoiled backwards for the sudden punch to his psyche. "Mac?" Samuel said, suddenly breathing hard as he patted his chest with one hand. "You need to know that for a guy as big as you are, you sure know how to sneak up on someone. Yeah, that is our Jeremy, and he is not in good shape at all."

"You know, I didn't want to tell you this before, but I knew that sometimes he could over indulge," Mac said, glancing down the alley at the paramedics hovering over Jeremy. "He is drunk, right?"

"Oh yeah, he is inebriated, but we called the ambulance because his pulse is faint, and he is having trouble breathing. Do you have any idea why he is back here passed out in the garbage?"

"No, I do not," Mac told him. "I would have told you. I looked out of my window," he said as he motioned with his hand, "up there when I heard the siren and saw your car and you two stooped over something. I kind of figured it was your brother. I came down out front where you saw me before and went around these houses to come out here."

"Mac, I would love to talk with you, but right now I really have to get over there to help."

"Hope he'll be okay," Mac said softly, and it sounded to Samuel that this Mac was not anywhere near the hard-core dude that he wanted people to think he was.

"Ah, listen," Mac said sounding uncertain of what he wanted to say, and then he stuttered a little before continuing. "You, ah, remember, ah…what you told me back there by your car? Ah… about wanting to get together me?"

"Yes, I do, and, Mac, I really would."

"Well, when this all blows over, I mean when you get some time, ah…would you give me a call? I got some things I would like to talk to someone about, and you, well, you look like someone who *does help people?*" Mac was trying to mimic the exact same manner that Samuel used when he said those same words to him. With that, he shoved a piece of paper with his phone number scribbled on it into Samuel's hand and just walked away not waiting for a response.

"I will give you a call, Mac," he spoke to the back of this monster of a gruff-looking man who appeared now to be as soft as a sugar cookie inside.

The paramedics were just lifting Jeremy into the ambulance when Samuel returned. Just then a squad car arrived and pulled forward to where Samuel had parked in the alley. *Odd*, Samuel thought. *They did not have their siren on or even their lights.*

"He is having trouble breathing," Rebecca told Samuel in answer to him asking, "and there is huge bruise on his side. They are saying it looks like he had been kicked. He is still out because of all the alcohol he consumed and—" She was interrupted as one of the police officers approached them and began to ask questions.

"What happened?" he started with and then, who are you, how long has he been here, etc. The other officer was already with the paramedics at the back of the ambulance, and Samuel noticed them pointing to the area where they picked Jeremy up. The officer then walked away from them in that direction. At that moment, one of the paramedics motioned for Rebecca that they had to leave.

"Don't leave without me," Rebecca almost screamed at them. "I'm coming!" She dashed away quickly to get in the back with Jeremy. She paused for a mere New York second, looking at Samuel. "Do you mind?"

"No," Samuel told her. "Go, go, I'll meet you at the hospital."

She rapidly climbed into the ambulance, and it looked like the lights and siren were on as they were moving almost before the door had closed.

Both officers had powerful lights they were using, and the one that was with Samuel asked, "You say you are his brother-in-law, right?"

"Yes, I am, what else can I help you with?" he asked the officer politely.

"First, let me start with his name and where he lives."

"His name is Jeremy Townsend, but all his other information should be on his driver's license, I think, wouldn't it?" he told the officer.

"Okay, well, my partner will be getting that I guess from his wallet." Then he went on with several questions.

The other officer joined them and asked, "Did you or your wife get a wallet from him?"

"No, we did not. He did not have his wallet on him?" Samuel questioned. "Really, are you sure?"

"He did not, and no identification of any kind either. The paramedic searched him just as they got him in the ambulance. Also, I have just looked all over the area where they said that they picked him up." The officer turned his head nodding to the garbage. "All over there," he told Samuel. "I found nothing at all. Did he have a driver's license?"

"Sure, he did. He always had it in his wallet, and he always tucked his wallet inside his Steelers jacket."

"Sorry," the one officer told him. "No Steeler's jacket either."

Samuel just stopped to think. "You're right," he said. "I did not notice because I was so busy trying to help. He did not have his jacket with him, but he always wore it."

"Don't know what to tell you, sir," the officer said.

Samuel gave the officers all the information he had on Jeremy and then his own name and contact information. Then he asked them if they were going to do something about Jeremy's injury or his stolen jacket. "Oh, and just out of curiosity, why didn't you have your lights or siren on when you showed up?"

"You can have your Jeremy file a stolen object form about his jacket if in truth it was stolen. That will be difficult to prove, though, won't it, in his drunken state. Anything could have happened to his jacket. He might have even given it away. We see that a lot with, well, situations like this. As far as his injury, that too will be difficult to follow up on. We will put it in our report that he 'appeared' to have been kicked, but that is about all we can do, and about our siren and lights? Well, that is another kind of story."

Samuel got the impression that these officers get called down here regularly on similar scenarios and have learned that pretty much nothing ever gets resolved. "Okay," Samuel said and thanked them.

"You good to go from here? I see you have your car there. They took him to Central Memorial," they told Samuel. "Is there anything else you need?"

"No, I guess that is all."

"Okay, then," the one officer told Samuel, so he left the police standing there, turned away, and walked to his car.

He drove off, praying for Jeremy and for Rebecca, "Oh yes, Lord," he continued, "for Mac as well."

He found Rebecca sitting at the registration desk at Central, working at checking Jeremy in. They had already taken him in for observation.

When they finished with the check-in, they looked for a couple of seats to wait. "Did they say anything at all when they looked at Jeremy?" Samuel inquired.

"Well, yes, they did. They said that they were extremely concerned about his breathing. That is why he got in so quickly. I think that they suspected something serious. Anyway, all we can do is wait. Want to give Pat a call now or later?" Rebecca asked.

"We should call her now. We said we would if we found out anything, so yeah. Do you want me to call her or do you want to?" he asked Rebecca.

"I'll give her a call," she said as she was already reaching for her phone.

"We found Jeremy," she told Pat. "He was passed out drunk behind Bobo's Bar and Grill. We called an ambulance and are at

Central now, waiting to hear how he is. It looks like he was kicked. We are not sure how bad it is yet, but he is being looked at as we speak."

Samuel could not hear Pat's side of the conversation, but Rebecca told her, "Be at peace, Pat, and you keep praying. This may be the one incident that will permanently help Jeremy turn around."

"Do you think?" Pat whispered.

"Yes, I think, Pat. Well, it certainly can be. It happened to me. Remember my story?" Silence fell between them as she sensed that Pat was weeping. "You still love him, don't you?" Rebecca said softly.

Pat could not answer at first, but then, "Yes, I do. I have never stopped loving him. I have been hoping for years that he could change, and we could be a family, but hope is all I have."

"God is a miracle God, Pat. Do not give up. Hang in there. In the end, the only thing that will change our Jeremy is when he finally gets rid of all that anger and his self-loathing and *all* that *only* gives way when he can ask for God's help, to finally forgive his father."

"That will be a miracle indeed, won't it?" Pat said. "You know how hurt he is, and how much his dad had done to him. I cannot see him ever forgiving his father."

"I can," Rebecca said. "I know it seems impossible, but let's just keep praying. We will call you when we know more."

They had to wait another half hour maybe when the doctor attending Jeremy came out to talk with them. He filled them in on Jeremy's condition. "He's doing okay, but you know that he is totally inebriated."

"Yeah, we know, but what about his breathing? How serious is that?" Rebecca questioned.

There is a large bruise on his side, so we think he was kicked. We ran some x-rays and saw that three of his ribs are seriously fractured and two more that are badly bruised. His one lung collapsed also, and for all that, he is having a pretty hard time breathing."

Both Samuel and Rebecca cringed at the mention of the collapsed lung. "Is he going to be okay?" she asked.

"Yes, he will," the doctor comforted them. "A collapsed lung is not that uncommon. It does sound bad, and he is going to be in a lot of pain for a while, but he will be fine. No work and no exercise or lifting of any kind. We are going to keep him for a while and see what he looks like when he wakes up." He asked them if they had any questions, and when they did not, he told them that a nurse would come out soon and talk to them about Jeremy's arrangements.

It was only a few minutes later when a nurse did join them. "He will not have a room," she announced, "but you will be able to visit him as soon as I get him situated. He is still unconscious, though."

"I want to be there with him when he wakes up," Rebecca told the nurse.

"No problem," she said. "I will get you a comfortable chair to sit in beside him."

"Unconscious, huh," Samuel said to Rebecca when the nurse walked away. "That's one way to say it." Then Samuel told her all of what had taken place with the police after she left in the ambulance.

"Why would he be without his Steelers jacket? Do you think someone stole it, or did he leave it somewhere?"

"Don't know," Samuel said.

"Maybe someone dragged him out there, kicked him in the side, stole his jacket, and left Jeremy for dead," she conjectured.

"That would be my guess, but Jeremy would not have had much money, if any at all, on him to steal," Samuel said, thinking out loud, "and certainly, no credit cards. He had nothing on him, probably, except his wallet with his driver's license and that jacket. The jacket was all a thief could have found that had any value, so why steal his wallet?" Samuel put on his detective thinking cap, "unless…since Jeremy always kept his wallet in his jacket pocket, not in his jeans like the rest of us do, the jacket thief might not have intended to steal the wallet. Having looked in Jeremy's jeans, maybe he just nabbed the jacket and ran, not knowing that he inadvertently had nabbed his wallet as well."

"Or unless he left the jacket in his apartment," Rebecca stated.

"Not likely," he told her. "But we can talk about that another time."

"Right," she said, "I am going to stay here with Jeremy till he wakes up."

"That's fine, but you know I have a nine o'clock," he reminded her. "What time is it now anyway?"

"It is almost seven," she told him. You go on home and get cleaned up for your meetings. I know you have a board meeting also, so don't worry about me. I'll try to get a little sleep before Jeremy wakes up, and I might even go down to the cafeteria to get something to eat later. Let me call you when I am ready for you to come and get me."

So Samuel said his goodbye and headed for home.

She had to wait only a little while longer when the nurse popped her head around the corner and motioned for Rebecca to follow her into a large multi-bed ward.

Rebecca investigated Jeremy's face and noticed that he looked much older than he really was. She could see that he was having great difficulty breathing. The raspy noises coming from her brother amplified her deep concern for him. "I will be here for you," she said quietly. "I will."

She was too tired to sleep and too tired to stay awake. Hours were going to pass before Jeremy would open his eyes having no clue how he got here. *This is going to be interesting*, she thought as she turned to eye the chair the nurse provided for her. It was not a large chair but looked very comfortable. "And that's a nice touch too, isn't it?" she said out loud. "It comes with a warm blanket."

CHAPTER 10

Sympathy?
Empathy?

S YMPATHY, SIMPLY PUT, IS HAVING compassion for someone else's uncomfortable situation, hardship, or pain. Empathy includes sympathy but often moves one to act on their sympathy with just a little more enthusiasm. Empathy evokes knowledge and experience of one's uncomfortable circumstance. That usually is the result of having had to live through the same thing or be involved with the one who needs care. Empathy always magnifies understanding, way in excess of just having sympathy. That then expands the desire to give much more toward the caring process. Occasionally, it even pulls out *all* the stops for the caregiver, who is wanting to help another at his greatest time of need.

Enter Jeremy's half sister, Rebecca, who knows, understands, and cares deeply for him because she too has had to face exactly what he is going through now. She too was brought into this same arena he is in now. She too was introduced to this same life-threatening pain via the same environment and by the same person. She too was just as close to being able to commit suicide, as he is now. But unlike Jeremy, *so far*, she was able to overcome that worst case scenario and, in the process, found genuine love, lasting peace, and freedom by truthfully forgiving their father.

It is because of that intense empathy she has for Jeremy now, that allows her to clearly see two potential outcomes pleading for her

68

half brother's life. One outcome will provide the same victory she has achieved while the other will continue to feed his deteriorating ability to forgive. That, she knows also, will only lead to bitterness, hatred, depression, and potentially death.

Jeremy woke to an agonizing pain coming from somewhere above his waist. Excruciating as it was, he could not identify it. He slowly raised from his bed trying to recall who was driving the truck that ran over him, but his instant second thought was, "Where am I?" he said out loud. He could remember nothing from the night before, and he had no clue how long he had been here, wherever here was. He tried to get up but physically could not and plopped right back down on his back.

"You're in Central Memorial, and you are very fortunate to be here," Rebecca said, as she stood up from her chair.

Jeremy slowly turned his head up to see who it was, and then a third reality basically nailed him back to his pillow. His head felt like a hand grenade had gone off between his ears but did not bother to kill him. He painfully tried to pull is hand up to rub his head but could not do that either. His side hurt more than his head.

Rebecca stepped up to his side, put her hand on his head, and gently began to rub. "Jeremy, honey, really, you almost died. Samuel and I found you passed out behind Bobo's and called an ambulance to get you here. That was around five this morning."

Jeremy groaned, "Found me? What do you mean found me, and what time is it now?" he uttered gruffly as he let out a pitiful whimper.

Rebecca looked for the time on her phone and told him, "It's after eight thirty now. We have no idea how long you were passed out over there, but you've been, well, passed out here for a few hours."

Jeremy turned his head toward Rebecca again, but it looked like he was laboring to focus on her. "What," was all he could muster, then he fell silent. His feelings were wrapped around many things at the same time. He had no memory of how he got here. "Central Hospital? Really?" he questioned.

"Central Memorial," she confirmed. "Yes. Do you know what happened to you last night?"

"I don't know *what* I did, or what happened to me, no," he told her. "I remember even less."

"That's pretty good right there," she responded. "You remember less than the nothing you don't know?"

Jeremy was not amused and looked away. "When can I get out of here?"

Rebecca spent the next hour trying to fill in some gaps for him, including the wretched smell from all the garbage that they experienced out behind Bobo's. She asked if he knew about the complete lack of street lighting in the entire neighborhood.

"Oh yeah, that," he told her. "Do not know why that is. We all just got used to not being anywhere but where we should be…"

"You mean like rolling in the garbage at four in the morning out in a dark alley behind a low-life bar like Bobo's?"

Jeremy shot Rebecca a discontented look. "Yeah, like that…but what does that matter now anyway?" he asked Rebecca crossly.

Rebecca ignored his temperament and went on to tell him all that she knew. "But we have no clue how you ended up back there sprawled out in the garbage." She did not mention meeting Mac at all. She did not even think about him. "What is the last thing you *do* remember?" she asked.

Jeremy looked up at her and said, "I don't want to talk about it." He plopped his head back against his pillow again, grimacing with pain. That seemed to bring more discomfort, so he turned his head away from her for the second time. Silence filled the room.

"How am I going to pay for all this?" he finally asked out loud rhetorically, "and where am I going to go when I do get out of here?" He looked at her again and confessed, "My rent was due a little over a month ago, and the landlord told me if I was late again that he would lock me out." Jeremy closed his eyes and quietly breathed out. "He may have already done that."

Rebecca just looked down but did not say anything to confirm or deny. She figured that he would find out soon enough.

Again, he tried to rub his head but again could not raise his hand to do the job, and he let out an anguished sigh. "You know that I lost my job again, but it was not my fault. They said that they could not keep anymore part-timers. I do not have a dime," and he stopped talking for a moment but then, "I even got money from Pat last night." He rolled his head away from looking at Rebecca as tears started to form in his eyes. Finally, he said, "You know, I was going to kill myself last night, but I even failed at that. I really am a loser, you know." Again, he just fell silent for a while, and Rebecca waited. "I went to see Dad last night. Do not know why I did that, but he told me again what a loser I was. And you know what? I have been a loser my whole life. He told me again that I was no son of his. You know, no matter how mean he is, at least he is not wrong about me. The only good thing I have ever done is prove that I am the best at being worthless. I really wanted to die last night. I still do."

Rebecca quietly surveyed her half brother and was unable to respond to him for the tears in her own eyes that she was attempting to choke back. *How can I help him get through this?* she thought, and in silence, she prayed. *Bring my brother to the other side of this healed.* Then just a moment later, she prayed for their father silently to herself. *Lord Jesus, when you were on the cross, you asked that Father God would forgive those who were crucifying you, for they knew not what they were doing. And when Stephen was being stoned, he prayed and asked that you not hold this against them for they too did not know. I am asking for our father that you can draw him to the understanding of Jesus your Son. I am asking that you bring Jeremy to that point where he will forgive our father because he, too, does not know. And that he will forgive in the same way that you will forgive him. The same way that you have shown me how to forgive our father.* She noticed that Jeremy was arching his back and moaning in pain.

"They said you have three fractured ribs," she told him. "Ah, you also have a collapsed lung."

"What the heck happened to me?" he asked. "Am I going to die?" he questioned but then added, "That may be the best thing anyway."

"You are not going to die, and the doctor told us that it is not that unusual of an occurrence to have a collapsed lung with an injury like this."

"How did I end up with three fractured ribs?" Jeremy grimaced.

"The doctor is saying that it appears that someone kicked you hard, and, well, here you are."

"Kicked? What, kicked? Who would do that?"

"We do not know, Jeremy, but we were told that you would be in a lot of pain for a while."

"Yeah, I get that," Jeremy said as he tried to arch his back again to alleviate some of the pain. "I am in a lot of pain right now. I cannot breathe well either. Is there something I can get for this pain?"

"I am pretty sure that you were not given anything to ease the pain yet since you were passed out, ah, well, inebriated, but let me call the nurse."

"I like the word inebriated…Drunk is the proper word," he told Rebecca. "But thanks for making it sound a little less offensive."

"I am betting they can give you something now that you are awake." Rebecca reached over and pushed the button to call for help.

After a few minutes, the nurse came in to check on him. "How's it going?"

Jeremy looked up at the nurse incredulously. "How is it going? I am glad you asked. This pain is intense. I feel like I have been run over by a truck. Can I get something for that? Oh, and maybe a jail sentence for that truck driver?"

She told him that she would get him something for his pain. "I can't help you with your truck driver, though. Let me take your vitals again first." He was almost begging for some relief but choked back his need to scream from the pain. After she had finished, she told him, "I will be back directly," she assured him.

"Jeremy," Rebecca said. "There is so much I want to share with you, but you need to rest, and you need to do your best to get well."

"Rest," he said, "I cannot even breathe properly. How am I supposed to rest? And why should I try to get well?" Jeremy shot back at her, again grimacing through his pain. "What have I got to get well for? My life is a train wreck, and you know it. In fact, everyone knows it."

The nurse returned then and gave him something for his pain and alerted him. "It will not be long for your pain to subside, and it also will not be long until you doze off. Have a nice rest, and I will check in on you later."

Rebecca leaned over closer to Jeremy. "Well," she said with the softest of tones in her voice and then paused, just looking at him.

"Well, what?" he asked.

Rebecca was stroking his hand like only a mother or an older sister could and continued in the sweetest of voices. "Jeremy, I know that you can't possibly understand right now, but I promise you that if you are willing, you will be able to see two vital things that will give you a life that you could only have dreamed of. A life full of peace, purpose, happiness, and even joy. Two things that you have been missing from the day you were born."

"Yeah? You don't know what I've been through," he said. "Well, not everything anyway, and you do not know where I have been," Jeremy groaned. "You do not know what I have done. I am sorry, but I cannot believe that anything good will ever come from me staying alive."

Jeremy could not keep his eyes on Rebecca and turned his attention once again to the wall opposite her. They stayed that way for a few very long minutes. "What two things?" Jeremy asked, keeping his gaze on the wall.

"Love," she said. "Love."

Jeremy still did not move or acknowledge her words until after another long silence, and then he asked, "That is one, what is the other?"

"Love," she said again.

"That was the first thing. You said that twice. I am asking what the second thing is," he said sarcastically.

"The first love is when you finally know that you are loved, and like I said, I know you cannot possibly see it right now, but I assure you that *you are loved*. The second thing is also love, but that will come when you are able to give real love to others." She fell silent, still stroking his hand, and she smiled as she loved the fact that he was not pulling his hand away from her.

"You're right," he said. "I cannot see that at all. Either one of those two things—love or love." Jeremy looked tired and yawned with a loud sigh. "Let me ask you a question. Do you know of anyone," and he stopped mid-sentence to yawn again, "who, ah, has had to live the way I have." He stopped to yawn a third time. He stammered lightly, trying to recapture his thought but then went on. "Ah, who has had to live through what I have had to live like, who can say that they have learned, ah…love? Ah, either love." He closed his eyes and looked like he was falling asleep, and he ended his sentence with another yawn. "Wow." He yawned yet again. "I guess that stuff she gave me is doing its job." That was the last conscious statement to come out of Jeremy's mouth, and he drifted off into a deep sleep.

Rebecca watched him lose consciousness and, for a while longer, just held his hand, staring into her brother's broken spirit, praying for him. She had no idea how much time had elapsed until she told him quietly, "Jeremy?" just above a whisper, and leaning very close to his ear, she answered his question. "Yes," she said, "I do know someone who has had to live through what you have had to live like and came out the other side knowing love and who learned to love others in the same way." She kissed him on his forehead as a tear dropped from her cheek onto his and whispered again, "It's me, brother, and I am praying for you to experience the same thing that I have experienced." She just gazed on his wearied face. "Sleep well, my brother. I will always be here for you."

Rebecca decided to stay with Jeremy because she knew that Samuel had back-to-back meetings and would not be able to come and get her for several more hours anyway. She walked out to the lounging area and laid down to sleep for a while. She dozed off for a couple of hours and then got up to go and check on Jeremy. Seeing that he was still out, she went down to the cafeteria to get something to eat. When she returned, she was told that Jeremy woke up once requesting more of "that good juice" he called it and was out again. She made herself comfortable, hoping to be there if he woke a second time.

CHAPTER 11

Mattie

I T IS NOT AN EASY task when you are forced to stay up all night, saving a life, then having just enough time to shower and head off to work. For Samuel to make his 9:00 a.m., he had to pay his dues to an additional discomfort. He had to grab anything within his reach for breakfast, in the one minute he felt that he had left, before racing off to his office. He eyed a banana and a donut left over from the day before and quickly mouthed his thanksgiving. "*My nourishment?* Not exactly what I would have wanted for my breakfast," he said, complaining. "However, I am a lot better off than Jeremy." Then he paused and chided himself yet again at the thought that he was also eating better than Rebecca this morning. He grabbed his briefcase, his keys, the banana, and donut, and was off.

It was Saturday, and his 9:00 a.m. appointment was for a class that he had developed in conjunction with the court's early release program for first-time offenders. He also had a 10:00 a.m. board meeting. He arrived at his office just in time to face off with his secretary. Mattie had been with the church for a dozen years and was a formidable woman with an impeccable sensitivity for being on time, and "there is never an excuse for being late." She always accentuated the word *never*, for effect. She was standing beside her desk with her hands on her hips when he walked in. Samuel looked at the clock to see that it read three minutes after nine. He was late, but he would have been late if he had arrived at five minutes before the hour. To her, one should always show up at least ten minutes early to anything, just to be sure you had all your ducks in a row. She certainly never scolded her fearless leader if he was late, but she never missed the opportunity to let him know, in one way or another, that he just stepped over the line. And…here she was standing in front of him like an Italian mother staring a hole in him, leaving no doubt that he was in the doghouse. Now one might think that Samuel ought to have a long talk with his secretary until they heard *the whole story*. Not only was she a class act keeper of appointments, the clock, the time in general, and the calendar, but also could qualify as the most efficient and competent secretary in every other area as well. Additionally, to say that she had his back would be an understatement. So now rather than to take the time to explain his being late was due to he and Rebecca staying up all night saving Jeremy's life, he chose a safer path. He raised his hands, including the one holding his briefcase, lowered his head in a submissive manner, and said with the most loving voice, "I am so very sorry I am late, Mattie. You are so correct to keep me accountable." He did have a slight *grin on his face*, though. "Thank you so much," he went on to say. He held that pose for a few seconds to prove his heart's attitude but then raised his head and raced past her through his open office door. "But I had better get going, they will be wait—"

"I already told them that you are on your way," she interrupted. "I set up some coffee and drinks for them, along with the cookies that were left over from last night's fellowship, and you're welcome," she said with a grin on *her* face. "Now get your act together. She chided so you can give them your best. Oh," she concluded, "I already prayed for you and them." With that, she just marched around her desk, sat down, and began to type.

Mattie only worked half days on Saturday twice a month. Saturday was the only day Samuel could be sure of having most, if not all, the elders present for the board meetings. Mattie was certainly needed for that, and she never missed. She always had Monday off and worked a half day on Friday whenever she came in on Saturday. On the Saturdays when there was a board meeting, she was requested to come in at ten and not at her regular working time, eight thirty, but she did anyway. She said that she could always find work that needed to be done.

Samuel spent just a minute in his office pulling out his notes for his class titled, "My responsibility in my relationships," and then he walked out of his door, past Mattie, and down the hall to one of the classrooms. He could hear Mattie clacking away on her keyboard a mile a minute as he left. *Man, was she good*, he thought. *I wonder if she dreams typing?*

The class was only scheduled for forty-five minutes, so he was back in the office at nine fifty. He walked in to find Mattie still typing and wondered if she ever took a break.

"Oh yeah, the class went well," Samuel said a little surprised that Mattie would ask when he returned. Then he stopped at her desk and went on, "like all our teaching we do here, some get it, some do not, some do not yet, but all are receiving some or a lot of good from our efforts."

"How about that Gary?" Mattie asked, leaving Samuel a little lost for words again. She hardly ever wanted to talk, and she continued. "He showed no interest in any of our classes. He is here only because the judge said it was either take these classes or go back to jail."

Samuel, really taking her interest to heart, kind of sat or leaned gently against the side of her desk, keeping his balance with his one outstretched arm propped on her desktop and smiled. "You know, I really think he is starting to realize that he only has a chance to succeed if he takes a better look at who God really is. His reaction to many statements I made last time and today indicate that his gears are grinding in there. I am hopeful that soon he will start to ask questions that will grease up the rest of those cogs. You see—"

"You see the time gear master?" she interrupted very abruptly, "you have a ten o'clock with the board." With that, she just started typing again.

That left Samuel looking stupid with his mouth hanging wide open mid-sentence, as if he were in the middle of a video and someone pushed the Pause button, capturing him frozen in a gesture with his other hand and staring wildly at his secretary. "Ah, sure," he said, and with that, he got up, smiled at Mattie, and disappeared into his office for a deep breath and a healthy laugh. He loved Mattie. She certainly had her ways, but he really appreciated her. He stopped when he got to his desk, and he chuckled again. But then he choked back a belly laugh, thinking about what just happened. He rushed back to his door to close it, attempting to keep Mattie from hearing his louder than it should be, uncontrolled laughter. He knew, if she heard him, that she would take it personally. "Okay, get over it and collect your thoughts, big shot," he whispered to himself. He grabbed his briefcase and headed back out of his office door to find Mattie already standing by the outer door with her notepad and tablet tucked away under her folded arms. She was not smiling and had that same "you are late" look on her face again. "You ready?" was all she said as she opened the front office door and headed out not even looking back. The gesture basically said, "Follow me."

He was about to tell her that he thought the meeting may take a couple of hours but did not get the chance.

"We'll probably be a couple of hours, I'll guess," Mattie said without even looking back.

Again, Samuel felt the urge to laugh out loud at this wonderful secretary God had given him. But, of course, he did not.

They had not taken more than half a dozen steps when Mattie flatly announced, "I did hear you laugh in your office. I assume that was for me?" She just kept walking and did not even look over her shoulder for any kind of response.

Samuel could not wipe the grin off his face all the way down to the boardroom. He looked up at the clock as he walked in. *Ten on the dot*, he thought. *I guess we are late again.* But as he looked around at all the empty chairs, he saw that only Frank Collins, the church "CFO" they all called him, was the only other one on time. But then he was a lot like Mattie. Everyone else shuffled in within the next five minutes. *But then they don't work for Mattie like I do*, he thought, grinning. He had to force himself not to burst out laughing at his own thought. *They don't work for Mattie like I do, indeed.*

Pastor Samuel took his chair at the head of their huge conference table, and Mattie sat tolerantly on his right. The meeting was called to order, and after prayer, Mattie read the minutes from the previous meeting, and a motion was made to accept the minutes, then a second was made. The meeting progressed as usual and ended with a discussion about the church finances. "Are there any other issues or programs that need mentioning?"

No one said a word until one of the elders commented, "Pastor, I noticed that you have not had much to say today. Is everything all right?"

There was a long pause, and then Samuel leaned forward in his chair and began to speak. "Well," he said, "everything is not all right."

"What's up, Pastor?" another elder questioned with concern in his voice.

For the next few minutes, Samuel gave them a short history profile on Jeremy, telling them briefly about his father, the way he was raised, and reminded them how and when they found out that he was Rebecca's half brother. He did not need to dig deep trenches explaining Jeremy because every member of the board had some knowledge about him already. Samuel had brought prayer requests for him often to board and prayer meetings. They had all prayed for Jeremy on many occasions.

"But," Samuel said and paused to capture his next best words. "Let me give you the close to our heart update on our Jeremy from last night." He went on to explain all that occurred the night before. "Basically, we found him unconscious in a dark alley in the wee hours of this morning. Just in time, I might add, to save his life. Well, we think anyway." Samuel glanced over at Mattie who he thought may feel at least a pang of understanding for him showing up late, but she did not. He went on to say, "Becca is still with him at the hospital as we speak."

"What would you like the church to do for him?" one of the elders asked, and immediately, several suggestions surfaced with ideas on what could be done.

"Jeremy, certainly needs help and lots of it," Samuel told them, and then mentally, he recalled all the times that some of the members of the board made their own private offer to come alongside Jeremy for a variety of things, but Jeremy had always refused. "Not only that, but he needs everything," Samuel said, continuing his depiction of his brother-in-law. He sat up a little straighter, looking really concerned. "See if you can grasp this picture. If Jeremy had been issued a ton of second chances, he has spent them all. Maybe even gone into debt for a few more tons of second chances and spent all of those as well. His car is broken down; he has no job and absolutely no prospects. He has no money and has had his wallet stolen. His landlord has padlocked his apartment for lack of payment, so Jeremy cannot get back in. His wife, ah, ex-wife, will not, ah, cannot let him in. They have been divorced for years now, and he has a son, Randy, that he pretty much has abandoned because Jeremy thinks he does not want to see him anyway. Jeremy does not even have a high school education. He has no friends at all that I can see, and he will be out on the street, well, in a day or two with not even a change of clothing. The Salvation Army is tired of him, and the Rescue Mission will only give him a meal once a day. He has used up his welcome in both those places long ago."

"Is there anything that you think we can do?" one of the elders asked.

"Jeremy is thirty-one," Samuel went on, "and he has nothing but the clothes on his back. To make this scenario even worse, I have never seen anyone so self-destructive or so bent on such a complete lack of confidence. He is absolutely locked between his rage for what his father did to him, and the thought that his dad is correct for telling him all his life that he really is completely worthless."

"Okay, so again we are asking, what can we do for him?"

"Here's the dilemma," Samuel told the board. "We have tried to help him in so many ways in the past, but he just does not want the help. Here is the reason I brought this all to the board. I thought about this as I was driving in. I have decided to ask Jeremy to come stay with us when he gets out of the hospital. We are hoping and praying that he will accept, and I am asking that you put your thinking caps on for Jeremy. If any of you have anything you think will aid in bringing Jeremy around to wanting to walk a different path, let me know. We need your prayers."

Silence consumed the room, but Samuel felt that their minds were already bouncing ideas off the privacy of their own thoughts.

"You know, we have been here before with Jeremy, Becca and I have," Samuel continued. "We have been up all night several other times, but we never actually had to pick him up from some dark alley, to save his life before. We are very concerned not only for his spiritual life, but for his physical life as well. I honestly think he is suicidal. There is some good news though. I think Becca and I are the only ones in the world he will trust. He does not want to take our advice about much, but he knows he can always come to our house if he is hungry, and he does do that. He has been doing that periodically for a few years now. So I am asking all of you to pray with us for Jeremy, and let's see what will happen. The world around us has given up on him a long time ago," Samuel told the board. "Jeremy has given up on himself long ago as well, but we know what God can do. Pray and ask for what we, God's ambassadors, may do to see Jeremy's life redeemed. Pray for his father also."

The board meeting broke up after prayer, and Samuel headed back to his office, walking beside Mattie this time and not behind her. "Wipe that grin off your face, Pastor," Mattie said, not even looking up to see if he really was grinning. "I know what you're thinking."

"You do?" he said incredulously.

"Yes, I do, and yes, I am sorry," she confessed. "I didn't give you time to explain why you were late." With that, she stopped and turned to face him. "You are a good man, Pastor Sam, and I am so proud to call you pastor. I know I am kind of stiff sometimes, and I am asking you to give me some grace." She just stood there staring directly into his face, waiting for him to respond.

"You always have my grace, Mattie, and the truth is, I need you in your position. You are my right arm. Not to worry," he ended.

"Thanks," she said as she patted her appreciation on his arm, then she just turned and moved on to the office. When she walked in, she had no more to say. She just sat down and began to type.

Samuel spent only about ten minutes in his office, taking care of some business that needed his attention. He remembered that Rebecca was going to call him when she was ready, so he decided to walk down to the kitchen in the fellowship hall to see if he could capture a snack. He eyed some leftover lasagna from their ladies

Thursday night carry-in. He fixed two plates and grabbed a Diet Coke for Mattie and a bottle of water and headed back. When he handed Mattie her plate and the Coke, she said nonchalantly, not even looking up from her keyboard, "I brought my own lunch," and she kept on working. So he just sat it down on the side of her desk and walked into his office. He closed his door but deliberately left it hanging open just a crack. He stood there peeping out silently at Mattie. He noticed that she kind of glanced stealthily over her shoulder before grabbing the lasagna. Samuel just walked away with a Cheshire-cat grin on his face. He knew Mattie as well as she knew him. "Enjoy, Mattie," he said to himself.

It was way past the time that Mattie was allowed to leave on her Saturday, but she always stayed for a couple of extra hours after the board meeting. That is why she brought her lunch. She deserved a medal for her loyalty and sacrifice. Many often told her so and often demonstrated their appreciation. However, Mattie had nothing else that she ever wanted to do that she felt was more fulfilling. Truth is, this was Mattie's life. No one, not even Pastor Samuel Kensley, had a clue as to what was really going on inside her mind or heart. Great woman, certainly, but she was holding something very close to her chest. Pastor Sam had known that for a long time, and he had a lot of discernment, but he could not pretend to figure Mattie out. She was always faithful and always on time. He knew so little other than that about her. She never gave herself away. She had never been married that he knew about and never talked about any of her family. Pastor and others over the years did inquire, but she always brushed their questioning off. She never looked offended in any way, she just seemed to carry a stoic—"I am who I want to be, so please leave me alone" kind of attitude. Eventually, they just quit asking. There were times, and today was one of them when Pastor Sam stopped to ponder again about this person God had given him as his secretary. When she stopped in the hall on their way back to the office and she confessed to being stiff sometimes and needing of his grace, it was the very first time she ever said anything like that. *Wow*, he thought at the time but did not expound on it. Now sitting at his desk getting ready to eat his lasagna, he was pondering on his Mattie again.

"What is that, Lord, is there something I am missing? Something that she needs?" He stopped and prayed for her before he ate.

When he had finished, Samuel turned his desk chair around to face looking out of the bay window behind him. There was a beautiful garden just a few feet away, and he just enjoyed that time while he waited for Rebecca's call. He prayed for Jeremy, and he also prayed for Mattie. He had no solutions for either, but he knew that God did. His phone rang, and he saw that it was Rebecca.

"Jeremy fell asleep after something the nurse gave him," she told Samuel, but I wanted to stay a while longer. "I did get a little sleep and something to eat, but I am ready to call it a day. What is it like on your end?"

He looked up at his clock on the wall and saw that it was late afternoon. "I am just leaving the office now. I will be there in about fifteen minutes. I had a snack of a little leftover lasagna, but I could eat, how about you?"

"Yeah, me too," Rebecca told him. "How about we stop and pick up a pizza, and we will chow down quickly and then go to bed?"

"You sold me," he said, "see you in a few. Why don't you call Pat and fill her in again?"

When Samuel walked out of his office, he saw that Mattie was just putting her jacket on. "You have a nice afternoon, Mattie, and thanks for all that you do," he told her.

"You too," she said without any emotion at all, but then she looked down at the empty plate that used to hold her lasagna. "Oh, ah, yeah, thanks for lunch also." She turned and left.

He watched as Mattie opened the door to walk out of the office the same way she always did. Head held high, exhibiting an attitude of complete confidence that could not be shaken. "Is that real," he thought, "or is she hiding something very large? Is there some other major hurt going on inside this wonderful woman that she has never let anyone know about? I am praying for you, Mattie," he said to himself as he watched her close the door.

CHAPTER 12

I Got You

S AMUEL PICKED REBECCA UP FROM the hospital, and they got
their pizza and headed home. They did not talk much as they
were both so exhausted, but Samuel did tell her that he had
committed to asking Jeremy to come and live with them. They
wasted no time devouring the pizza and, after, prayed for Jeremy.
Before going to bed, though, Samuel had to go over his sermon notes
for the next day, and Rebecca needed to spend time with her children's church material. As exhausted as they were, that turned into a
real chore.

"No problem, though," she told Samuel. "How does the old
saying go, 'A pastor's wife's work is never done'?"

"No, I think it goes something like a pastor's work is never
done." They both grumbled out a sarcastic laugh.

"Well, the upside," Samuel told her, "is that it is still really early,
so we'll be able to get to bed in time to get some good sleep."

"I'm with you on that," she agreed.

When Rebecca finished her work and slowly braved the steps
to their bedroom, she found that Samuel had finished before her
and had already fallen asleep. She showered and was climbing into
bed, as she looked at the time on her phone. "Eight thirty? Are you
kidding me?" she asked herself. "Earliest I have been to bed in years."
She turned her phone off, not caring even if the president of the
United States wanted to talk with her about some national emergency. "Leave me alone," she commanded, pointing at her phone as

she laid it face down on her nightstand. She just rolled over and, in minutes, was oblivious to anything connected with consciousness.

Morning came early for them, but they had over nine hours of sleep. They were grateful for many things, but the biggest thing this morning was that Jeremy had been found and was alive.

They got to church at least an hour before everyone else, except for Mattie. She always had the bulletins set up and was ready to help the greeters when they arrived. Samuel headed for his office to do his last "look-see" over his sermon and wait for the elders to show up to pray for the services. Rebecca headed for the different rooms where they held children's church for different ages to set up the appropriate teaching material.

They had two services. One at nine thirty and one at eleven. Almost always, someone would invite Pastor Samuel and Rebecca for lunch after the last service, but this Sunday, they declined. They were in a such a hurry to get up to see Jeremy that Samuel even cut his visiting time short, asking their head elder to "finish up."

When they arrived at Jeremy's ward, they were told that he "just up and left," the nurse informed them.

Rebecca looked at Samuel with a totally shocked look on her face. "Where does he think he can go? Not only does he have nowhere to go, and with no transportation at all, but how about his ribs? Can he walk?" she asked, turning back to the nurse.

"Well, good enough, I guess," she said.

"Did anyone try to stop him?" Samuel asked with surprise written all over his face.

"I was told that he just, well, kind of left. I am not sure that anyone saw him leave," she answered.

"Well, do you know about when he did leave?" Samuel asked.

"Not sure about that either. He was gone when I came on my shift, and I came on at noon. Could have been any time from, wait." She paused to look at his chart. "Let's see, his last stats were taken at eleven, so sometime after that. His clothes were gone, so I guess he just decided to leave."

Samuel and Rebecca turned and headed to the front exit of the hospital. They stopped at the reception desk to see if anyone had noticed him walking out. The woman on duty said that she had not seen him. Then Samuel asked, "Can someone, what, he had to be on crutches or something, didn't he? I mean can someone just walk out of here injured like that without anyone seeing him?"

"There are three other exits to the hospital," she said, "but on Sunday, they are locked, so anyone wanting to enter the hospital would have to come in through here. Someone leaving could get out any one of those other doors, but as injured as you say he is, it would have been very difficult for him to push those heavy doors open. He would have needed help to do that. I came on here at noon, but the person who was on duty before me would have told me if an injured person tried to leave without proper release papers. If he is not in the hospital and did not leave by one of those other doors, he would have had to 'sneak' out right here. This is not a prison, and we are not glued to our station here, so if someone really wanted to get out without being seen, it is not that difficult. I am sorry."

After a lengthy time to come up with some solution to their disappointing quandary, they gave up, walked out, and headed for their car. "How far do you think he can get with three busted up ribs?" Samuel asked Rebecca. "And a collapsed lung," he added.

"Not far, I'll bet," she said, but suddenly stopped in her tracks. "Not far at all," she said a second time. "Actually, less than a hundred feet, I would guess, like maybe as far as one of those park benches over there just off the parking area," and she pointed, "like that one?"

Samuel followed her pointing, and sure enough, he saw Jeremy slumped over, half sitting half falling off the bench, moaning with excruciating pain.

Jeremy did not see them until they were standing right in front of him, but then he looked up with a "what the heck are you doing here" look on his face. "What!" though, was all that came out... crossly.

Samuel knew that most people would not pass the temptation to berate him with something like, "What do you mean what? Don't you know we were up all night trying to save your life?" Jeremy was about to find out, however, that there was no one more equipped to give him the full measure of grace that God had in store for him than

Pastor Samuel Kensley. Instead of any kind of condemnation, Samuel knelt on the sidewalk right in front of Jeremy, put his one hand on Jeremy's knee, and looked up at him. He gently said, "We are here because we genuinely love you. We really do, Jeremy." Samuel paused for effect and then continued, "And God loves you even more than we do."

Jeremy did not say anything for a moment, but then he looked up at Rebecca. "Did you tell him to say that?"

"No, Jeremy," Rebecca said softly as she too knelt next to Samuel. "I promise you. He came up with that on his own."

"Because that's what you told me yesterday just before I was drugged out."

"I know, Jeremy," she said. "What we want you to believe is that this is real. We do love you."

"Well, that's nice," but that was all he said for another moment as he just sat there thinking. "Really, that is nice, and I do not want you to think I do not appreciate your words, but that does not help me right now. I need to get to my apartment and get some things. I think the landlord is about to lock me out. Then I will need to try to find somewhere to hang my..." He stopped mid-sentence. "My Steelers jacket. Was it with me when they brought me in here?"

Rebecca stood up, bent over slightly, and wrapped an arm gently around his neck. "Jeremy, we were the ones who found you, and your jacket was not anywhere near you from then until now. And your landlord already did lock you out."

"Great," he said. "That's just great. What am I supposed to do now?"

"Well, we would like you to come and live with us for a while," Samuel said. "We have that spare room, and you will have your own bath. I think you will like it well enough there."

Jeremy did not say yes or no, and they waited in silence for him to answer, but he said nothing. Jeremy disliked the idea of moving in with them for a couple of reasons but did not want to tell them what those reasons were. He had no idea what else he could do, so he just sat there, desperately trying to come up with any other plan.

"Jeremy?" Rebecca questioned after several minutes of silence.

"Yeah, I'm thinking," Jeremy said kind of angrily. "I'm thinking."

"Take your time," Samuel said.

Jeremy knew that this was not only the best choice he could make but also his only choice. The reason he did not want to say yes was because he believed he would lose all his freedom, but he had no money, no job, and no place to live. "So," he said, "I guess I…" but then he fell silent again. It looked like he was going to say yes, but just then he remembered his car. "Can you drive me over to get my car?" He was thinking that he could just sleep in his car and figure out what to do later. He had done that multiple times in his life, but he did not tell them what he was planning.

"Sure," Samuel told him. "We can get you to your car, but you need to know that in addition to your Steelers jacket, you did not have your wallet on you either. That means that you do not have a driver's license."

"That's not a big deal," Jeremy confessed. "It's expired anyway."

Samuel stood up not knowing what else to say to Jeremy about coming home with them but suggested, "How about us going back into the hospital there and get you checked out properly?"

"I guess that is the smart thing to do," he agreed, so Samuel helped him up and even helped him walk.

When they took care of business in the hospital, they got Jeremy in their car and started to leave. "I'm not positive where my car is, now that we're about to go looking for it," Jeremy announced from the back seat. "I think it has to be—"

"Jeremy," Rebecca interrupted, "we do know where it is. During our search for you, we saw where you parked it."

They were driving the same route they had taken to find Bobo's before. When they turned onto the one-way street where his car had been, Samuel instantly saw that it was gone. Samuel stopped where Jeremy's car had been. "Oops," he said as he looked at Rebecca.

"Why did you stop?" Jeremy questioned. "What's wrong?"

"That"—he pointed to the empty parking space—"is where your car was the last time we were here."

"No, it wasn't," Jeremy said in disbelief.

"Yes, it was Jeremy," Rebecca said sorrowfully. "I'm afraid it really was."

"Could have been someone else's car you saw that looked like mine? Maybe?"

"Not likely, Jeremy. You have the only car on earth, I will bet, that is missing your front and rear quarter panels on the same side of the car. Could have been stolen, though, I guess," Samuel said.

Jeremy just sat back in his seat and tried to fold his arms across his chest but grimaced in pain. Then he grumbled out a complaint, "That's just insult on injury. No," he said, resigning to the facts, "that had to be where you saw my car. Probably towed. The plate was last year's too."

Samuel drove up to the end of the block and found a place to pull over, and he turned the engine off. He turned around to face Jeremy and asked him again if he would be willing to come home with them.

Jeremy knew, without being told, that if he agreed, they would have "house rules" that he would be asked to follow. He had made up his mind from his thirteenth birthday that he had had enough of anyone's house rules, but he was stuck between a very hard rock and a very tight spot. "What do I *have* to do?" he finally asked with an emotionally pained look on his face. "You know, if I do agree to come live with you?"

"What you *have* to do," Samuel told Jeremy, using the same, but comical tone of voice, "is let us love you. We will ask that you eat your meals with us. That you spend some time with us each day more than just at those meal times. That you take it easy on yourself so you can heal, and lastly, that you show us respect."

"Doesn't sound so hard," he murmured.

"No, it doesn't," Samuel said. "I do have a few things I would like to see you do, but that is on my wish list for you, and we will get into that in time. Right now, though, let's just concentrate on that small, easy to succeed in, *have-to-do* list. What do you say?"

"Not sure," he said.

Rebecca reached around to comfort him. "It's okay. Let us get you home. We will help you in every way we can to help you feel better, and well, you can start over."

"Start over," Jeremy shot back in anger. "I am sick and tired of starting over. Truth is, though, I never once in my life got started so that I could 'start over,'" he said sarcastically. "You know what you can do for me." It was not meant to be a question as he spat the words out. "You can drop me off back there at that park," he said as he pointed with his thumb over his shoulder. "I will make my own way. I have done that before...lots of times, and I can do it again."

"No, Jeremy," Rebecca pleaded with him. "Come home with us. Give it a working chance at least. I will promise you that if you do, things will start to look up quicker than you think."

Jeremy was done talking, and he reached over and opened his car door and started to climb out, but he could not maneuver his body successfully without severe pain. He stopped part way through the process with his body twisted half in and half out of the car. Then because of the pain, he tried unsuccessfully to get back into the car. He leaned his head back in agonizing pain and let out an angry frustrated scream. "I cannot even get out of the back seat of a car. Why didn't I die?"

He did not see, but Samuel was already standing beside him outside the car and was gently lifting his thin body up to alleviate some of his pain. When Jeremy finally became aware of him being there, he yelled at Samuel, and then cursed at him. "Why are you doing this? What do you care what happens to me?"

Samuel was a strong man, so this task was not as difficult as Jeremy thought it was. He ignored Jeremy's curses and quietly spoke to him. "I got you, Jeremy, I got you." He smiled a smile at Jeremy that could only mean one thing. Jeremy did not hear Samuel say it, but internally he felt its implication. "I forgive you, my brother, for yelling and even for cursing at me," was what his emotional radar was picking up. Jeremy relaxed to allow Samuel to help him, but all the while just fixed his stare on Samuel's face. It was the first time in Jeremy's life that he could remember anyone more interested in him than themself.

It was going to take time for Jeremy to believe that he was truly loved, but this day was the beginning for proof of that. He would need even more time to learn how to love others with that same selfless attitude he was receiving from his sister and Samuel. The real bottom line for Jeremy though, Samuel knew, was that until he could learn how to forgive his worst enemy, his father, he would never learn how to truly love others selflessly.

His pain subsided enough, with Samuel's help, that he could slip back into the car and bring his legs up to a sitting position again. Once again, Samuel squatted down just outside the car to be on the same eye level with Jeremy. He was silent for a long moment but then smiled at Jeremy and asked. "What do you think, big guy? You willing to give us a shot? We are not only interested in helping you, Jeremy, we are interested in you, period. We really want to get to know you." He waited again for Jeremy to speak.

Finally, Jeremy agreed. "But no rules, right?" he tossed back at Samuel.

"Jeremy, lying to you now would not help either of us. Yes, we do have some rules, as you would call them. But in truth, they are not 'rules' at all. What you will find out is that everything we will share with you are honest, simple to understand, healthy guidelines meant to bring out the best in Jeremy. Nothing that I have in mind for you will hurt. I promise."

Jeremy did not say a word, and it became a standoff between the two of them until Samuel took the bull by the horns, so to speak, and threw a cookie at him to tempt him into saying yes. "Okay, here's the deal, Jeremy. How about a fantastic home-cooked meal every night?"

"I can do that," Jeremy said, smiling at Samuel. "Yeah, I can do that, thanks."

Samuel placed a mild manly slap to Jeremy's one good shoulder, signaling his understanding of Jeremy's acceptance. They both let out a chuckle, and Samuel closed the door, walked around, and got into the car and drove off.

Samuel did not miss thinking about Mac as they turned the corner leading away from Bobo's and made a mental note to remember to call him.

When they did get home, Samuel helped Jeremy into his room. He went and got a change of clothing, telling him, "I know these are not your size, but they will do until we can launder what you have. We will get you some new clothing." Then he gently spoke into Jeremy's spirit with a wide smile on his face. "Welcome home, Jeremy. You get cleaned up, and Becca will call you for dinner."

CHAPTER 13

Real as Rain

URING THE FIRST COUPLE OF weeks that Jeremy lived in his sister's home, he discovered for the first time what *living* really meant. There were no angry words, no yelling, no name-calling, no domineering, no suspicious looks, and no unexpected expectations. It appeared that they did not even know what an argument was. The disagreements that he did experience really seemed to be exercises in coming to an agreement. This really was the very first time he had ever seen real peace demonstrated, and it looked like it was genuine, and that it was not going to end.

Not all news for Jeremy was good news though. He did find out that his car had been towed. They also discovered that the car was not safe or legal to drive anyway. Well, Jeremy already knew that. Almost every mechanical or electrical part needed repair or replacement, rendering the car nothing short of rolling junk. Samuel paid the towing bill and the fine for the out-of-date plate, and they sold the car to a salvage yard. They did not even recoup the cost of having it towed, though. Jeremy was grateful for Samuel's help but sad as well because he was now without transportation. It was just one more checkmark on Jeremy's "can't do" list that made him dependent on someone else, and that loss of freedom was what he feared the most.

Jeremy showed concern for Pat and Randy as he asked to use Rebecca's phone on occasion to call her. "That was very thoughtful of him," Rebecca told Samuel, but between the lines, she could tell that Jeremy was wanting to be out on his own as soon as possible, healed or not. Two weeks was about as long as Jeremy was interested in staying anywhere if it meant sharing life with anyone. "This isn't bad at all, though." Jeremy would confess to himself before he went to bed every night, but then he would follow that thought up with a question. "So why do I feel so trapped?" He had no answer.

Samuel had developed a pattern with Jeremy from his second night living with them. Each night after dinner, he would invite his brother-in-law into his study for a "man to man" he called it. Jeremy thought that was a bit corny, and he did not find it particularly entertaining at all...at first. He thought he would rather have escaped to his room. But then he also thought, *What the heck am I going to do in my room?* so he obliged.

At first, Jeremy could not come up with much to talk about, except, "My ribs, my lung, my doctor's appointment, what's going to happen to me next, I can't stay here forever." Samuel just allowed him to talk. He wanted Jeremy to have all the room to say whatever was on his mind. When he seemed to run out of something to say, Samuel would ask him questions like, "So what do you think about that?" or "That's interesting, anything else?" but then he would just wait for Jeremy to pick up the pace again. Of course, that often led to him asking Samuel, "Well, what do *you* think about that?" That, then, was when Samuel had more to say. But Samuel always avoided any topic that was not interesting to Jeremy. After several nights of these conversations, it unlocked Jeremy's heart and mind to feel free enough to say anything that he previously, for whatever reason, did not feel confident enough to talk about. It was only about one week into their meetings that Jeremy started looking forward to their time together.

Jeremy became bolder, talking about things that, "I just do not understand how..." or what or who or when, etc., but they were not questions. They were rhetorical statements that Samuel knew were not deserving of an answer. Samuel just listened. Jeremy, though, had two main I-don't-get-it topics that really set fire to his attitude. The first one was about his *father*. Jeremy's thought processes almost always filtered through his idealistic beliefs that basically stated, "That is what's wrong with this world." That then almost always ended with a major complaint about how he, Jeremy, ended up the way he did. That then led him into his rampage over his never-ending hatred for his father. He was never shy about unloading angrily at his father, as if his father was right there listening. Samuel always prayed silently for him whenever Jeremy dove into that understandable yet dysfunctional pool of hatred.

The second I-don't-get-it topic that Jeremy was not shy about unloading on was *religion*. That is what he unashamedly named Samuel's faith. He never attacked Samuel outright, but he made it clear that he could not understand "how seemingly smart people could believe what they believed about God."

Samuel never tried to correct Jeremy when he wanted to talk about "religion," he just listened. He did, on occasion, let Jeremy know that he was not in agreement with something he said, but overall, he just continued to show interest in whatever Jeremy wanted to say. Samuel knew that his self-controlled patience in listening to Jeremy continually, night after night, was earning him the right to teach Jeremy later.

That was Samuel's deliberate plan from the start. He wanted Jeremy to just talk himself out. For him to be allowed to voice his thoughts on every aspect of what he called *religion*. Samuel knew that rather than for him to get sucked into a debate he was not going to win at this stage, he just allowed Jeremy to ramble on. It was kind of like giving him enough rope to hang himself. So he just continued to take the blunt end of everything Jeremy wanted to throw at him on his topic of religion.

One night, as they readied themselves for bed, Samuel told Rebecca, "I have not tried to upset Jeremy's apple cart, not even once so far. That was on purpose, just to give him all the space he needed to commit himself to whatever he thinks a great picture of reality is. That, honestly, is not much different than the way many people operate their lives, though. They just 'think' themselves into many truths without trying to discover what the 'real' truth might possibly be. Anyway, tomorrow night is the night I am going to take over. It is going to be Jeremy's turn to listen."

"What if he doesn't want to listen and just wants to take it back over from you?" she asked.

Samuel just brought his "you have got to be kidding me" glare to bear on her without saying a word.

"Oh, ah, yeah, sorry," she said. "Got it."

So that next night, when they finished dinner and headed to Samuel's study, Jeremy was the first to speak. "I was listening to the news earlier," he began, "and you know what really gets me." He went on for a couple of minutes complaining until Samuel slowly raised his right hand and left it frozen in the air while staring directly at Jeremy. He did not say a word.

Jeremy stopped talking. "What?"

With a stern look on his face, Samuel asked, "Do you remember the day we picked you up a couple of weeks ago from the hospital?"

"Yeah, I remember," he agreed.

"Good because I have a question about that day for you, Jeremy," Samuel stated.

Jeremy thought that maybe a lecture was on its way. "Oh, boy," he said. "What did I do?"

"No," Samuel quietly assured him, "no, I just want you to answer this question for me."

"Okay, what is it?" Jeremy asked a bit put out.

"Since that time, just after you woke up in the hospital, and Rebecca told you how much you were really loved, and then me the next day when I told you he same thing—"

"Yeah," he interrupted Samuel, "I told you that I remember."

"Okay, well, here is the question. Can you say with certainty that we have, since that time, demonstrated what you could identify as real love for you?"

Jeremy looked surprised, almost shocked, but smiled at Samuel. "Oh...well, yeah, no doubt. No doubt whatsoever. Sure, you have. Why did you think you needed to ask?"

Samuel, rather quickly, pulled his wheeled office chair up close to Jeremy as he "took over" the conversation. "Because my young, hopefully 'ready to start over' brother-in-law, who said that you were sick and tired of starting over, and the truth is, you said also that you never once in your life got started in the first place so that you could start over." He took a deep breath from his exaggerated elongated sentence but did not give Jeremy a chance to comment before he continued. "You need to learn some *things* you have never learned so that you can start over for the first time in your life, and I can help you do that...Interested?"

Thunderstruck is a great word to describe Jeremy's entire body language. From his face to his knees, he looked like someone just stole his Thanksgiving prize turkey but replaced it with a whole refrigerator full of fun things to eat.

Jeremy literally could not respond. "So," Samuel continued, "if you can clearly see our love for you, it should be easier for you to accept the *things* I want to...*need to* teach you that are *real* truth and not just opinion. Especially on what you call religion."

Jeremy sat still gawking at Samuel for several seconds seemingly shell-shocked. "Okay," he finally said sheepishly.

"Jeremy, I want to teach you those *things*, but to do that, you really *need* to listen."

"Okay," Jeremy said again looking like he might be just a little frightened, "I get it. I will listen."

"But, Jeremy, you first need to learn *how* to listen."

At that, Jeremy pulled his head back slightly with a "huh" look on his face and frowned.

"Let me encourage you with this," Samuel told him. "You are no different than any of the rest of us, but for you to succeed at anything, you need to first learn how to listen with your heart, not only your ears." Samuel paused briefly, but then in a very compassionate, softened voice, he continued. "Jeremy, you never have had anyone who loved you enough or who themselves knew enough to teach you so many *things*. You were left to your own devices, and you floundered. I have listened to you for almost two weeks every night now, and I have learned *from you* who the real Jeremy is. I have also learned *from you* what you really believe. Jeremy, it is your turn to not just hear my words but allow your heart to hear truth in my words. Learning to hear with your heart fundamentally means that you get deathly serious about what your ears pick up so that your core beliefs become accurate and are based on proven truths and not opinion. Your core beliefs will place you and keep you on your chosen life's path. Basically, your core beliefs will end up controlling almost every decision you make on just about everything in your life."

"Wow!" Jeremy mouthed quietly. "Wow!" he said a second time.

"I would like to bring truths to you that you have not yet considered to be truth. Some truths that you have distorted, believing instead what only makes sense to you. Also, just to add another layer to this quest, it will require you to unlearn many *things* that to date you have bought into that honestly are flat-out wrong, and here is a real kicker. I am asking that you accept these truths I am going to teach, first giving them a chance to make a difference in your life before you kick them out because *it just doesn't make sense.*"

Jeremy looked at Samuel with a renewed sense of awe and respect. "You know, you and Rebecca *have* shown me love I have never known," he conceded, "and I think it is as real as rain. I cannot think of any other reason why you would take me in like this. I think that I would like to learn, and I will do my best to listen."

"You have a good heart there, Jeremy," Samuel encouraged him, "and thanks for listening so far."

"So where or how am I supposed to start, I mean listen or learn?"

"The Bible, Jeremy, is a proven truthful source where you can gain absolute truth, and it is completely reliable." Samuel snickered a little as he pulled his chair back. "You know, Jeremy, reading and believing what is written in the Bible might just be how, even smart people, can believe what they believe about God."

Jeremy laughed at himself. "Cute. I kind of thought that that might come back to haunt me."

"Sorry, I just could not resist, but honestly, the Bible contains answers to questions, help in times of need, and is an overall light to guide our path through life. It will alter the way you evaluate everything you do hear with your heart from the moment you do believe what is written there. Jeremy, so far in your life, you have been evaluating almost everything based solely on what makes sense to you at the time. In your defense, though, you did not have anyone to help guide you any other way." Samuel fell silent to give Jeremy a moment to think about what he just said, and then… "But…now you do."

"Okay," Jeremy said out loud. "So…what, I start reading the Bible, and then what, I will be different?"

Samuel did not answer, nor did he take his eyes off Jeremy. Silence filled that small office for way too long, and Jeremy could not take it. "What?" he asked, but Samuel kept quiet. Then a smile creased Jeremy's face as he raised his hands a little frustrated and asked a second time, "What?" but the silence got even louder. "Samuel, please," Jeremy besought him. "Talk to me," yet Samuel maintained his silence. "Okay," Jeremy said, giving up, "what am I missing?"

Samuel gently leaned forward in his chair and, ever so softly, told him, "Nothing can begin in regards to learning to have faith in the Bible until you believe that Jesus also is as real as rain. That Jesus is God's only perfect Son, and that he did die in your place so that you can have your sins forgiven. Until you really believe that, the Bible will offer you the same silence that I deliberately demonstrated a few minutes ago. What you are missing, Jeremy, is Jesus."

"Jesus," Jeremy said out loud. "Yeah." He too leaned forward in his chair with his head down. "I have heard all that before, you know." He looked up at Samuel. We had to sit through chapel at the Rescue Mission before they would let us eat. Mom told me that she believed in Jesus before she died, but I never gave that much credibility because of the way she died. She did say that she believed, though. I noticed that in these last couple of years, it seems that Pat, and her mother too, started to believe in Jesus." Jeremy sat thinking for a few minutes and then… "You know, there was this preacher at the mission, and I do not remember what he said exactly, but it really made me stop and think about Jesus. Nothing more ever came of that, but I never forgot how it made me feel. I guess that I—"

"Jeremy, God never made it difficult," Samuel interrupted. "Let me ask you a few questions, and you need to answer them honestly. Do not tell me what you think I want to hear, just answer them truthfully, for your sake. Can you do that?"

"Sure, I can," he told Samuel as he shoved both his arms up gesturing a genuine surrender to the request.

"I know that you know you have done some things wrong in your life, but there is a distinct difference between calling your wrongdoings errors and calling them what they really are…'sins.' Can you call your wrongdoings 'sins' and just to amplify the real truth about it all, can you confess that your sins are really against God?"

"Well, yeah, sure I can. No question about that. It would take a fool to say that they have never sinned."

"But don't you know," Samuel went on, "that there are some who view their sins as just mistakes or human error or poor judgment, and that they are simply normal, etc. But to your credit, what you just confessed tells me that you do believe in God. So take a moment to think about this. Along with confessing that you have sinned against God, can you honestly confess that you, from your heart, believe that Jesus is God's Son? That he died in your place to pay for your punishment due you because of your sins, and that God raised him from the dead?"

"You know, that just reminded me," Jeremy said with excitement. "That is almost exactly what that preacher at the mission asked, what, maybe a couple of years ago. I left that half hour chapel believing all that, but nothing ever happened."

"You did not follow it up, Jeremy, but you can now. So would you like to?"

"Wow," Jeremy said with awe all over his expressions. He sat thinking again, but finally he said, "Sure, I guess so. I mean what do I do to follow it up?"

Samuel's solemn gaze said it all, but he did quietly announce, "You just did, Jeremy. You just did." Samuel led him in a prayer where he confessed Jesus as his Savior, asking God to forgive him all his sins. Samuel went on to explain what just had happened to him in detail. "And I have a gift for you, Jeremy." With that, he opened his desk drawer and pulled out a new Bible. "This is yours, and I would like to start teaching you," he paused with a slight smile on his face, "if you are willing to listen from your heart."

Jeremy smiled back at Samuel. "You bet, and again, I thank you for being patient with me."

Samuel was thrilled that Jeremy had accepted Jesus as his Savior, but he knew that Jeremy still was going to have to face the heart-wrenching dilemma of learning to forgive his father. He knew that that was going to be seemingly impossible for Jeremy to grasp, but he also knew that he would not move forward very far until he could do that. Samuel kept that thought to himself, though, for the time being.

"Let's go into the living room," Samuel said, ending their discussion, "we have a pretty big surprise for you."

When Samuel and Jeremy entered the living room, they found Rebecca already camped out there. "What's up?" Jeremy asked.

"Well, like I said, we have a great surprise for you."

"Okay, what is it?"

"There is a man in our church," Samuel told him, "who owns a large factory, and he is always in demand for good workers. He said that he would give you a chance if you are willing to work hard. It is a good job, full-time with insurance. Pays pretty good, and I think you would fit in nicely there."

Jeremy could not contain himself. "That *is* a great surprise, but it cannot be that simple. I have been looking for a full-time job like that all my life, and now one just jumps up and parks itself right here in my lap?"

"He has a requirement, though. If you would be willing to tackle that one thing, he is willing to give you a try. It is a requirement that you have a high school diploma. I told him that you did not graduate, but he is willing to wave that requirement if you sign up for GED classes."

"That leaves me out then," Jeremy said, "I did not only drop out of high school, but I literally failed every course I took up to that time. I can read. I can add and subtract a few numbers, but that is just about it. I am serious. That is all I know. I feel like I am just stupid or something."

"You are not stupid," Rebecca encouraged, "nor are you a loser. That is just a lie you have been led to believe. We have already checked into everything. All you need to do is want to try. We will help you with your studies, and I know you can do it. All you need to do is get up every morning, go to work, and do your best for just that one day."

"Okay," Jeremy agreed, "when am I supposed to start?"

"That will depend on your doctor's appointment on Friday," Samuel told him. "My friend at the factory knows about your injury, and he told me that you could start out on light duty work."

Jeremy smiled and commented, "It looks like I have just been given a couple of gifts tonight."

"Okay, what was the second gift you were given tonight?" Rebecca asked, hoping, as she eyed the new Bible sitting in Jeremy's lap.

"You tell her," Samuel encouraged him. "I know she will love to hear it from you."

"I am not sure I can tell it correctly, but I prayed and asked to be saved."

Rebecca looked like she was going to burst with excitement. "Really, I mean, really you confessed, like all of us, that you are a sinner, believing that Jesus died on the cross for you? Jeremy, you honestly believe?"

"I did, I mean, I do, but I am not sure what all that means yet. I guess Samuel will dial me into more later." He looked at Samuel and asked, "Do I have to start calling you pastor?"

"No, Jeremy, not at all. You can call me Samuel or Sam, for that matter, if you wish, but it has been a long day." So, with that, Samuel stood and announced, "It is way past my bedtime. We can talk about all this tomorrow."

Jeremy agreed and was off to bed himself, feeling better than he ever had.

"All's well that ends well," Rebecca told Samuel after they had gone up to their room.

"He still has a very difficult bridge to cross, though," Samuel said. "He is not going to understand how, let alone why he should ever forgive your father. But until he does, he will not experience any lasting peace."

"This has been a wonderful day, though," she told her husband. "Just think about what has happened here tonight!"

Samuel gave up his negative thought and confessed, "You are right, this has been a great and beautiful day today, for us, but mostly for Jeremy," he agreed as they turned out the lights.

CHAPTER 14

Four in the Morning?

JEREMY KEPT SAMUEL ON HIS toes daily with questions and a multitude of what-ifs about Christianity. He had stopped calling Samuel's faith "religion" and he did "try," he said, to listen with his heart to all that Samuel was teaching him about the Bible. To Rebecca, it appeared that Jeremy wanted to learn what it meant to be a Christian. Samuel, however, maintained a slightly different attitude about him. When Rebecca questioned him on that, he told her, "I am sure that Jeremy meant it from his heart when he asked Jesus to be his Savior, but he absolutely refuses to even entertain any thought of forgiving his father. That has left him straddling a fence, where on one side is him accepting forgiveness from God for all he had done, and the other side is him not forgiving anything his father had done to him. He will never be able to grasp the full grace of God that way. He will not be completely free until he is able to get off that fence, and Jeremy, at this stage, will not be moved. As much as I understand and have compassion for him, he just cannot let go of the hurt."

Samuel and Rebecca both were, on occasion, as busy as maybe young parents might be...back and forth to Jeremy's work for him and getting him enrolled in his G.E.D. classes. Not to mention having an extra body in the house to care for that they were not used to. "Just keep pedaling," he told Rebecca. "That's the ticket." So they did. They went to bed some nights, though, whiney through their weariness.

During one of those late-to-bed grumblings, Samuel thought of Mac. "Hey, Becca, you remember Mac? That bigger-than-life, mean-looking man who owns Bobo's?"

"How could I forget?" she piped. "I'm not sure I have ever seen a man that large!"

"I told him, well, he asked me, to call him when we were set up with Jeremy. I feel bad that I have not contacted him yet, but I think I will give him a call tomorrow. It is Saturday, and we do not have anything on the calendar this week, do we?"

"That is a really good idea," she said, "and no, we have nothing on the calendar. Love to find out what he is up to, but more importantly, what makes him tick. Remember the first time we met 'Mr. I am not sure if I am going to shoot you or not' waving that gun around?"

"Yeah, I do," he told her but then sat in silence for a moment, recalling the dark alley where Mac just appeared like a phantom out of nowhere. How he shoved a piece of paper into his hand, quietly saying in what seemed to be a way out of character, almost begging voice, "When this all blows over, give me a call."

So, the next day, Samuel figured it was time to do that. He waited until after noon because he knew that Mac would have worked late the night before and wanted to give him a lengthy time to sleep in. "Don't say anything to Jeremy that we spoke to Mac the night we found him face down behind Bobo's," he instructed. "Or that we even know who Mac is for that matter. I know that Mac knows him or at least knows about him. It is a possibility also that Jeremy knows something about Mac, though it may not be enough to make any difference. Either way, Jeremy has a lot to think about at this stage, and I do not want to throw another loaf of bread onto his plate for him chew on."

"Wow, thanks for saying something," she told him. "I had not thought about that, but you are right. I will not even bring up Mac's name."

When Samuel called, he immediately recognized Mac's harsh gruff voice. "Mac!" he answered his phone in his imposing voice. "Who's this, and what do you want?"

"Mac, this is Pastor Samuel. Me and my wife Rebecca met you the night we found Jeremy, Rebecca's brother? Just thought I would give you a call and maybe set a time so I could come and visit with you. What do you think?"

There was an extended pause from Mac's side of the conversation and then, "Pastor Sam, yeah, I remember you. You were sneaking around my front door in the middle of the night." Again, Samuel was experiencing that very mean aggressive attitude. "What do you want?" Mac commanded.

"Well," Samuel began again, "you told me to give you a call when we had everything worked out with Jeremy, so I was calling to see if—"

"Yeah," Mac interrupted, "well, changed my mind," and hung up.

Samuel was left holding the disconnected line with a half surprised, half wondering sense of "what?" on his heart. He grabbed his jacket and headed for the front door like a man on a mission.

"Where are you going?" Rebecca asked.

"Mac," he half shouted. "Mac needs me. He did not ask, and he does not know it, but he needs me, and I am going."

"Good luck," she said to Samuel's back side as he negotiated the front door like an Olympic speed skater.

Mac was busy, seemingly content wiping off his bar when Samuel walked into Bobo's. Mac froze instantly at seeing him. He did not appear to be angry, but he did have an "are you kidding me" look on his face. "Okay," Mac finally said, showing off his 'I am a really big man, you know, and I don't appreciate your busting in here' attitude oozing from his demeanor. "You found the door coming in, so I know you can find it going out." He just stared at Samuel, looking like he expected him to leave on the spot, but when Samuel did not respond, Mac continued. "I see you cannot take *no* for an answer either." He walked slowly around the far side of the bar. He looked like he was saying, *You are not hearing me. I do not want you here*, without saying it. Mac had a seriously frightening look on his face that Samuel remembered seeing the first time they met. He honestly was not sure what Mac's next intention was. Mac stopped just a few feet from Samuel, looking down at him like a gladiator ready to strike. Samuel did not say a word, but waited for Mac to make the next move. He felt the need to seriously fear him, but something in the way Mac was steadying himself left Samuel believing that he could be reasoned with "maybe," he thought. Again, when Samuel did not respond to what he later labeled "the fear factor," Mac finally spoke. "Look, Pastor Sam," he said and then paused like he was thinking on what to say next. "Look," he said again, "I know I asked you to call me, but I honestly don't know why I did that." He turned slightly toward the bar and furiously threw his cleaning rag down hard on the bar. So hard, in fact, that it almost bounced back up. "Look," he yelled, turning back to face Samuel, "I do not need any of your God talk right now, and I know that is why you are here. I have changed my mind about talking to anyone, about anything, so you can leave. I am just fine the way I am." Again, he just gazed into Samuel's face with that same angry look, waiting impatiently to see if Samuel was going to obey. At that, Samuel was believing that either his life was going to end or, at a minimum, was going to need medical assistance if he did not leave…very soon. He held his hands up in the same way he did the first time they met. Samuel knew something very serious was plaguing this man, and he wanted to help. He presumed that whatever it was had been a giant stabbing to this big man's heart for a very long time. So with kindness written all over his actions, he investigated Mac's face, and he neither moved toward or away from the front door. Then, after what must have seemed like a prolonged period of stalling, he ever so gently said, "No problem, Mac." He intended for it to come out with the utmost of compassion and respect. "No problem at all," he told him again. "I would like to talk with you. Not for my sake but for yours. Let me give you my card, so then you can call me anytime you want if you change your mind. I will come, Mac, and I will listen." Samuel slowly reached into his pocket, leaving one hand in the air and held out his card, waiting for Mac to take it. Looking straight into Mac's face, he started to move slowly closer to this angry mountain of a man, not away from him, and said again, "Mac, I will come, and I will listen."

"Okay," Mac said quietly and slowly, "I got it," but now his voice had changed. Samuel remembered hearing that same gentle voice when Mac shoved his phone number into his hand that first night a month before. Mac just stood there, seemingly speechless, seeing clearly that he did not frighten this pastor standing in front of him into leaving. Samuel saw, again, that this apparent beast of a man had two distinctive sides to him.

Both men just faced off with each other for a long moment, and Samuel could not help thinking about a game show he remembered from mega-years before, and at that, he thought, *Would the real Mac please stand up?* He was so encouraged by the fact that this larger-than-any-man-should-be with an apparent attitude larger-than-any-man-should-possess would under any conditions call him "Pastor Sam."

Finally, the ice seemed to have been broken because this gladiator of a man reached out and took Samuel's card. He looked at it very briefly, but then Mac did something that surprised Samuel almost speechless. He reached out gently and grabbed Samuel's hand to shake it like he had been his friend for ages. When Samuel reciprocated the handshake, Mac cupped his second hand over Samuel's, signaling at least to Samuel's interpretation that Mac was in desperate need of a brother-type friendship. "Pastor Sam…wow," Mac said and even smiled at him.

Mac used the word "wow," but Samuel heard the word "wow!"

Mac motioned for Samuel to sit at one of the tables. "Can I get you something to drink, ah, water or a soda, I mean."

"No, Mac, but thanks." Mac sat down across from him.

Mac just sat there fidgeting with Samuel's card, unable to say anything, and Samuel just waited patiently until Mac opened up. "Yeah, I, ah, I will call you, and, ah, we'll talk."

"What about if we talk some now?" Samuel encouraged and waited again.

"Oh well, ah, yeah. Sure, I guess," Mac said, not even looking up, and it was apparent that he was very uncomfortable.

Again, Samuel had to choke back a smile at the sight of these two opposite personality sides Mac could so convincingly demonstrate at will.

Finally, "I honestly don't know where, or even how to start," Mac stumbled out a few words. "Also," Mac continued, "I'm open for business right now, and this really isn't a good time." There was no one in the bar, so Samuel assumed that Mac was just stalling. But then Mac continued, "And I am not just trying to get rid of you. I just know that people could start coming in any time now. I do not have an office or back room. This is it."

"Again, no problem, Mac," Samuel agreed, "and I do believe you. What would be a good time?"

"I don't have a good time," he told Samuel. "I live a nightlife because of my bar, so a good time for me is a time you don't want to do, I promise you," he said sarcastically.

"Try me," Samuel told him.

Mac just gawked at Samuel but not with his angry face. He finally said again sarcastically, "How does four in the morning sound?" and he chuckled, shaking his head. "See, I told you that you wouldn't want to do that, so what—"

"What day is best for you?" Samuel interrupted.

"Are you kidding me? You mean that you would drive down here at four in the morning to meet with me?"

"Why not? It was four in the morning the last time I was here," and he chuckled, "but yes, I will," Samuel told him with emphasis. "Just tell me which day."

"I do believe you, Pastor Sam," he told him. "But the truth is, I would not let you do that. Like I told you before, this is one of the worst neighborhoods in the city to be anywhere outside after dark, let alone at four in the morning. You might be okay occasionally, well, like you were before, but sooner than later, it will catch you. No, we will figure out other times."

Other times! Samuel thought to himself. Those words told Samuel that once Mac decided to trust him, he was intending to make Samuel his friend. "Okay, Mac, but let's not let this get cold. I will come, even if it is four in the morning. Are there any nights that you can take off like the night we first met?'"

"Yeah, occasionally, but I never know in advance when those nights are going to come knocking on my door. The bar closes on Sundays. I cannot stay open in this state on Sunday, but you have church on Sunday, right?" Then before Samuel could ask, and Mac knew he was going to, he sat up straight in his chair and announced,

"No, I'm not going to start coming to church," but he did smile at Samuel.

"Okay, how does Sunday afternoon work for you?" he asked Mac.

"Don't you have other, ah, church business to take care of then?" he questioned.

"No, I really want to meet with you. How does two in the afternoon on Sundays sound?" Samuel did not pass up the opportunity to make it plural. "We can start tomorrow if that will work for you?"

"Yeah, I guess that's okay," Mac said. But then he hung his head and continued. "I have never shared with anyone except my mom what I need to talk about. Not sure even now if I will be able to with you when you come."

Samuel leaned closer to Mac. "I know it will be difficult at first, but please trust me. Everything you tell me will be completely confidential. Also, I know from many years of experience that only positive things, and good results will come from this no matter what it is that you need to talk about."

Then Mac changed the topic to help bring a conclusion to this first awkward visit. "So how is your Jeremy doing anyway?"

"Pretty good so far," Samuel said. "We got him to the hospital that night on time. Rebecca and I are putting him up at our place. He has a decent job for the first time in his life, and I think he is trying to get his life together. But, like the rest of us, he is a work in progress."

Mac rolled his eyes and breathed an identifying sigh. "Boy, you got that right. Me too! You are a good man, Pastor Sam," Mac acknowledged.

"You know," Samuel said with the seriousness of a judge who was about to acquit a falsely accused man, "I'll bet you are too."

"Don't push it, Pastor Sam. Remember I have a reputation to keep up," but he said that this time with a huge grin on his face.

Samuel held up both his hands in a mock surrender, but he added, "Mac, like I said, you look like a good and honest man yourself, but I know that there is something very hurtful going on inside you, and I know that you will never find any peace until you let it out. I will be praying for you and our meeting at two tomorrow."

They stood up and shook hands, and as Samuel moved to slip out of Bobo's front door, a couple of very unsavory people were walking in. Samuel turned to Mac and waved a friendly goodbye.

"AND DON'T COME BACK AGAIN!" Mac yelled with that recognizable hurtful mean-spirited voice at Samuel. When Mac saw the two men who were entering his bar turn their heads to see what Samuel was going to do with that, he grinned from ear to ear at Samuel behind their backs and waved his goodbye to Samuel. Silently, though, he mouthed the words, "Don't tell anyone."

Samuel had to control his funny bone, keeping his laughter to himself. He wanted to be faithful to Mac. He quietly turned and walked out. On his way home, he prayed for Mac and gave thanks to God for this meeting with him.

"Tell me, Sam, I can't wait!" Rebecca begged Samuel that night.

"Patience, my dear Rebecca," he told her. "I have never met anyone like Mac, ever. He possesses the most unique ability to perfectly project either one of two distinct and opposite personalities at will. He can turn each one of them on or off instantly. He can show you this monster of a man who seemingly could snuff out your life and not have the slightest regret. On the other hand, he can be as gentle as a kindergarten teacher leading a boy who got lost in the hallway to the bathroom."

"Do you think he is schizophrenic? I mean do we need to look out for Mac?" Rebecca questioned.

"No," Samuel said instantly. "Absolutely not. The only thing wrong with Mac is that he is very guarded, very protective, and it is the sweet side of him that is the real Mac, I am sure of it. That hard core 'don't cross this line for fear of your life' Mac is an act. A very good act, but I am sure I will find out what that is all about during our upcoming visits, starting tomorrow afternoon, by the way."

"Okay, so he agreed to open up," she said. "That is great. But why the charade? Why the mean guy attitude? Does it have something to do with where he lives?"

Samuel fell quiet, thinking, and he pulled his feet up onto the bed as he leaned back against the headboard. "Yeah, I guess that must be part of it, but I suspect that there is a lot more to that side of his life than we know at this time. Mac is hiding something. Something very personal, very hurtful, but let me share some of what I discerned today, and you will see why I know that it is his gentle side that is the real Mac. And how I know that the 'kill you with no regrets' Mac is only an act. Mac is as sane as you and I," he told Rebecca.

Samuel did not share any in-depth details from his first visit with Mac, but he did relate how this apparently belligerent mean man ended up so responsive. He told her how Mac shook his hand, and how that "gave me the feeling that he was looking for someone to become a friend as close as a brother. Someone who he could really trust. I think that is why he called me his Pastor Sam." Samuel ended his recap for Rebecca by sharing how Mac yelled at him to never come back and how he smiled from ear to ear and mouthed silently behind their backs, "Don't tell anyone." And they both laughed.

"I still would like to know what that tough guy act is all about though," she told Samuel. "He is very intimidating, and would be even if he was only a four-foot midget, but since he is, what…six foot seventy something? Yeah, I would love to hear the rest of his story."

CHAPTER 15

Moving On?

S AMUEL HAD MAYBE AN HOUR after they got home from church
to ready himself for his two o'clock with Mac. He let Rebecca
and Jeremy eat lunch without him, as he secluded himself in
his study, closing the door indicating he wanted no interruptions.
He allowed his thinking to zero in on his two new, "Ah, disciples?"
he asked himself out loud. "Can I even call them disciples yet?" He
knew that Jeremy, although he had prayed to receive God's free eternal gift, Jesus, was still hiding behind a huge wall that needed to be
broken. He knew that it was only a matter of time until a spiritual
war for Jeremy's heart would force him to *choose*. He would have to
choose between being healed by forgiving his father or *choose* to slip
back into his "I am worthless, and I hate everyone" lifestyle. It is easy
to understand why it is so difficult for anyone to forgive those who
hurt them so seriously, but…it still comes down to choosing. "We
just get hung up on remembering only what *they* did to *me* and not
emphasizing the importance of what *I* did to *you,* God," he said out
loud to the walls of his office. "God still loves you, Jeremy," he kept
speaking softly, "and your sins against God are forgiven, but until
you really forgive your father, you will struggle much. Very much,
and choosing that path could end up dragging you deeper into that
pit you are trying to get out of."

"And what about my new friend Mac?" he continued thinking
out loud. Samuel was so encouraged about how this guarded street
warrior let him penetrate his armor the way that he did. He gave
glory to God for that because he knew that it was a simple matter of

being in the right place at the right time. He could not wait to see what was going to unfold with this huge man.

Samuel looked at his clock and saw that it was about time to leave. He went out and found Rebecca and asked that she pray with him for Mac and for their first meeting. When they had finished, he headed for the door and was off.

Samuel did his now familiar zigzag around the Sixth Street Park on the last leg of his journey to his first scheduled meeting with Mac. As he passed the park, he once again noticed people who chose, or for any number of reasons were forced, to live their lives this way. He made a mental note to bring to the church board an idea that just at that moment struck him like a lightning bolt. "That's good stuff, that," he said out loud. "An outreach to this Sixth Street Park population."

He turned the last corner that led to Bobo's and could find no place to park on either side of the street. So he drove unsteadily around back, down that incredibly unwelcoming alley. He parked on the same concrete slab where he found Jeremy passed out a few weeks before. He did not know what else to do, so he banged on the back door of Bobo's. After a short time, he heard a window open on the second floor of the building attached to the bar, and Mac stuck his head out and told Samuel, "I'll be right down."

Mac led him through the bar and out the front door. He locked it and turned toward a second door several feet down and to the right.

"This is my apartment," Mac announced. "I constructed my door this way on purpose. I do not want any surprises when I am at home. This thing will hold off a tank." Once in, they climbed a flight of stairs and then through another steel security door. "Come on in," he told Samuel, "and make yourself at home. I like coffee, want some?"

"Sounds good, just black for me, thanks." Samuel sat down.

While he waited, Samuel began to look around the room. Then he inadvertently noticed something that looked like it was way out of place. It was like finding a used horseshoe in the middle of your small fenced-in backyard. "What the blazes?" He got up to investigate. As he got closer, he saw a diamond engagement ring that looked like it was forced over a tiny football that was attached to an outstretched arm on a football trophy. "I thought that's what I was seeing," he mouthed silently to himself. "Wonder what that's all about?" But then he noticed a large plaque that read "State Champions 2006." Then he noticed, right next to the plaque, that there was a photo of Mac in his high school football uniform holding the trophy. Right next to the photo was the trophy itself with the ring on it. Samuel did not want to pick it up because of all the dust that had accumulated on it. He felt leery about disturbing it, so he bent over and read the inscription. "Larry Macpherson, Most Valuable Player, Class A Football State Champions 2006." Samuel was in awe of what he had discovered. "Wow, MVP," he said under his breath but then straightened up and said again out loud, "MVP? Wouldn't that mean…?"

"Ah, you found one of my secrets," Mac announced as he returned with their coffee. "Boy was that a long time ago. Now you might be wondering if our team went to State and won, and that if I was awarded MVP, wouldn't I have been given a scholarship to any college I wanted to attend? Well, I was," Mac continued without waiting for Samuel to answer. "I got offers from universities all over the country." They sat down and Mac took a sip of his coffee. "So you may also be wondering, why didn't I accept? Or did I accept? Well, simply put," again without waiting for a response, "it is like anything else. If there is an immovable wall that you cannot climb over or go around, sooner or later, you just give up and go another way."

"So," Samuel asked, "just out of curiosity, what was the immovable wall that prevented you from attending university?"

"Okay, well to start with, just the pressures of surviving here"—Mac gestured, waving his arms around indicating the area of the city he lived in—"took the front row seat for my decision. Dad died just a year before, leaving Mom, me, and my older brother Buck to run the bar, and he did not handle that well at all. He needed me to give him everything I had to help. Also, no one in our family had ever gone to college, so they did not understand why I should either. Then there was the money factor. Even though the tuition and books would have been paid for, there were still some costs where funds were just not available. But the real hurdle was that when I graduated from high school, everyone figured that my football was over. It was only an extracurricular activity at best anyway, they believed, so 'just give it up, and go to work' was the bottom line. They could not wait, especially my brother, for me to get old enough to take over the bar from him. So as they say, that was that."

"Mac, I am so sorry about what happened to you," Samuel sympathized. "How are you doing with all that now?"

"Oh, good, very good," he told Samuel. "I do think about it sometimes. I mean how it would have all turned out if I had gone to college, but in the end, when all is said and done, I am good, I really am."

"You know, you sound like you could have done well in college. You appear to have a lot more on the ball than most people who know you might believe," Samuel mused.

"Oh, I do," Mac agreed. "And I have an associate degree in business to prove it."

Samuel's eyebrows instantly raised in a "kudos" kind of way to affirm Mac. "That is fantastic. How did you accomplish that, ah, without going to college?"

"Well, just after Mom died, let me see, that was a little over ten years ago, I found myself all alone with only the bar to keep me company, so I started taking classes on line. Well, don't you know, about three years later, I was handed a degree. It has helped me out immensely even here in this miniscule bar business."

"And your brother? Obviously, you did take over the bar from him, and at an early age, I suspect. What happened to your brother?"

"My brother? Wow! My brother Buck. Well, he was about four years older, and he was a hothead. He hated the bar and made no bones about it. He was a drinker too, and he did not take any guff from anyone. He would push his boundaries to the limit. One night, in a fit of anger over something very trivial with one of the customers, he invited the man out back to settle the score, and the guy shot him. Well, we think it was that guy who shot him. Anyway, that man just disappeared, and Buck died. Whoever it was never saw justice, that I know of. There is a lot more to that story, but maybe some other time."

"All right Mac," Samuel said, looking a bit confused, "you have proven to me that you can do anything you set your mind on to do. MVP, State champion, and college. You are young yet, and you are alone," Samuel hesitated to ask. "You are alone, I am guessing from the things you tell me. I mean are you married? Or do you have a permanent, ah—"

"Girlfriend," Mac finished his sentence. "No, not married, and no one special at all. It is just me."

"Okay, well, you told me that you are not in love with this bar or this neighborhood, so why have you chosen to stay here all these years in this bar? In this, ah, this, well, ah this—"

"DIVE?" Mac shouted the conclusion to Samuel's statement. Then he smiled that huge ear to ear grin again. "Yeah, it is a dive, you can say it. But..." Then Mac's mood got serious, and he looked away and down. "Yeah," he continued without looking up. "There is a reason. I guess there are a few reasons why I have stayed, but really, only one good reason."

Mac's demeanor instantly changed, and Samuel knew that he had inadvertently opened a deep wound. "Mac, I came here to give you my ear, but if you are not ready, don't worry, I will wait."

"No, it is okay. This is why I wanted to talk to someone." Mac just stared at the carpet as he was thinking on how to proceed. "Well, let me see," he began, and it looked like an act of simple determination as he just lifted his spirit to continue. "It isn't the money, I can assure you of that," and he grinned out a laugh. "What to tell you..." He stopped for a moment to think again. "Okay, here it is. The upside is that I own Bobo's, along with this building my apartment is in, so I am pretty much debt free here. I have not made a lot of money but have managed what I did earn well. If I moved now, it would mean that I would have to sell this, ah...'dive' and, well, who would buy this place? And...well, I guess," he said sadly, "what is the difference where I live anyway?" Then he stopped. He looked like he had more to say but just clammed up.

"Is there another reason why you have chosen to stay here, Mac?"

"Yes, there is, but I'm not ready to spill that can of beans," he told Samuel. "Maybe next time we meet."

"No problem, Mac. You just let me know when, or even if, you want to talk about it."

"Thanks," was all he said to Samuel.

"You are a marvel, though," he said to encourage Mac. "Really you are, and I mean that as a compliment, but I was wondering. Could you fill in a few blanks for me on something else?"

"Sure, I was hoping that we would get into a lot of things today," Mac proclaimed. "Shoot!"

"Thanks, well…ah, I just wanted to ask you… It's your *act* of being a really mean man. Your 'you are probably going to die right here and now if you make another move' show. That is because—"

Mac leaned forward in his chair, chuckling. "Well, mostly because of this neighborhood. I am telling you it is rough. Someone shot and killed my brother right out back there," and he pointed, "as proof of that. There are a lot of people who would not hesitate or who really are 'you are probably going to die right here and now if you make another move' kind of people. And some of them are not only not kidding, but most likely have done exactly that, maybe more than once. The only respect that most of them know is what I show them. It has saved my bacon a bundle of times. Yeah, mostly the neighborhood."

"That is kind of what we figured, but you need to know, you are very convincing. Wow, you nearly scared the life out of Rebecca that night."

"Not you, though. You seemed to take it in stride," he told Samuel.

"No, I was taken back plenty myself, but you are right. Not as much as Rebecca. Do you mind if I tell her what you just told me?"

"Naw, that'll be okay," but then he snickered, as he put on his tough guy act again. "Just do not tell anyone else. I have this reputation you know," and they both laughed.

"No problem," he told Mac. "My lips are sealed."

Samuel could easily see that Mac was harboring a hurt bigger than Texas for something he was finding very difficult to talk about. He did not know what it was, though he was starting to suspect. "Have you got room for another item on my 'I'm puzzled list'?"

Mac was apprehensive as if he was able to guess what was going to be asked, but he agreed. "Sure, I guess so, Pastor Sam," but he said those last words 'Pastor Sam' in a different tone than he thus far had shown.

Samuel did not say a word at first. He only lifted one hand, as he stared directly at Mac. Then slowly, he moved his hand sideways across his chest, pulling a finger up into a pointing position. He could see the curiosity building on Mac's face as he stretched out his arm. He never took his eyes off Mac's as the crescendo reached its peak. "That diamond engagement ring," he said slowly as he pointed directly at it, "precariously caressing that trophy's football at the end of the player's outstretched arm?" He lowered his hand and waited for Mac to respond. When he did not, Samuel went on. "Been there a long time, Mac. I can tell from all the dust. I must assume its importance is off the chart for you. I want you to be at ease talking about it, so if I have crossed a line I am not supposed to cross, just tell me and I will not bring it up again." Samuel sat still and waited.

Mac's big frame collapsed backward into his seat, as he just stared back at Samuel.

"Mac," he assured him again, "it is okay if you are not ready to talk about anything, but I surmised already and now know that that ring represents something very huge in your life."

Mac shifted his gaze from Samuel to the ring, and he just fell silent as the grave. "It does," Mac finally confessed, as he sat up straight again. "It really does. That ring embodies the biggest issue, ah, hurt in my life, and I have had way too many of them. That," he said slowly, "is the can of beans I was not willing to spill...*yet*. Wow, I cannot believe that I have been stuck for all these years on that." He pointed to the ring. "That ring signifies the biggest reason I have stayed here. It has been years ago that I should have moved on, but, like so many other things, time just slips away, doesn't it? That ring is the reason I gave you my phone number and asked that you make some time for me." He lowered his arm but just stared at the ring. "Well," he finally conceded, "we're into it now, so let me tell you the story."

"Okay," he told Mac. "How about another cup of coffee and I'm all ears."

"You got it," he said and got up to fetch a second cup for them both.

When he returned with the coffee, he told Samuel that his story began a long time ago. "I hope you do not think me completely off my rocker for still wondering and worrying about it after all these years. I know I should be 'over' this, but I am not. My mind just will not pull the plug on it. My hope is that you will help me finally get rid of it. To bury it once and for all."

Samuel leaned forward with his 'I'm your man' look on his face. "Whatever it is, Mac, I will do my best to help you bring closure to it…permanently."

"Okay, here goes. I was eighteen and was just beginning my senior year football season, and I met, well, *the* most beautiful girl in the universe. She was a senior too, and from our very first meeting, both of us knew that we knew. Know what I mean?"

"Yes, I do," Samuel agreed.

"Her name was," Mac stumbled slightly over the word *was*, "ah, I mean *is* Anita, but I called her Annie. Anyway, we met at a football rally a week before our first game. She was hanging around with some of her friends when I came out of the locker room. We met, talked, and I walked her home after the rally. So we liked each other, and there you go. The start of a beautiful thing.

Dad had a stroke when he was only fifty-seven and died. That was only the year before, and Buck had taken over the bar. He was forever grumbling about having to run it. He really hated it that he had to do that, but we needed it. That was all we had. Buck could care less about me or my new girlfriend, but Mom really liked her. Not the case in reverse, though. Annie's mother pitched a fit when she found out who I was. You could have heard her in Connecticut the way she went off. She just flat out did not like me. As soon as she learned that I was the boy whose family owned Bobo's, it was all over. I was despised from that moment on. I believed that it was over with Annie and me before it even got started. She did not exactly avoid me after that but kind of made it clear that it would not work out. Later, she told me that she backed off to spare me and to give me the opportunity to find a "normal" girl. Well, that was not going to work. I tell you what, Pastor Sam. She had my heart from hello, as the saying goes. So I kind of bullied my way with her until she agreed to start dating me. We could not go on real dates, and we could not normally date on Friday nights, like some of the other kids."

"Because you were on the football team and a star to boot, right?"

"Yep, but there was an advantage in that because she was allowed to go to the games, and there were many times after those games that we had maybe an hour. That worked out well. Also, when we had an away game, she set it up where she would go with friends, and after the game, I worked it out where I could go home with her and her girlfriend and her girlfriend's boyfriend. We double-dated like that several times. We also were able to get together sometimes during the week when her mother went to bingo or a movie, and I would walk over to her house. I met her grandfather a couple of times, but her mother ruled the roost. Her grandfather seemed to like me but did not have much to say about anything.

"Okay," Samuel said, "so what happened?"

"Gets sticky from here. Pastor, I fell in love with her. Plain and simple."

"How did she feel?"

"Same, I am sure of it. She convinced me that she really did love me as well. She made that clear dozens of times. We were truly in love with each other." Mac stopped talking for a moment before going on. "You know what? Herein lies my problem. Even now after seventeen years, I think I might still be in love with her, and to put a real wrinkle on this mess I have made of my life, I still am holding onto the last thing I remember her saying, 'I will always love you,' she told me."

"I am almost afraid to ask," Samuel said, "but I will. What happened next?"

Mac hung his head at the memory. "She left me," he said sadly, and he held his hands up in the air like he had no answers. "She just left me. But...I do not blame her. I blame her mother," he said in anger, and when Mac said that, Samuel saw the real *lookout* Mac come out. He could tell that it was not an act when he got up and ranted his hatred for Anita's mother for a few minutes, and he silently feared what Mac could do. After that few minutes, though, Mac did calm down, sit down, and quietly apologized. "I'm sorry," he said, "but, boy, that woman really got me back then, and as you can see, she still gets me today. I blame her for breaking us up. I truly believe that she ruined our chances to have a great life. That, I think, is why I need your help."

"I'm assuming that you were going to propose to her?" he asked Mac.

"I did propose to her!" Mac said, getting excited again. "I did, and she accepted, and I put that ring on her hand," he said as he pointed to it again, "though she only wore it when she was with me."

"Mac, I am so sorry. I can see that this is hard. Please go on."

"Well, okay, here is the rest of the story, and this is the biggest reason I am being held hostage by my own thoughts. She got pregnant. She came and told me about a week before graduation. No problem, I told her. We will just get married a little sooner. But she would not quit crying. I told her that I would be faithful and that she need not worry about having a baby, that I would be there for her. She told me that it was not the baby that worried her, it was her mom.

I asked her what was going on, and she told me that her mom absolutely refused to allow her to marry me. So I told her that after we graduate, we can do whatever we want. I knew that my mom loved her, and that she would let Annie and me stay here as long as we wanted. Then she told me that she was so afraid to tell her mother that she was pregnant. I told Annie that we will just elope and be done with it, but she told me about her mother's vindictive side and warned me that she could do anything and, in other situations, had done unbelievable things."

"Okay, what happened next?" he asked Mac.

"What happened next was, I did not see her at all until graduation day, and she seemed to be avoiding me. She was there with her mother but just seemed to shun me. I finally caught up with her for a moment when her mother was not looking, and she quickly told me that she would come over the next night to talk."

"Did she?" Samuel asked excitedly.

"Yeah, she did. She would not quit crying again though, not even for one minute. She stumbled through her thoughts with great difficulty. She told me that our wedding was off, and she gave me back my ring. She told me that she had told her mother about her pregnancy, and that her mother was so angry, and that she just refused to allow her to marry me. She pushed the ring into my hand and asked for me to give her a week or so to think. 'Please,' she pleaded. The last thing she said to me was, 'I will always love you,' and then she left."

"So then what happened?"

"I waited for a week like she asked, not hearing from her at all and then just had to find out, so I called her, and a message said her phone had been disconnected. I went over to her apartment, and she was gone. They moved. I had no forwarding address and no phone number. She had had a cell phone, but I did not. We could not afford one back then. She and her mother just left. I tried dozens of times during the next year to locate her with no success at all."

"What's her last name?"

"Doesn't matter," he told Samuel. "I know where you are going with that, but that failed also. I gave up on that after trying every listing with her last name in the book. I never did know her mother's first name. Her grandfather lived with her too, but his name never came up. She only called him grandpa. You know, I even tried once about five years ago using the internet and got zilch. She is probably married by now anyway. I really did run that to ground. I am sure no one can come up with some suggestion that I have not pursued. No, she was and is gone."

"Do you have any photos of her?" Samuel asked.

"Like I said, I did not have a cell phone to take pictures like they do now, and I did not think of hauling Mom's camera out to take a photo of her. She was going to give me one of her senior pictures, but that never happened either. She took pictures of us and our friends, but I never did. No, no photos, sorry."

"Okay," Samuel spoke softly. "So you are looking for help to be healed from these memories so that you can finally move on, right?"

"Not sure anyone can help, but yes, that would be my hope," Mac said. "I have never looked for another woman to marry. I guess

I was still hoping that my Annie would just walk back into my life again someday and say, 'Honey, I'm home!'" They both chuckled at that. "Fat chance, that," Mac went on, "and my son or daughter must be what, sixteen by now?" Mac looked totally dejected. "I know there is no hope of finding Annie or my child, but if you could help me put this all behind me, like you said, once and for all, that would be fantastic," he confided. "Oh, and I might add, that if you pray, you would pray that I would not hurt her mother if I ever cross her path again."

"Do you think that you could hurt her?" Samuel asked, seriously wondering.

"No," Mac said. "Certainly not. Saying that is just me getting even with her in my brain. No, I am not that type of person. I would not hurt a fly unless it was swimming in my soup. My brother would have, though."

"Mac, it may take a while, but I am confident that if you will follow my lead and commit to some easy to commit to ideals, you eventually can be set free from all this."

"I will say it again, Pastor Sam. I believe you, and I will trust you. This is what you do anyway, right?"

"It is, and I'll do my very best."

Samuel looked at his watch and saw that it was going on six. "Oh, Mac, I must get going. Are you okay for another visit then?"

"Absolutely," Mac said truthfully. "I have gotten a lot out of our time today, thanks." Then he raised his eyebrows as he commanded Samuel, "Do not ask me to go to church, though." Then he smiled at his Pastor Sam, "Next Sunday at two?"

"I will be here, Mac. I cannot wait. Do you mind if I pray for you before I go?"

Mac just folded his hands, closed his eyes, and bowed his head, and Samuel prayed for him. Mac led him out and through the back door of the bar to his car. He said his goodbye, and Samuel was off.

On his way home, he could not stop wondering about Mac just folding his hands, bowing his head, and allowing him to be prayed for. "He has been there before," Samuel concluded.

When he and Rebecca closed the door to their bedroom for the night, she was super inquisitive. "How did it go?" She sat down on the side of the bed and waited.

Samuel did relate some of the things Mac shared with him. He gave her his explanation about Mac's *mean man act*, and why he knew that Mac was, "As sane as we are." He did not get into some of the more sensitive issues like the diamond engagement ring, but he did tell her about the MVP trophy, and that Mac's team had gone to State and won. He told her about Mac's parents, his brother, and his associate degree in business. "There is a lot more that Mac told me, and I am going to help him win over some issues plaguing him from his past." At that, he warned her several times. "Mac is a very private person, and for whatever reason, he has chosen to bring me into his arena. He needs to overcome a very deep hurt in his life, and we need to be faithful to keep anything he tells us completely confidential. Please remember that you cannot talk about anything remotely related to Mac no matter how insignificant it seems to be. I want him to be able to trust me as we meet again and again."

"I got it," Rebecca confirmed. "Trust me, I will not breathe a word of any of this to anyone," and she paused thinking, "well, except Mom, of course. And the ladies' group at church, and, of course, Madelyn, she is my best friend. Oh, and maybe Belinda, our neighbor. We tell each other everything. That's okay with you, isn't it?"

Samuel did not even respond. He knew how faithful she had always been and was going to be. He smiled at her knowing she was trying to pull his chain. He just got up and walked to the bathroom to get ready for bed. "Love you too," he said, walking away.

CHAPTER 16

No Way

I T HAD BEEN A COUPLE of months that had come and gone with Samuel mentoring his new friend Mac. It appeared that a marvelous escalation of hope had been imparted into Mac, but things were not looking so great on the home front. Jeremy was showing more signs of restlessness. Rebecca was faithful to help him with his GED studies, but that was not working out. Part of the problem she was having with him was expected because of his background, but the biggest problem was that Jeremy seemed to lose interest in trying.

Samuel continued to invite him to his one-on-one meetings, but Jeremy did not seem as interested as he had been. Their Bible studies all but stopped because every time Samuel got started, he saw that Jeremy did not bring his Bible, or he did not look up the Scriptures he was asked to read in advance. Jeremy left nothing to doubt. He was just not interested. He became critical and even began to refer to their meetings as Samuel's *religion* again.

The nightly sessions were turning out to be once-a-week sessions. He had also stopped going to church. Up until very recently he had not gone out drinking, but he started that up again. He had made friends with someone where he worked who would pick him up. He did not stay out any night late, though, and he never drank at home. His apparent alteration back to the old Jeremy, however, was alarming. Then they noticed that his obstinate, rebellious attitude had returned. Samuel and Rebecca both, on various occasions, confronted him on his change of pattern.

"Hey, it's just me being me, okay?" he would tell them. "A man has to live a little, right?"

"Where do you think this will all end?" Rebecca asked Samuel one night in the privacy of their bedroom.

"Only one of two ways as I see it," Samuel said. "Either he will finally come to his senses and give up this path of destruction he is headed for…again or give up wanting to be a follower of Christ and return to his vomit."

When he said that, Rebecca just sat down hard on the bed with her shoulders bent forward. "I know," she said, "and I fear for which way it will go."

Samuel remembered trying to teach Jeremy on various occasions. *Listen up, my wonderful young brother-in-law new friend. The biggest reason for forgiving your father, and I know he does not deserve it, is that it will set you free.* But all Jeremy heard was, his father did not deserve forgiveness. Samuel also remembered telling him that "the world's ideal and God's ideal on the topic of forgiveness are found on two *totally* separate pages," but Jeremy was not listening to that either.

Samuel sat down beside her and lifted his arm over her shoulder. "What Jeremy has not yet grasped is that he is stuck between two open doors, and he can only walk through one of them. The first one is not that difficult, though he is refusing to regard that possibility. That one leads to him forgiving his father and finding peace beyond his wildest dreams. Of course, by making that choice, he will have to give up his right to being right, and let God deal with his father. The second door leads him simply to settling on not forgiving his father and living in agony. The benefit to him, if one could call it a benefit, is that choosing that door will give him the justification he needs to beat up on his father mentally again and again because that is what his father deserves. That choice will ultimately lead to his self-destruction. It will also provide him the excuse he will need to say, 'It was not my fault that I ended up this way.' That then will easily lead him back into a life that could be even worse than where we found him a few months ago. Reality," he concluded, "is that he will either give in to the biblical stance on being forgiven and forgiving, or he will continue to live with the bitterness that comes from a 'pushed to the curb' life outside of Christ."

"Boy, you sure do have a way with words, my wonderful husband." She pushed her head up and under his outstretched arm, wrapping her arms around him for comfort. He pulled her into him as he hugged her hard. "All we can do for him is pray, and we will."

It had been a couple of weeks since the last night Jeremy had agreed to meet with Samuel, and this night, Jeremy was filled with contention. Samuel's intention was to address again the topic of Jeremy forgiving his father. He suspected that it was not going to go well. At the same time, he knew that this was the only teach that could possibly help Jeremy. He needed to hear this because Jeremy was stuck and could not move on, period.

"Jeremy," he began, "I want to tell you again how proud I have been for you being a great worker and for giving the largest portion of your earnings to Pat. That is not only the biblical stance, but also the mature manly stance." Samuel could not mask, however, that he had his heart's desire fixed on something very serious. Nor did Jeremy miss the difference in Samuel's demeanor and voice inflection.

"You are going to bust me on my lifestyle change again, aren't you?" Jeremy blurted out.

"In a way, Jeremy. It is like the statement, 'You are what you eat,' or 'You are what you wear.' What a person puts on, like T-shirts with explicit sayings on them, tells anyone looking that that must be what they are inside."

"So," Jeremy said very disrespectfully, "you are telling me that you can read someone's mind?"

Samuel knew that he had lost the battle, but he tried just the same. "Jeremy, God has given all of us who really believe in him and his Word the Bible, an insight that does help us to see. It is called discernment. What it means basically is that your actions will tell us what you really believe, what your values really are, and what it is that is most important to you in life." He paused briefly and then continued. "Jeremy, your recent actions, your vocabulary, you not wanting to go to church any more, or continue to study the Bible, and your lack of respect for Rebecca and myself leaves me with only one conclusion."

"And what is that?" Jeremy said with a revolted look on his face.

"Jeremy," Samuel said in kindness. "Up until about a month ago, you and I had a great relationship going, I thought. Becca and I have done everything we know of to bring you love and kindness. Honestly, I believed that all was going well. You made some wonderful turn arounds in your life, and I meant it when I told you that I was so proud of you. So tell me, what happened to change that? I first noticed it maybe a little over three weeks ago."

Jeremy just hung his head in sadness and spoke so quietly that Samuel had to lean forward to hear him. "You won't let up on me about forgiving my father," he said.

"I do understand, Jeremy. Honestly, I do." Samuel just sat in silence with him for a few moments before continuing. "Jeremy," he said, and his voice was loaded with nothing but compassion, "I asked you several times in these last few months if you trusted me. Do you still trust me?"

Jeremy remained totally silent, so Samuel asked, "Please allow me to share with you this truth one more time. If you will at least consider its value, it can set you free from all the hurt that you are experiencing."

Again, Jeremy just sat still as a stone with his head down. Without hearing anything from Jeremy, Samuel went on to expound again on forgiveness and unforgiveness. "Jeremy, I know that your father does not deserve your forgiveness, but we do not deserve God's forgiveness either. You or me. I am not expecting you to just jump on board with all this right now," he told Jeremy. "But I am asking you to at least remember all that we have gone through from your first day here. Please give it some time."

"Is that it?" Jeremy sat up in his chair with an angry look on his face, and Samuel knew that his young brother-in-law had not even tried to understand. He was just so angry at his father that he had no room for anything else. "I told you that I could never forgive him. NEVER!" he almost screamed at Samuel. Then before Samuel could respond, Jeremy jumped in again. "Look, you cannot dictate anyone's life for them. I am a Christian now, and I am doing just fine. I am making money, and like you said, I am supporting my family, and I, well, I just want to have some fun from time to time. To just be myself, and I do not see the first thing wrong with that at all, so get off my back, okay?"

Samuel started to say something, but Jeremy interrupted before he could utter even a syllable. "Do you hear me, Mr. Samuel?" Jeremy said very disrespectfully, as his anger escalated. "You—"

Samuel instantly interrupted. "Look, no matter what else you think, we do not deserve your disrespect," Samuel told him, showing a little attitude of his own. "We do not deserve the way you have treated Becca and myself these last few weeks. Jeremy, at a minimum, just calm down."

"Well, it's your fault," he said in his miserable attempt to bully Samuel. "Because all you want for me is to live like you live. To do your religion like you do, and it is not me."

"I don't have a religion, Jeremy, I have told you that. I have a faith in God and his Son Jesus, and I get all my direction from the Bible for everything in my life. Where does your direction come from?"

"My own self, that's where," Jeremy shouted.

"Jeremy," Samuel said, pulling his chair up close to his, and once again, he spoke very calmly. "Please listen to me. This is vital for you to hear."

Jeremy pulled back hard and stood up. "I told you," Jeremy's voice raised again. "I can't do that. I just cannot. Why do you keep hounding me on that? You know I cannot. Tell me something else I can do." And Jeremy just stared at Samuel, waiting for some answer.

After a long silence had invaded them both, Samuel filled in the awkward pause, although he thought he knew before he opened his mouth how Jeremy was going to react. "Jeremy," he began again as he too stood up, "honestly, I do understand, and you have my heart on this, but…there is no other way for you. You do not need to accept everything quickly. Give yourself time, but you need to let me help you forgive your father. Can you trust me for—"

"*NO WAY!*" Jeremy shouted. "You know what he did to me. You know that someone like that could never be forgiven, and do not you tell me that God would forgive him either." For the next twenty minutes, he continued to rant and rave and to rake his invisible father in the room over an imaginary hotbed of coals. Rebecca came into the room, but her and Samuel together could not calm him down, even for a second. "You've just been setting me up for this, haven't you?" he yelled at Samuel, but then, almost instantly, Jeremy stopped and put his hand out toward Samuel. "No, I, ah, I didn't mean that, I'm sorry, but if that is what I have to do to be a Christian, I'd rather not." He turned to leave but then spun around with one more accusing question. "Tell me! How in the world could anyone *ever* forgive him?" He turned again not waiting for an answer and stormed out, slamming the door as he exited the dearest living conditions he had ever known.

Jeremy did not come back that night or any night after. Samuel called his friend at the factory the next day and was told that for the first time Jeremy did not come to work. He had had an exemplary record up to that time, and his friend asked Samuel what had happened, but all he told the man was that Jeremy really needs prayer. During the next couple of weeks, Jeremy continued to miss days and was late the days he did come to work. He ignored the warnings and write-ups, and his attitude was only sad to angry continuously. He even started producing much less than quality work. Eventually, they had to let Jeremy go.

Jeremy's unforgiveness of his father had pulled him once again into that same hole he had been in all his life. He had chosen a path that would once again lead to his destruction. "But...it's my way," Jeremy would say. Everyone knew, though, that it really was no way at all. Many tears were shed for him. Rebecca and Pat wept bitterly for their Jeremy. Samuel kept his cool, though.

"I have faith that with all he has been exposed to, and that he confessed and asked that Jesus save him, he will eventually find truth. I will not give up on him."

The added hurt for Jeremy, they knew also, was that he would be evaluating his situation again the way most people did. And that would be the world's *normal, idealistic way* of looking at his father. Jeremy would likely think that he should *never* be expected to forgive his father in the first place. End of discussion. The commonly understood *proper stance* on this *idealistic forgiveness platform* the world at large leans on was that Jeremy's father was never going to deserve to be forgiven, so what's the problem? The truth, though, was that Jeremy's unforgiveness was killing *him*, not his father.

Jeremy just disappeared into an oblivious world of more pain and hurt. He stopped hanging around Bobo's also. "He must have found a new hole to crawl into," Mac told Samuel during their next Sunday session. Mac often asked about Jeremy, but Samuel just told Mac that Jeremy was a hurting man, and that he had moved out.

Rebecca and Pat were often on the phone with each other from the night Jeremy stormed out. Pat had had her hopes up for the first time since they had been divorced. For a while, she was sure that Jeremy had finally turned a page. He had made some wonderful moves to show her that he really did care, and she was starting to hope that she would get their family back on track. She even noticed that Randy had started to warm up to him too. She knew that Jeremy could be a good man and thought that all he needed was some real support and a break, and he got that living with Rebecca and Samuel. "He had everything he said he ever wanted," Pat would cry to Rebecca. "I do not understand. How could he just throw that all away?" She shed a lot of tears after he left. Rebecca did her best to help Pat deal with her pain, but she knew that it was going to take time. What Pat did not know was that Rebecca was hurting almost as much. She too needed some encouragement but did not want to let her guard down for Pat's sake.

Samuel tried to help them both understand. "Jeremy is only on the first chapter leading to his healing. He does not want to hear it, but he really needs to learn how to forgive. Not only his father, who is what he thinks is his only problem, but he also needs to learn how to forgive…period! I know it looks bad now, but keep the faith. Remember this, though," he warned them, "what he seriously needs now is tough love, and that might be very difficult. He has burned many, if not all his bridges, and, most likely, he will need a handout very soon, depending on how he handles his last paycheck. We need to be strong, especially you, Pat, because it is most likely that he will seek you out first. He may need to hit a bottom he has not yet experienced. I know it will be hard, but if he does come to you, you will need to deny him. Do it softly, do it with understanding, and do it telling him that he is loved, but do not give in. If you do give in, it may prolong what needs to happen for him to finally overcome. You can tell him that we told you that if he needs help, he can *always* come here, and we will feed him. It has been my experience that people have their best chance of finally overcoming whatever they have to face when they hit their absolute bottom." Samuel could not resist the temptation. "Just say no," and he half-laughed until he saw that they did not think that was funny. "Seriously, though, if he comes around needing anything, tell him to come here. I will not see him starve."

With that encouragement, Pat and Rebecca made Jeremy their most important mission, as they became daily prayer warriors for him. Samuel had settled back into his normal groove of pastoring his church. Although his heart, like theirs, was deeply concerned for Jeremy, he still had other people to minister to, like Mac.

Rebecca's hurt over Jeremy came mostly from the knowledge that statistics had shown that some will spend a lifetime trying to conquer this real problem of unforgiveness. She hurt also knowing that although Jeremy was a victim, he also had made victims because of the hurts that had been levied on him. "It makes no difference in the end, though, does it?" she concluded. "Who hurt who the worst, or whose fault it is anyway." To conquer this unforgiveness problem, Jeremy would have to submit to something so much bigger than himself, and to date, he was not willing to do that.

CHAPTER 17

Getting to Know Mrs. Macpherson

MAC WAS AN ABSOLUTE JEWEL to mentor. He had a serious load of hurts to overcome, but his spirit was never broken like Jeremy's had been. Now, after three months of meeting with him, Samuel could clearly see the fruit from all those hours and days of his teaching. Since that first revealing conversation they had, Mac had no problem sharing anything. It ended up that Mac did view and respect Samuel like the older brother he never had. Their conversations often drifted back to his Annie, though. "But I am moving on," he would tell Samuel. "She is long gone, and that is that. I will always love her, but she is gone." He was able to pry the engagement ring off the football trophy and pack it away, along with his photo, but after dusting his trophy, he placed it on a shelf to display it. "Not that anyone will ever see it," he conjectured.

Eventually, Samuel did get Mac to agree to start a Bible study with him, and like Jeremy, he gave him a new Bible. When asked, Mac did confess his belief in Jesus. He even acknowledged that the Bible was "probably correct on most everything, I would guess, but going to church? Not going to happen."

Although Samuel invited him periodically, Mac always respectfully declined. "Can I ask you why?" Samuel finally asked him, but Mac just joked it off with a variety of statements like, 'God was everywhere, so it did not make any difference.' But during this session, Samuel pushed back. "Mac, you and I have been meeting for a long time now, and you have been able to tell me everything. Why would you not tell me why you will not come to church?"

Mac sat thinking for a while, and then he said, "Look, I know you pastor a church, and I know you think church is the answer to a lot of things. Why else would you do that? I did not want to tell you how I felt about church because of that…BUT!" Mac hesitated to go on, half smiling, half frowning.

"Mac, you know you can tell me anything."

"I did not want to make you feel bad," he blurted out. "But here it is. Mom was a believer, and she went to church. She got up Sunday mornings when Buck and Dad were asleep, but I was always up. She asked me to go with her, and I did…once, but I did not get a thing out of it. I admit that I was only maybe eleven at that time, but Mom was faithful to go every Sunday. I am not sure Dad even knew. It seemed like she had to hide that from him and from Buck after Buck took over the bar. I found Mom's Bible about a year after she died, and you should see it. It did not look new like this new one you gave me. Anyway, the bottom line is this. It did not do anything for our family or for her that I could see, so, sorry I do not want to start going to church."

"I would love to see that old Bible of hers. Would you mind?"

"No, not at all," Mac conceded as he got up and disappeared into another room. He returned with his mom's Bible and handed it to Samuel. "Don't know what you will get out of it, though, she scribbled on a lot of the pages. I kind of glanced through it once, and some of the pages are folded over, some even look like they are about to fall out."

Samuel opened it to the inside of the front cover and started reading the handwritten notes that were penned there. After a while, he turned to the back of the Bible and began to read the overwhelming number of her personal notes that she had scribed there.

After way too long sitting in silence, Mac had to ask, "Uh, what are you doing?"

"What I am doing," he told Mac, "is reading about Mrs. Macpherson. I am reading some about your family history, but most importantly, I am reading a lot of what was in your mother's heart. I have learned that your mother's name was Janet, and your father's name was Earl, and that Buck was born on a Tuesday, and you were born on a Friday. I learned that she became a Christian only a couple of years before that one time you went to church with her, and that you were thirteen, not eleven. She prayed for you that day, and from reading this, it is most likely that she prayed for you every day after until she died. I learned that she had assigned two Scriptures to you that same day, and that they were Romans 10:13–15 and Proverbs 3:5–6. I learned that she endlessly prayed for your father, your brother Buck, and you. I learned that she was almost broken the day your father had his stroke and died, and that her hurt was probably double that, the day your brother Buck was killed."

"Okay, wait…you telling me she wrote all that?"

"Oh yeah, she did, Mac, and more. Much more. She even mentions me in her notes."

At that, Mac smiled, and he said, "Boy, you had me going until you said that. My mom died over ten years ago, and I only met you a few months ago. She could not have mentioned you in her notes. What, is this your way to get me to come to church? Cute and nice try, but—"

"Let me read it to you," Samuel interrupted, as he pulled the Bible around so that Mac could see it too. He opened it to the page and told Mac, "I will start with the inscription she wrote the one time you went to church with her." Then he hesitated and said to Mac, "No, I think you should read it. Will you?"

Mac took the Bible from Samuel. "This is kind of weird," he said, "reading what Mom wrote about, ah…you?"

Mac squinted some at his mother's handwritten notes, although it was legible. He began to read.

"Out loud," Samuel requested. "Out loud, Mac, please. I want to hear you read it out loud."

Mac complied. "Larry, your first time ever in church. You just turned thirteen a month ago, and I know you are not impressed. If ever you read this, though, please look this up in my Bible. Romans 10:13–15. I am praying for you to believe and understand who Jesus really is. I am also asking that in your life, God will send a true man of God to come along side of you to help your faith in Jesus grow, and that you, one day, would become a true man of God yourself. Please also read Proverbs 3:5–6."

Mac was silent for a moment before saying, "Wonders never cease. Why did I not read any of this before?"

"You were not looking for it," Samuel explained. "It is as simple as that, but here it is. She wrote so much, Mac, and I think it would profit you to read it all."

"That is her handwriting, but why do you say that she was talking about you, Pastor Sam?"

"Not me per se, Mac. Her heart was so interested in you learning what faith in Jesus meant that she prayed for *some* man of God, *any* man of God, not specifically me. One who would find his way into your life and guide your faith in God and, more importantly, to guide you into following Jesus. I think God answered her prayer by allowing me to come into your life. Do you know of any other papers that your mother would have written that you also have never read?"

Mac just froze, and his expression told it all. "Yes…I do. She had a couple of notebooks that I opened once. It looked like some kind of diary. I did not bother reading any of it."

"I will bet you, Mac, if you go back now and read those notes, you will get a picture of your mother you never knew. I will also bet that in those notes, she will mention praying for you special because you were all she had after Buck was killed."

"Any other predictions while you are on a roll?"

"Yeah," Samuel said with confidence. "You will probably find that she was praying for you to find a good Christ-centered church that you would not only attend but want to join."

Mac just studied Pastor Sam's face and finally told him, "That's why you want me to go to church!" It was a statement of fact, not a question.

"I know that we have only started getting into the Bible, but you will learn, if you trust me, that going to church is important for many reasons. You are right when you say that God is everywhere, but one of the most recognizable places where He is is in church. I will not lie to you either. Even Christ-centered churches all over the world are filled with all kinds of people. Some are not even believers. There are hypocrites and who knows what else. The majority, however, are humble true believers that Jesus is their Savior and are mainly interested in three things as they attend church. They come to offer worship to their God…they come to learn more about their God, and the third thing is that they come to share in fellowship with like-minded believers. Church, Mac, is a very good thing."

It was on that day that Mac understood more about his mother than he had ever known. He also understood more about why one should go to church than he had ever realized. "Okay," Mac announced. "I guess I'll start going to church."

Samuel told him that he would pick him up early the next Sunday, "Like seven forty-five? I have a service at nine."

Mac was obviously not liking that. "You know I work on Saturday night, and I don't ever get to bed before five in the morning."

"We have another service at eleven, but I can't break away to come and get you—"

"Just tell me where it is," Mac said. "I'll find it."

"That is great, Mac. I am looking forward to seeing you in church."

"Bet Mom would be too, if she were here."

"Next Sunday then," Samuel said. "Come about ten minutes before, if you can, and thanks for listening."

"No," Mac said as serious as a judge. "Really…thank you."

CHAPTER 18

No Sin Too Great

MAC'S FIRST TIME IN CHURCH was interesting. Samuel had a lot to do, being the pastor, but he did notice that Mac seemed to fit in, like he was trying on a shirt he had always admired but previously never worn.

After that first eleven o'clock service that Mac attended, Samuel and Rebecca took him to lunch, hoping to encourage him to come back a second time. "I was shocked," Mac told them. "I have only been in one other church service ever, but this was a totally different experience. Well, I think so anyway. I cannot remember much as I was only thirteen at the time, but what I do remember about that other church was that it seemed to be much more formal or something but here! Wow, I have never seen such a group of friendly people. It was almost like they already knew me. Is it like that all the time?"

"Oh no," Rebecca scoffed, "not at all. Sometimes, it is a lot more friendly." And they all shared a good laugh.

Mac did not disappoint, as he also came the following Sunday. "It was encouraging to see Mac back for the second time," Rebecca commented, "but did you notice the response some of them had when they saw the biggest man they had ever seen? They had that 'you can't shock me with anything' shocked look on their faces. I did not say a word, but I had a good chuckle when I saw that. I wonder if Mac noticed it."

"Mac does not miss much, but he didn't say anything to me about it," and then Samuel smiled, "he is a big man, though, isn't he?"

Samuel was so pleased for Mac. He really was coming to life. He appeared to be progressing perfectly on his quest to bury his thoughts for his Annie and his child. Mac still struggled much with the thought of forgiving Annie's mother though. "I just can't get there," he would say at times, but he understood why he should. Samuel was faithful on so many occasions to teach what God's answer for us was on the topic of forgiveness. "Give it time," Samuel would encourage him, "and it will help when you think about forgiving her, how much God has forgiven you."

As joyful as he was for Mac, he was that fearful for Jeremy. Samuel's faith was strong, though, and he was simply believing that Jeremy would, at some point, make a turnaround. Jeremy was his prodigal, and Samuel allowed his concern to shift to worry only on rare occasions, so he just waited and prayed.

While Jeremy was looking everywhere he should not look for answers and Mac finding answers without really looking, there was now a new squall on the horizon. Samuel knew something was seriously troubling his secretary. Mattie had been the church secretary for twelve years and had been faithful, almost to a fault. Her skills were never in question, and she was disciplined, organized, and professional…but she so rarely exhibited joy. Now that was Mattie, pure and simple. Samuel, over the years, had on many occasions attempted to find out why or maybe what happened in her life. He had invited her into his and Rebecca's confidence, but…she had always refused and did so with an "is there anything else" kind of comment, just before quickly slipping away.

However, something very different had occurred recently that implanted an "I better find out what's going on" crinkle across Samuel's brow. One Sunday morning, she just did not show up for church. If it had been anyone else, he would not have thought much about it but Mattie! She had not missed a church service even once in all her dozen years as secretary that he could remember. Missing coming to church was just one thing, though. Mattie did not just miss church…Her norm was to show up early to set up teaching materials for Sunday school and children's church, communion when they were to offer that, bulletins, and make the coffee for the elder's prayer time prior to service. She was always there for several other self-imposed duties that she felt were hers to perform. She also stayed for both services and was not always, but often, the last one to leave the building. Mattie just did *not* miss church, so when she did, and without warning, something was seriously wrong. Samuel knew, and the bells and whistles were going off in his head like a four-alarm fire.

Samuel called her even before the first service that morning to check on her. When she picked up the phone, she simply told him, "I am fine. I will let you know when I get sick." He recognized her calm but indifferent voice.

"Okay," he told her, "I was just worried for you because—"

"I'm fine," she snapped back, and her voice changed to an almost angry tone. "I told you, I'm fine." Nothing more was said. Silence filled the line for a long moment until Samuel finally heard the identifying "click" of her disconnecting.

What really brought the curtain down on her "just-leave-me-alone, very self-protective" act was that she did not come to church the next Sunday either. So on Tuesday, when she came to work, he let her get settled at her desk, but he did not wait long before coming out of his office to talk with her. It startled her because he was rarely there before she was.

"What are you doing here so early?" she asked nonchalantly, as she turned back to her desk.

Samuel pulled up a chair and sat facing her. He had never ever done that before, and it created the effect he wanted. She looked confused. "Mattie," he told her. "Something is wrong. My intention is not to pry. I do not want to pry, but you have missed church these last two Sundays. I would not even think a thing about it if it were anyone else, but—"

"I told you I am fine," she pushed back. "What is the big deal? Lots of people miss church occasionally."

"Mattie," he told her, "you missing church is like the pope missing mass. Honestly, I do not want to come across like I was your father or big brother, but, Mattie, I am your pastor and a friend. A trusted good friend I might add as well. I have proven that to you for over a decade, and I really do care about you." He waited for her to answer, but she did not. "Mattie, what is going on?"

"I told you!" she said angrily. "I will let you know when something is wrong."

"Really?" Samuel asked as he folded his arms in protest and just stared at his secretive secretary.

"Really!" she said, but Samuel was in no way convinced, especially when she looked down and away seemingly ashamed. She knew that she had just given herself away but quickly regained her composure.

"Mattie, I am not talking to just any old somebody in need of help. You have been working with me for a dozen years, and you know that everything you tell me will be kept confidential, and you also know me well enough that I am not going to give up on this... on you because I care," he told her again. "You need to tell me something...anything," Samuel said and waited for a response.

After just a moment to regroup, she looked up with her well-practiced expressionless mask on her face and told him, "I will be, ah...fine...I...I will," but it sounded like she was trying to convince herself. She then did something that she had never ever done. She got up and walked out.

Samuel waited for over half an hour, and when she did not return, he thought that she may have gone home. He went out to the parking lot and saw that her car was still there. He turned, went back into his office, and called her. He hung up when he heard her phone ring because it was in her purse sitting on the floor beside her desk. He figured that she was in the lady's room. Being a Tuesday morning, there was no one else in the building, so he thought that he should go and knock on the lady's room door to see if she was all right but changed his mind. "She already thinks that I have invaded her private life...probably." So he just waited. After another worrisome few minutes, he called Rebecca. He shared with her the basics of his confrontation with Mattie to gain her perspective.

"Well," Rebecca replied, "we cannot force anyone into telling us what, or if, something is wrong. Basic common courtesy dictates also that we just stand by and wait until they want to talk about whatever is bothering them. Sometimes, that even means watching them sink in the process of waiting. Look how much trouble we have seen people get into by 'thinking' they know what is wrong with someone else, diving in with both feet, and then finding out that they caused a relationship problem that was not there before."

"Okay, but what is more painful for her?" Samuel asked. "For me to respect her privacy and watch her die on the vine or jump in with both feet upsetting her sense of fairness to try and help? Becca, I just cannot stand by and let her drown without throwing her a line."

"I get that, and I agree with you," Rebecca went on. "I was just giving you a good look at the other side of the coin. The difference here is that you are not just someone who thinks something is wrong with Mattie. You represent her employer, you are her pastor, and you have known her for a dozen years. Besides, I think it is more your style to jump in with more than just both your feet, Sam. Is there anything I can do to help?"

"Yeah, there is," Samuel said as it appeared that he suddenly knew what it was that should happen next. "She is still here...I know because I saw that her car is still here. She will have to come back sooner or later to get her purse, and I want to, as kindly as possible, get her to open up. I think that she would feel more comfortable doing that if you were here. Can you come over right now?"

"Sure, I can. I will be there in about fifteen minutes. See you in a few."

When Mattie finally did return, she found Samuel waiting for her, sitting on the chair he pulled up earlier.

Mattie walked around him, sat down at her desk, and prepared her computer for work, not even looking at Samuel. He started to say something, and she cut him off. "There is nothing to talk about," but then she not only fell silent but suddenly motionless as well. She did not look at him but kept her gaze on an invisible spot on her blank computer screen. "What do you want to talk to me about?" she finally asked. Then, as if someone just pushed the Play button, she composed herself, put on her familiar 'I am in control' face and said yet again, "I am fine, Pastor, really. I do not want to talk about anything." She reached over to pick up a stack of paperwork to begin to work.

Samuel slowly reached over, trapping her hand on the stack of papers and pushed them back down. "Mattie," he gently said, "we need to talk. If what I am seeing in you was not such a huge thing, or if you were a brand-new employee here at the church, I would certainly respect your desire for me to leave you alone, but as it is…"

"I told you," she began but could not finish her sentence, and this time, her voice was just above a whisper. Samuel could tell that she was consumed with hurt.

"Mattie, you know from your twelve years of working with me that I am only interested in your well-being." He paused just briefly. "You are not fine, and both of us know that, and I think you need to talk to someone about whatever it is. Will you please trust me?"

She pulled her hand back and looked away, as she mumbled out a sentence, "I, ah, don't know, ah…what to do, I ah, I feel like…" Her hands had begun to shake, and he noticed that she had started to sob ever so slightly but uncontrollably.

Samuel knelt on the carpet next to her. "I am not sure exactly what you need to talk to me about, but I am as sure as anything I have ever been sure of that you know precisely *what* you need to talk to me about. Please trust me, Mattie, I can see that it will hurt you to talk about it, but I think it will hurt you so much more not to talk about it, and I think you know that too."

Samuel waited for Mattie to respond, but she did not. She did not get up either. In fact, it looked like she could not get up. She slowly pushed her office chair backwards, leaning over at the waist. She pulled her hands up over her face and just bawled like a child.

That…surely is not my Mattie, Samuel thought, and he began to pray for her, and just then, Rebecca came in and joined Samuel as he prayed. After about a minute, Rebecca let Mattie know that she was there and began to comfort her. "Mattie, you are so important to us, and we really do care about you. Do you know that?"

Mattie sat up and nodded convincingly. "I know that is true. I just have something so awful to…" She began to weep again.

Samuel stood up and invited her and Rebecca into his office. Have a seat there, Mattie, on the sofa, and I'll get us some coffee." She sat down on the couch but could not stop sobbing. Rebecca got her a box of tissues and sat down beside her. She wrapped an arm around Mattie, giving her a gentle hug. That was a first for Rebecca because Mattie was not a hugger. Samuel returned with the coffee. He sat down in a chair opposite the sofa. He tried to encourage her. "Mattie, whatever this is all about, I know that God can work it out."

"Not likely," she mumbled through her tears. "I cannot see any light at the end of *this* tunnel," she said, reaching for another tissue. "Boy, does your past have a way of coming back to haunt you or what?" She took a deep breath and looked like she was beginning to calm down. She took a sip of her coffee, but suddenly, her emotions grabbed her ability to reason, and she burst out in tears again. She stayed that way for a couple of minutes.

Finally, Rebecca told Mattie, "We have no idea what you are going through or what is wrong, but you have the best of friends right here with Sam and me. You need to know that, and that you can trust us completely."

She looked like she was unable to say anything but did utter a "yes," although she could not stop crying.

Mattie gained control again, blowing her nose, and sat up like the stoic secretary Samuel had gotten to know for the last dozen years. She sniffed out the last of her crying jag and leaned back against the sofa.

"Wow, I've got to tell you, Pastor," but then she fell silent again, thinking. Then, "I always figured that one of two things was bound to happen. Either I was going to be able to hide *this...*, forever, or it would just pop up right in my face one day, and I would be forced to tell it all. I guess I now know which way it's going to go."

"There's no rush," Samuel announced, "just take your time. When you are ready to talk, we are all ears."

"You want to know why I've missed the last two Sundays? You want to know why I have been so guarded, not just recently, but all these years? I know you figured that it was just my personality. Truth is, I tried to make it look like that so I would never have to, well, end up like I am today. What really brought all this to a head was something that happened suddenly three weeks ago."

Samuel and Rebecca were as curious as two toddlers on Christmas Eve who just could not wait to open their presents, but they did not let on.

"You just tell us what you want to tell us. We are here for you, Mattie," Samuel told her.

"You know that big man who came to church three Sundays ago for your eleven o'clock service?" Mattie opened with.

"Yeah, what about him?" Samuel quizzed.

"That man," she began but could not finish her statement. Finally, when she was able to speak, she began again. "That man is the father of my child."

Samuel and Rebecca could not begin to hide the look of shock on their faces, although Mattie could not possibly know *why* they were so shocked. She had no idea how much Samuel instantly knew about her because of all the counseling he had had with Mac over the past several months. Samuel was a pro at disguising his feelings, but he could not even pretend to hide this one.

"I know," Mattie said. "It would be a shock for anyone to find that the church secretary had a past like I do. And you thought you heard it all," she said sarcastically between a couple of sniffles. "That man, Larry is his name, and I were in love a long time ago. We were going to get married until my mother put a stop to that. I got pregnant and…" Mattie once again dropped into an uncontrollable crying jag.

Rebecca wrapped her arm around Mattie again to comfort her, and they waited. Mattie had put her head down and buried it in her hands again, looking totally ashamed. Samuel just stared at Rebecca for a moment with a knowing look. Samuel thought, *Wow! Right here it is. Mattie is Mac's Annie! It is the rest of Mac's story. How on earth am I going to tell him that the love of his life, who left him all those years ago, has been my secretary for the past twelve years? He is just now working toward forgetting that she ever existed so he can go on with his life.* Samuel also wondered, *How on earth am I ever going to help Mattie, knowing that she has no clue how much I already know about her?* He also instantly knew that he could not use her name Anita or Annie. *And,* he also thought, *why is her name Mattie to us and Annie to Mac? Wow!* His head was reeling with all this new information, but he tried to stay focused on Mattie, right here, right now.

Mattie finally regained her composure again and started to finished her sentence. "I got pregnant, and we were going to run away, but then my mom, aagh! My mom!" Mattie kind of shouted in anger. "My mom made it clear that she would do anything it took to break us up. I had already told Larry that I was pregnant, and he told me that he would be faithful. He said that we would just get married earlier, and, of course, I believed him. I told Mom that night that I was pregnant, and boy did she hit the roof! She told me that since I was only seventeen, just one month short of my eighteenth birthday, that she could see to it that Larry was arrested for rape, and that I had nothing to say about it because I was a minor. Stupid me, I believed her. I could not see him again until graduation day, and I told him that I would come over the next night to talk. That is when, because of Mom's threat, I told him that the wedding was off, and I gave him back his ring. He would not give up, so I asked him to back off for a couple of weeks because of my mom. That upset him, but he agreed. I did not discover until the next day that Mom had my phone disconnected, and to my surprise, she just up and moved us almost overnight. We lived in this small semi-furnished apartment, and I guess she did not have a lease at all, so we just left. She packed the few things that we owned, put them in the back of Grandpa's pickup, and we were gone. She took us to live with her sister clear out of state. I did not get a new phone for over a year. I was going to get back over to see Larry and try to explain, but I did not get the chance. Mom made sure of that."

"I need to know something," Samuel asked. "Why didn't you call him after you did get a new phone?"

"Why didn't you ask me about my child?" she retorted, swelling up for a new bout of tears.

Samuel was going to follow that up but did not get a chance. Mattie simply lost it, and she could not be consoled.

In all the years that they had known her, and especially Samuel who worked with her almost daily, they could not believe what was happening to Mattie.

Again, it took a long while of waiting, and both Rebecca and Samuel trying to comfort her, but finally, Mattie calmed down enough to be able to speak.

"Okay," she started again with difficulty. "Here is the most difficult part of my story to tell. Mom knew that I was not *able* to contact Larry. Then with more threats, she coerced me into aborting our child, and after that, I certainly could never face him again. So when I did get a new phone, I just started to brush him out of my mind, hoping that he would find someone else. What am I supposed to do with that now? I know he could never forgive me for just leaving him with no answers, let alone forgive me for aborting his child without him even knowing. Heck, I cannot even forgive myself. I know what the Bible says about God forgiving all our sins, but I have always wondered about that one. I was not what you would call a Christian back then, but I did know that what I did was wrong. Even though Mom coerced me into it, I still was the one who did it. I think about that all the time and ponder what Larry would say if he ever found out what I did."

"There is no sin too great that God cannot forgive," Samuel assured her.

"You know, I certainly cannot boast that I was doing okay the way I was," Mattie told them. "But then, *'Bam!'* She sat still for another moment. "So there I was in perfect gloom, and Larry just shows up on our church doorstep one day. You did not know that I left that first Sunday, did you? I took one look at him, and I was out of here."

"Tell us what happened to your mother," Rebecca asked.

"Mom and her sister fought like cats and dogs daily. Grandpa was no help and did not want to be anyway. He and I stayed out of the way. It was his Social Security that we lived on mostly, and I think he just gave up and died. After that, since Mom did not have much to offer my aunt, she asked us to move, and we ended up back here. That was about a year before I started coming to church here, and as you know, you needed a secretary, and I filled the spot. Mom lives with me still. She has nowhere else, and although she is a beast to live with, I cannot throw her out. She is such a controller. She is still the same today as she was then, but now she tells me all the time that it was me who ruined *her* life. She tells me that her dream for me was destroyed because I was the tramp who got pregnant, and the best thing she ever did for me was to talk me into that abortion. I have never forgiven her for that. I never will, and she knows it."

"God loves you, Mattie," Rebecca told her as she leaned over and gave her yet another hug. "Let me tell you again. There is no sin so great that God will not forgive."

"You know," Mattie said, "I have not seen Larry since that day that I gave him his ring back, well until he just strolled in here three Sundays ago. Do you think that he is going to continue to come here to our church?"

"Well," Samuel said, "I don't really know, ah, for sure," he stumbled on his answer because he knew what Mattie did not know. "I mean I cannot tell him to go away, can I?"

"What am I supposed to do then?" she asked. "I cannot face him."

"Mattie," Samuel just said her name and waited.

"Oh, please do not tell me that I *have to* face him. Please, I am too ashamed. Please." She began to cry again.

"Why don't you take the rest of today off and think about all this and pray," Samuel comforted her. "We will do the same, and we will come up with something."

Mattie agreed and slowly got up and walked to the door. She turned abruptly and thanked Rebecca, but, to Samuel, she took the time to say, "Thank you, Pastor Sam."

She had never called him that before. She just wanted him to know that she really was, maybe for the first time ever, willing to submit to his leadership. She had no idea, though, that that is exactly how Mac identified his Pastor Sam.

Rebecca waited and made sure that Mattie had left, and even went to the front door to look out and down the hall in both directions before mouthing her first words about what they had just learned. "Are you kidding me?" she said in her most surprised attitude. "Who could have called that? Not in a million years!"

"Not in a billion years," Samuel added. "Mattie is Mac's long-lost love," and after saying that, Samuel stopped to think.

"What's up?" Rebecca quizzed.

Samuel held up a finger as if he had just captured an earth-shattering idea and headed to Mattie's filing cabinet. He opened the folder labeled Church Personnel and pulled it out as if on a mission. When he slapped it down on Mattie's desk and opened it, Rebecca asked, "Are you looking for Mattie's file?"

"I am, but look at this," he said.

She read the name on the file he had pointed to and asked, "Who on earth is A. Matilda Sanford?"

"It appears that she adopted the nickname, Mattie, from her middle name Matilda. I have always only known her as Mattie. That is all she ever wanted to be called, and that is why I never put it together that Mac's Annie is our Mattie. Mac told me that the girl he fell in love with, the girl that was pregnant by him, the girl that he was going to marry, and the girl that left him cold seventeen years ago was named Anita. He called her his Annie, but never, not even once, did he mention her last name, Sanford. Also, I think he may have never known what her middle name was, or if he did, he would not have known that she didn't even use her real middle name but went by her nickname, Mattie."

"So how did you find her file when you only knew her as Mattie?"

"Simple, I knew her last name was Sanford, but like I said, Mac never once mentioned her last name. Until just this morning, I say again, I had no way to put his Anita and our Mattie together. Mac never knew to tell me any more than he did, and I did not know anything at all to tell him. Neither of us had the slightest suspicion at all until Mac agreed to come to church, and Mattie saw him. Another reason I could not know anything is because I think that Mattie deliberately chose to use her nickname for just one more barrier to hide her past."

Rebecca sat down to allow her thoughts to dice up this unusual scenario, but her "what-if's" had put a blockade on her ability to produce any kind of a solution.

"Wow! I do not know if you can see it," Samuel finally said, "but I can. This could end up being the best thing that has ever happened to Mattie and to Mac. Wow," he said again, "you can't make this kind of stuff up!"

They just recapped several things for a few minutes and then Samuel announced, "I cannot take the day off myself, though. I have some work that just will not go away. See you at home later."

"So you are just kicking me out then?" Rebecca asked as she kissed her pastor husband on the cheek and waved her goodbye over her shoulder.

"Pastor Sam?" Samuel repeated Mattie's words after Rebecca left his office. "She called me her Pastor Sam. Hmmm, imagine that."

CHAPTER 19

What to Do?

"**G**OT ANY IDEAS ON HOW you will tell Mac about Mattie?" Rebecca asked Samuel as he arrived home from the most revealing of days they could remember ever having.

"I have not gotten past the 'are you kidding me' let alone how I am going to tell him anything, but how does this sound? 'Hey, Mac, you know that girl, what did you say her name was, Annie? I am so happy that you are finally getting over her, but here is a real kick in the pants for you. Guess what? Your Annie has been my secretary for the last twelve years, and her name is Mattie, by the way, not Annie, and I do not think that she wants to see you.'"

"Cute," she told him. "How about you make your own dinner tonight."

"Sorry," he said. "Of course, I did not mean that. I am just at a loss as to where I can begin. If I had known from the start, I would have handled all this differently, but hindsight is always twenty-twenty, isn't it? We have two precious souls in our care, and I want to make sure that both of them will find success, joy, happiness, peace, love...and...and—"

"And," she said, finishing his sentence, "not to mention Jeremy, Pat, Randy, and Mattie's mother. Looks more like six precious souls that are in our care."

"That there, my wonderful wife, is true," he said as he turned to face her. "But you forgot one."

"Yeah, and who might that be?"

Samuel put his arms around her shoulders and softly said, "Your father."

Rebecca fell silent but then hugged into him as she agreed. "Yes, my father. I can clearly see why you included him in our group of precious souls, but Jeremy cannot."

"Okay," he asked, changing the topic. "Anything else happen this afternoon after you and Mattie left the office?"

"No, but Pat called, and we were discussing the last time she saw Jeremy. It's been a while now, so we were wondering again what had happened to him. She remembered telling him what you told her to do. She recalled how that hurt for her to have to do that, but she said that she understood. I remember her telling me at the time how he really pitched a fit when she told him what you had instructed her to say about him coming here for help. Do you think he will come here for help? At least a meal?" Rebecca said pleadingly.

"I surely hope so, and if he does, we will feed him. I will not bargain with food. I would give him all he needs, including a great meal, a bath, and a warm bed, and—"

"Really?" Rebecca interrupted. "What was all that stuff about tough love?"

"You did not let me finish. I would do that for him for only one or two nights. Then he would have to convince me that he had finally discovered the error of his ways, and I mean convince me and be willing to really try to learn, or out he would go."

"You could do that?" Rebecca quizzed Samuel.

"I do not want him to suffer, certainly, but I also do not want him to continue his downward path full of excuses having a soft bed to pad his hurts. I do want him to finally cross that bridge I have been leading him to for months now. Well, more like the last several years, but mainly these last few months, and I know that he probably will not get there until there is no other way. Tough love is tough on both parties. I know that he did not initiate his hurt, but he is perpetuating it using the excuse that he did not initiate it."

"There's a mouthful," Rebecca commented, "but you are right. Our instinct is to just continue to feed him and continue to try and teach him, but there is a time, isn't there, where you have to, for their sake, just let them go…That is tough."

"I am hungry," he said, changing the topic again. "What's for dinner?"

"Don't know yet," Rebecca said kind of apologetically. "What sounds good?"

"That's a great question," he told her. "And the only thing that comes to mind is Swiss steak with mashed potatoes, whole kernel corn, a salad, a hot dinner roll, and a piece of hot apple pie ala mode."

"That does sound great, but that is not going to happen here in this house tonight, my hungry husband. I know you are talking about Candles Restaurant, and I am with you on that, just let me get my jacket."

They spent the better part of two hours at Candles Restaurant discussing possible ways to proceed with Mattie and with Mac. They recapped the information Mattie had given them and compared that to the information that Samuel learned from Mac during the months of visiting with him. "Wow!" Samuel expounded. "Like I said after Mattie left the office this morning, *you just cannot make this stuff up.*" They did not come up with a definitive solution, but it did help that they had all their eggs in one basket.

Samuel and Rebecca readied themselves to leave. He paid their bill, and as they were walking to their car, he told her, "Becca, I would like to figure out how to do this without hurting either one of them, but I don't think that is possible." They climbed into the car and Samuel continued, "I know I said that this could end up being the best thing that has ever happened to them, but boy are we going to have to do our best light-footed dance on some very thin ice to help that end up being their outcome."

"I'm with you on that," Rebecca agreed. "Mattie is such a dear woman. Her character is beyond reproach, but she has been wounded way past any kind of understanding. Her anger and unforgiveness are on two fronts. First, her mother, who basically, selfishly, ruined her relationship with Mac, the love of her life, and secondly, that her mother coerced her into an abortion. She did agree to do that, but honestly, just seventeen? She had no other path that was apparently available to her back then. How often have we seen that? Oh, and there is another issue about her anger and unforgiveness, now that I think about it. She cannot forgive herself. Here she is, having all this brought fresh back into her life when she thought that Mac was long gone. Surprise…he just shows up one day, but she cannot face him to work it all out. And what about Mac—"

"Mac," Samuel interrupted, "has spent the last seventeen years obsessing over Annie, the loss of the love of *his* life. Oh, and his constant wondering what ever happened to his child. You know, the biggest reason he stayed right there in that bar was because he always hoped that his Annie would just waltz back into his life with his all but grown-up son or daughter in tow. Not only was that not reasonable to believe, but now he will learn that his child had been aborted. And," he went on, "to put an ugly accent on all this, I have finally convinced him how to rid his life of his Annie and his child altogether. What do you think he will say when I tell him that not only is she not really gone, but that she has been my secretary for the last twelve years?"

"We are certainly at a major crossroad here, aren't we?" she said, leaning closer to Samuel.

"It is not going to be easy, that is for sure," he agreed.

"Oh, and here is something else," Rebecca brought to his attention. "You say that he is well on his way to really forgiving Annie's mother, who he blames for their life being ruined. What do you think he will do when he finds out that not only has his Annie been found, but that evil woman, he calls her, is alive and well and living with Mattie, I mean Annie? Boy, when you are right, you are right, Sam. You just cannot make this stuff up, but there it is, and here we are."

Just when they walked into the house, Rebecca had an idea. "What do you think about putting Nancy and Mattie together?"

"That is a great idea," he said enthusiastically. "She has been with the Crisis Pregnancy Center for years. They minister to women just like Mattie. They do so much for women who have had abortions. Remember some of Nancy's success stories? I know that she can really help Mattie. Maybe you could talk to her and even make an appointment for her. It would be fantastic if you could even go with Mattie, at least the first time, if she agrees?"

"I would love to do that," she told her excited husband.

"Mac will be a different issue," he told her. "The last few months have been so productive in teaching him how to 'move on with your life,' and he has been almost completely successful in that venture. His whole demeanor has changed, and basically that is the reason he agreed to start coming to church. But, Becca, my own words are echoing in my brain right now as we discuss all this. I remember telling him, 'She has been gone for so long now, Mac, and don't you know that we all need to face some serious situations that will never have answers? You most likely will never know what ever happened to her or your child. So now after seventeen years, you need to learn to let it all go, Mac! Trust me, this is the best thing you can do for your life.' Now? I need to help him do a one-eighty, reintroducing him to the woman he has just learned how to...*let go.*"

With that, they did pray for each of these *cheated-in-life people*, and headed up to their bedroom sanctuary, hoping to accomplish more hours of sleep than sleeplessness.

CHAPTER 20

You Are Not the Author of Confusion

SAMUEL HAD GONE TO BED forgetting to turn his phone off, and he now was going to experience the consequence for that. He snapped out of a deep sleep and groped for his phone to answer before it woke Rebecca up. In his fumbling, it continued to ring several more times before he could silence his enemy that was demanding his attention. "What," he spoke into the phone trying to be quiet.

"Samuel, it's me, Mac. You up yet?"

"Sure," Samuel said comically, "why not?" He got up to walk into the bathroom to talk. Over his shoulder, though, he heard Rebecca ask who it was.

Samuel pulled his phone into his chest. "It's Mac." He looked at the clock and saw that it was just about time to wake up anyway. "What's up?" he asked Mac. "What can I do for you today?"

"Nothing, really," Mac said. "Well, yeah, I just wanted to tell you that your sermon on Sunday really helped me realize how important it will be for me to finally move on. I will be in the process of trying to sell the bar." Mac was seemingly waiting for some kind of kudos from his mentor. He had reached that decision and was anxious to share the good news with his Pastor Sam, but he heard nothing. "Ah, you still there?" he asked.

"Yeah, Mac, sure I am. Listen, I am just crawling out of bed. Can I call you back in about an hour?"

"No problem," Mac said. "Talk to you soon," and he hung up.

Rebecca followed Samuel into the bathroom. "What did he want?"

"He said that my sermon on Sunday really helped him make up his mind on how to finally move on with his life. He is going to put his bar up for sale. You know what, Becca? I have no clue at all how I am going to speak to Mac, but I need to know within the next hour. That is when I am supposed to call him back. Here is the up side to it all, though," he said with a confident grin on his face that could sell ice to an Eskimo, "God knows, and I am praying that He gives me all that I need for Mac's sake before that one hour has become the past."

They got themselves ready for the day, ate their breakfast, and drank their last cup of coffee when Samuel looked at the clock. It was time to call Mac back. He paused to pray with Rebecca and dialed Mac's number.

"It's your dime this time," and he laughed. "I got to tell you, Pastor Sam, I am having a wonderful day. Like I told you, I have decided to sell the bar, not that that will be easy, but it is probably the most positive step I have made yet. That is good stuff right there, isn't it? What do you think about that?"

"That is good stuff, Mac, and I am proud of the way you have been working through all that you have had to face for so many years. I have a request, though. Is there any way that I can come by, oh say about lunch time today, maybe earlier? There is something important I need to run by you." Samuel cringed at the thought of what he had to tell him.

"Sure," Mac said. "Wednesday is not my slowest day, but I never get customers in here, well usually, before three or four in the afternoon. What, noonish?"

"Sounds good, Mac. See you then."

"Wait," Mac said. "Can you give me some hint?"

"No," was all Samuel said. "I'll see you around noon."

"Okay, I guess I can wait," Mac said, but Samuel could tell there was a huge 'what's up' going on in his voice.

When Samuel arrived at the church, he saw that Mattie had already started working. "I missed yesterday, so I thought I would come in a little early to catch up," she informed him.

He told her that he had to leave around eleven thirty for an appointment, and she pulled out her notepad to write it down. "Who's it with?" she asked.

"Oh, just a friend, that's all," so she put her pen down but did not go back to her typing the way she always did.

"You know, Pastor," she just started talking, "I want to tell you that I am so blessed that you and Rebecca were here for me yesterday. I do not have a clue what I am going to do next, but I am relieved for having opened up about everything. She took a deep breath and went on. "You know, I really loved that man, but I betrayed him. I cannot even come up with a good excuse. You always said that one must get into it to get over it. 'Face your giants,' you always quoted. Well, not this time. I meant it when I said that I will never be able to face him." She paused again, and Samuel just marveled at how much this 'I do not have time to stop and talk' secretary of his was so talkative. "I also have made up my mind to not come back to church for fear of running into Larry."

"Mattie," Samuel told her, "I do understand, but you said that you trusted me—"

"I do, Pastor," she interrupted, "but this just can't be fixed."

"Mattie, can you remember all the counseling sessions I have had that started out with a 'this just can't be fixed' problem? Only to see that, in most of them, it did get fixed?"

Samuel just waited for an answer, but Mattie sat there quietly until she told him, "You know you should have been a pastor." She smiled, which was a very rare sight. "Do not quit your day job," and she ended with, "we all need you."

"I won't," he told her, "and I won't quit on you either." He walked into his office, thinking, *I wonder what she would say if she knew I was going to meet with her Larry in a couple of hours?* He prayed for Mattie and for himself and his meeting with Mac. "I trust in you, God," he said out loud this time, "for you are not the author of confusion."

CHAPTER 21

"WHAT?"

"**P**ASTOR SAM," MAC BEGAN AS he was opening the door for him. "I tell you I am so excited about how everything is working out. Come on in. We can talk down here today instead of going upstairs. Boy, let me tell you, if you had not come around like you did a few months ago," and he paused, "well, I think that I would still be in that limbo state of not being able to forget my Annie. I am wondering now how many more years would it have taken me to get right here where I am now. I cannot thank you enough. Oh, and here is another thing. I have been wondering lately, how long I can continue to push booze through this bar of mine. I never did really want to do this for a living, but now, well, I am feeling like it might not be the best thing that I could do for my life. Do not know how to quit, though. Maybe you can help me with that too, but like I said, I am in the process of putting the bar up for sale." He could not contain himself and wrapped one of his huge arms around his Pastor Sam. "Just got to thank you again. Well, sit down and tell me what is so important that you had to come by special today."

"Mac," Samuel said seriously, "you need to sit down for this."

"Good heavens, Pastor, what on earth is it? Are you about to ruin my unruinable day?" He just stared at Samuel like the world was about to come to an end.

"Ah, not kidding, Mac. Really, you need to sit down, and yes, this will ruin your day. Know this, though. This is the hardest thing I have ever had to do."

Mac took his advice and plopped down hard in one of the chairs, looking very worried. He raised both his hands looking for understanding, "What the hey, over," he said, being lost for any other words.

"Mac," he began but could not continue. He just looked down as if trying to come up with words that he did not have.

"Pastor Sam? Look, just come out with it," Mac fired at him, getting frustrated. "Whatever it is, I can take it. Did someone I know die? Your Jeremy maybe or something like that?"

"No, Mac. No one died. It is kind of the opposite," Samuel said, leaning in toward him. "It's about your Annie." Samuel fell completely silent as he looked hard into Mac's used-to-be-confident now ashen face. Samuel had not only fallen completely wordless, but also looked as if someone had just shot his best friend.

Mac mouthed out one single word. "What!" He glared a hole through his Pastor Sam and waited for his mentor to go on.

"Mac, I will share the whole story with you, and as I hope you know, you can trust me. I will leave nothing out at all, but you need to prepare yourself for a couple of for real deal bumps. I not only know where she is, but I know all about her. I give you my word, though, I really knew absolutely nothing about any of this that I am going to share with you, nor did I even suspect any of this until yesterday. Mac," he emphasized loudly, "honestly nothing until yesterday."

"Okay, I got it, you knew nothing. Get on with it. What about my Annie?" He crossed his arms and steeled himself for what he may be faced with next. "Wait!" he demanded as he stood and walked to the front door. He locked it and headed back to the table. "I do not want to be interrupted." When he sat down again, he held his hand up to halt Samuel from speaking and kept his hand in the air, giving the understanding that Samuel could only continue when he lowered his hand. Finally, Mac dropped his hand with a slap against the table and announced, "Okay, go for it, I am ready."

"Rebecca and I spent the better part of two hours talking with her in my office yesterday."

"In your office?" Mac questioned incredulously. "In your office?"

"Yeah, Mac, in my office, and I guess that is the first thing that I need to tell you about. She has been my secretary for over twelve years now."

"WHAT?" Mac yelled as he stood up. "How can you say that you only found out yesterday when you have heard my story about her over the last three months? What, her name did not ring a bell?" Mac began to pace and seemed to be perspiring angry beads of sweat from his brow. He began to mumble to himself.

Mac's outburst left Samuel wondering if he was going to act out his anger this time. He remembered seeing Mac demonstrate his most convincing 'you are dead meat if you cross me' act without even looking back, but this time, he saw a genuine 'hurt first and ask questions later' demeanor in Mac.

Samuel waited for him to cool some and then gently continued. "Mac, she never went by her first name, Anita, in all these years, so, no, her name could not ring a bell. You never once told me her last name. Look, she is the most competent worker I have ever known, but she is also very secretive. Until yesterday, I never questioned or felt the need to question her on any personal level. She only ever went by the name Mattie."

"Mattie!" Mac repeated, "Who the heck is Mattie?"

Samuel continued. "It was not until she shared her story with me yesterday that I put it all together. Please try to relax and let me tell you the whole story. Please?"

It took Mac a minute or so, but then he wandered back to his chair and plopped down, crossing his arms again. He just stared at Samuel with what could only be interpreted as a 'this better be good' look on his face.

"Mac," Samuel said compassionately. "The name she gave when she was hired twelve years ago was A. Matilda Sanford."

"Yeah, Sanford," Mac agreed, but then the truth hit him like a brick. "Oh, I got it. You asked me for her last name, and I never told you. If I had, would you have put it together before yesterday?"

"Probably, although her last name came up very rarely at church, but I suppose I would have, yes. Anyway, she adopted the nickname Mattie from her middle name Matilda. I think that she has been hiding from everyone since her earliest days. That, of course, would have been long before she came to work at our church. So she had been very accomplished in her disguise mode even then. She simply did not want to be found, especially by you, I found out yesterday."

At that, Mac lowered his head and softly said, "So she never loved me after all."

"No, Mac, please hear the whole story. She not only did love you for real back then, but it is highly possible that she still does love you now. I believe that she has tried to stay in that 'I don't want anyone to know who I really am' camouflage mode all these years out of shame."

"Shame?" Mac blurted out as he straightened back up in his chair. "Shame for what? What could she possibly be ashamed of?"

"Mac, I am pretty sure that she has even been hiding from herself as well. I think you will get it by the time I am finished telling the whole story. Mac, listen. I know this is hard, but please be patient and listen to all the story, okay?"

Mac agreed to calm down and listen. "I cannot believe this, though. After all these years, wow! Anita, or what, you say she goes by Mattie? Wow," he said again, but with that, Mac's face seemed to twist into a question mark, "Wait," he quizzed, "do you think that she will even remember me now?"

"Yeah, Mac, and that is the next thing I want to lay out on the table for you." Samuel paused and let out a light chuckle. "Interesting that you would ask that question." He leaned into the table again to continue. "Mac, that is *the* reason why all this information about her, well, and you, came out yesterday. She did recognize you, instantly, I might add, the very first time you came to church. And when she did recognize you, well, she dove headfirst into her 'you are not going to find me' practiced syndrome. That would have been your first visit to the eleven o'clock service three weeks ago. Now I knew something was seriously wrong because she never, and I do not use that word lightly, missed church. We did not know that she went home that first Sunday you came, but she was nowhere to be found the next Sunday. She did, however, come to work on her next scheduled day, so I knew that she was not sick. Same thing happened last Sunday.

So yesterday, with God's help, Rebecca and I confronted her, and it all came out. So here I am today."

"Pastor Sam," Mac questioned in his most settled down voice, "it sounds like she doesn't want to see me. Why is that? I mean, you say that she did love me, and you think she still may. It has been over seventeen years, and she knows that there was no way that I could have found her, and you know I have tried..." Mac's last words just fell off, and he looked like he was deep in thought.

"And you are wondering," Samuel finished his thought, "if she still really did love you, why she did not contact you once in all these years. Also, why she did not just walk up to you that Sunday, and say, 'Hey, Larry, you remember me?'"

"Yeah," Mac said quietly as he slumped over in his chair. "Yeah," he said again, "something like that. I mean, what is that all about, and what in the world am I supposed to do now?" But then suddenly, another question dominated his whole existence. "What about our child?"

"I know you have a hundred questions, and I will answer all of them. I promise, but how about a cup of coffee?"

"No coffee down here, but I can get you a cold soda or how about a water?"

"Water will work, thanks."

Mac got up and walked behind the bar and was fumbling for a bottle of water, which was exactly what Samuel needed. He was stalling for just a little time to figure out how to tell the rest of the story.

"So what about our child?" He became very intense staring accusingly at his Pastor Sam. "I have to assume that you know."

"I do," he told Mac. "But again, I am asking you to be patient, and I will tell you everything, including the story about your child."

"Your child?" Mac repeated. "I must assume that since you did not refer to my child as a him or a her, that my child is either dead or has been adopted...what?"

"Mac," Samuel hesitated, and then, "yes, your child did die. I am so sorry."

"How did, ah, my child die?"

"Mac, please let me get it all out the only way I know how. Can you honor me with that?"

Mac unloaded his guns, figuratively speaking, mellowed out, and assured his Pastor Sam, "Yes, of course, I can. You have been so faithful. I will not interrupt you again. Thanks for all you have done so far, and it looks like what you are trying to do here again is help. Please tell me the rest."

Samuel breathed a deep starting line breath, as he endeavored to unfold this complex record of events for Mac. "Before I continue, let me warn you again, herein lies two of those for real deal bumps I was talking about."

Mac nodded his affirmation.

"What happened was this…" He went on to inform Mac what Mattie had told him and Rebecca. That Mattie's mother had her phone disconnected and moved her out of state. That her mother had convinced her that if she ever went back to Mac, she would see to it that he was arrested on rape charges, and that Mac would spend at least thirty years in prison. And if he was able to escape the charges, she would see to it that Mac's reputation was ruined beyond repair. "That, of course," Samuel told Mac, "would destroy your scholarship offers to any college. Mattie had no idea at that time that you were not going to accept one of them in the first place, so…" Samuel went on to explain that that was the reason Mattie was so afraid to contact him again. "She told us that she had seen her mother do some other things," Samuel explained, "that sounded unbelievable but got away with it. That reinforced the threat that not only would her mother do it, but it gave your Annie the belief that she could get away with that also. That is why, on your behalf, and because she really did love you, well, she bit the bullet and just stayed away."

"Oooooh…that woman," Mac seethed. Would I love to bust her. How can she sleep at nights? But here is another question for you. When Annie realized that her mother could never have gotten away with that allegation, why didn't she come to see me then?"

"Mac," Samuel once again seemed to be at a loss for words. "Okay," he endeavored, "here is the hard part for you and for your Annie too. Her mother knew, I am sure, that your Annie would try to reach out to you at some point, so she planted another poison in her thoughts. She told Annie that since you were gone from her forever, that the best thing she could do was to allow her to make an appointment for Annie at the women's clinic for an abortion. Now Annie did not initially agree to that, certainly, but with her mother's constant nagging and time passing quickly before it was too late, Annie finally was coerced into agreeing to abort your child."

Mac stood up as he shed some tears. "What a horrible thing this is. How can I ever forgive her for this?" He was not angry as much as he was simply hurt and sad.

Samuel stood also and asked, "Forgive who, Mac? Your Annie or her mother or both?"

Mac spun around rapidly. "What do I have to forgive Annie for, ah, Mattie for? It is her mother who deserved the worst punishment. Annie did not do anything. Well, okay, she did agree to abort our child, and I know that was wrong, but look at the circumstances."

"Mac, we can discuss guilt later. But you see, *that* is the reason she never came back. *That* is the reason she feels so ashamed, and *that* is what she needs to overcome, even if she never sees you again. But here is the good news. You are in the position and have the power and all else that is needed to be the one who helps her finally overcome *that* for the rest of her life."

"Me?" Mac said, surprised.

"You willing to tackle that?" Samuel asked.

"Cute, Pastor Sam, did you read what position I played at State when I was given the MVP award? I was a defensive linebacker. Am I willing to *tackle* that? And you know I am not a quitter. You know if you tell me that you think that this is the best move for Mattie, ah, Annie, I will put my uniform back on. Do I get to throw her mother to the dirt when I do *tackle* this?"

"No," was all Samuel said, and he did not laugh. "Okay, first let's tackle this name problem. She is Mattie to me and Annie to you. We both know who we are talking about."

"Got it," Mac agreed.

"Mac," Samuel said as he put on his most serious face again. "Please pay very close attention to this because this may be the last for real deal bump you will have to live with. This will be for you as well but mainly for Mattie. I believe that the only way you can permanently help Mattie is to lead her through a dark tunnel, metaphorically speaking. We can name that tunnel 'this way to forgiveness.' The tunnel might be filled with every condemnation you can think of, and all of them meant to break down yours and her emotions. It will grab at your sense of fair play. *Your* strength leading her through that dark tunnel is the key. You will need to resist the temptation for revenge. In order that Mattie exit that dark tunnel healed, she will need to forgive herself. And for her to forgive herself, she will need to forgive her mother, and do it in the same way God has forgiven her. Now, here is where your strength and leadership come into play. For Mattie to reach that goal, you will need to forgive Mattie. And even though I believe that will be easy for you, she will need convincing that you not only *say* you forgive her, but that you will forgive her in a way that makes her feel as if it never happened."

"I can do that!" Mac boasted. "Honestly, I think I can do that. That does not sound difficult to me at all. I know it will be much harder for Annie, but I will be there for her."

"I'm not finished, my wonderful friend Mac," Samuel announced. "There is one more, let me say, vital element to this becoming a success story, instead of a lifelong story of regret."

"What's that?" Mac asked but then quickly followed with, "I think I know."

"In order for Mattie to reach those goals, *you* will need to forgive her mother also before you can truly convince Mattie that you forgive her. And I might add…"

"I know," Mac said, "and forgive," he paused, "that, ah, woman in the same way God has forgiven me."

"Right," Samuel confirmed. He just looked at Mac and waited.

Mac sat back down again with his arms across his chest and fell silent. Samuel sat down next to him. "Wow, it all comes down to who do you love more," Mac confessed. "My sweet Annie or my own pride. And based on all the other things you have already taught, I cannot just say 'I forgive you' to her mother, I have to clear that with God in my heart," and he paused again, "or it's nothing."

"You *have* been listening, haven't you?" Samuel agreed. "I will confess that it is not the easiest road to take. Our natural self wants to get revenge, but if you are willing to take God and his Word to task, there is nothing we cannot overcome. We can forgive the way God has forgiven us because of what he has done for us first. We can succeed at things that we thought otherwise we could not...but that is where the word maturity comes into play, doesn't it?"

"I'll say it again," Mac stated with confidence, "I am willing to tackle this with a new heart, including learning how to forgive her mother," Mac thought for a moment and then, "I hope that there isn't anything else to this story that I haven't heard." And he looked at Samuel for confirmation.

"Oh, ah, did I tell you that Mattie said her mother hasn't changed?" he told Mac.

"Well, I figured that, but I can just start by seeing Annie by herself, right? I mean when she is ready. I do not have to *see* her mother..." Mac still waited for confirmation from Samuel but got none. "Right?" he asked the second time. "Well?" He projected that last word to Samuel as a command.

"Mac...that will be difficult. Her mother still lives with Mattie."

Mac could not say a word. He just stared into his Pastor Sam's face for a moment with a wide-mouth grin and then burst into a for real deal belly laugh. When it lightened up after a moment, he wiped the laughter from his eyes and said, "Still liv—" He broke into laughter again. Finally, "Well, is there anything else?"

Samuel just shook his head and said, "I am going to meet with Mattie tomorrow, and I will tell her that you and I talked. Mac, I honestly believe that when *she* knows that *you* know, her heart will soften. When she truly believes that you *want* to meet with her, and that you have already forgiven her, she will want to meet with you. Maybe not right away, but that ball will start to roll downhill from now on. Make it your priority to pray for her and yourself. Trust in the Bible's teachings on developing the skill to truly forgive, in the same way that God has forgiven you. You do that, and you will earn a second MVP." Samuel chuckled, and when Mac asked what he found so funny, he told Mac. "There probably will not be a plaque or a trophy for this one, though."

CHAPTER 22

When Secrets Are Not Secret

S AMUEL DID SPEAK VERY BRIEFLY with Mattie on Thursday, but as it turned out, he just set a meeting with her for the following Saturday after their board meeting. Mattie was not keen on another meeting but was not objecting to it either. It seemed to Samuel that she was disoriented and searching for what she was going to do next.

When Samuel arrived on Saturday for the board meeting, she did not seem to be any more collected with her emotions. "You okay?" Samuel asked as he met her in the office prior to making their short walk to the board meeting.

"Yeah, I guess so…maybe," she muttered.

Samuel prayed, and she put on her 'I am all business' front, so none of the elders could presume anything was amiss.

He had arranged for Rebecca to meet them in his office after the board meeting so that all three of them could settle into a 'this ought to be interesting' meeting. Rebecca told Samuel that morning, "She has no clue, or even a need to think that there would be a clue, about what we know or what we are about to tell her, does she?"

"You are correct," Samuel agreed, "and I do not want to warn her in advance. She will simply be walking into all this exactly like Mac had to do."

When Mattie, Samuel, and Rebecca finally sat together around the small conference table in his office, Samuel began. "I have known you for a dozen years, Mattie. You and I have worked side by side all these years, and although I could not boast, until last Tuesday, about how well I really know Anita Matilda Sanford." Mattie looked seriously shocked when he announced her full name. "I can boast about that now."

"What an opening," Mattie said. "I had a few ideas why you wanted this meeting, and I am willing at this point to listen to anything, but you need to answer a question for me."

"Sure, what is it?"

"You said that you can *now boast* about how much you really do know me. Now I will grant you that I let a lot out of the bag on Tuesday, but I would be interested in finding out what you think you know about me other than that. Oh, and my name? I assume you dug that up from my file, but what made you look for that anyway?"

"Mattie, we want to, no, we need to tell you about a lot of things we know and how we know what we know."

"Okay," Mattie said, "this ought to be interesting."

Samuel started with, "You told us that you recognized, ah, your Larry, when he came to church that one Sunday three weeks ago. Wouldn't you like to know why it was that he chose this church to start attending?"

"Yes, I would. I have been asking myself that since that day. I was wondering what an odd coincidence that was."

"I know the answer to that question, as well as the answers to many other questions you do not yet know to ask, but let me start with that, ah...coincidence. I want to take you back to that one board meeting, probably four months ago now. You remember, when I told everyone how just the night before we picked Jeremy up in the middle of the night and got him to the hospital?"

"Sure, I remember, but what has that got to do with the price of prunes in Brazil or wherever they grow them?"

"Brace yourself, Mattie," Samuel said. "You are about to hear what they say is 'the rest of the story.' Do you know where we found

Jeremy that night?" he asked. "It was right outside the back door of Bobo's Bar and Grill."

"No!" Mattie said as she stiffened and pulled her hand up over her mouth in shock and just stared at them. Then, ever so softly, "And you met Larry that night."

"It was pure chance," Rebecca chimed in, "and we had no idea who he was, what he was, or how all this was going to unfold. Samuel, being Pastor Samuel, and again by God's grace, pursued him and eventually became his friend."

"I have been mentoring him ever since," Samuel confided, "and naturally, I invited him to church and voila, here he is."

Mattie was speechless but finally told Samuel, "I wish I could say 'good job,' but look what you stirred up."

"He scared the life out of us that first night," Rebecca added. "We met him, rather he found us, at gunpoint I might add, about four in the morning, and he told us his name was Mac."

"Yeah, everyone, well except his mom and me, called him Mac. I always liked to call him Larry, you know like he was only mine or something."

"Anyway," Samuel went on, "it was maybe a couple of weeks after that night that I started meeting with him at his place every Sunday afternoon. For the first several weeks, he shared everything with me about himself and about you. So now after all this time, I have gotten to know you pretty well without knowing it was really you. All that came together when you finally shared 'the rest of *your* story.' He never knew you as Mattie. He only referred to you as 'his Annie.' I never knew you as Anita or Annie, and that is why I never put the two of you together. Of course, after you shared your story, I was able to put two and two together, so I looked your name up in our files to be sure and bingo."

"How much did he tell you?"

"Pretty much everything he knew about you up until you disappeared. How you met, how you dated, how he found out you were pregnant, your mother, etc. I needed him to share it all with me so that I could help him overcome his seventeen-year mountain of hurts. I was trying to help him to be set free from all those regrets and to get on with his life. I convinced him that his Annie, not knowing that she was you, Mattie, most likely was never going to come back, so the smartest thing he could do would be to erase his Annie from his memory."

"You've known him all this time, but you didn't even mention his name," Mattie sniffled out through her tears.

"What was he supposed to say?" Rebecca kindly asked in Samuel's defense. "He had no idea until last Tuesday who Mac was to you, or what this was all about. He could not suspect that your Larry was his Mac. Plus, his counseling with him was confidential."

"Mattie," Samuel told her again, "you need to brace yourself for even more. Mac had no idea either about any of this," and he paused to gain eye contact, "until Wednesday this week. Until then, he was completely content to put you out of his mind forever."

"What? You met with him after we met? And what, you told him everything?"

"Yes, I did, Mattie, and I know that sounds like I broke confidence with you, but think about it. I am his mentor, and I had knowledge, all the knowledge that he has been looking for, for almost two decades. I was the one who was trying to help him put you completely out of his life. Then you showed up, like some angel, he had always hoped you would. I could not just pretend that I did not know the rest of *his* story. I was obligated to tell him everything. It should have come from you, but all three of us in *this* room know that that would have not happened for a very long time...or at all, maybe. and," Samuel emphasized, "if I had not opened that can of stew, each of you would still be licking your wounds looking for bandages that did not exist. Remember this also. I am telling you *everything* he and I talked about for the same reasons. I told him I would, though."

"Did you tell him..." She began to cry. "Did you tell him?" She started over, "About...ah...the...ah...our child?"

"I did, Mattie," Samuel said, "yes, I did. But you need to know that he holds *nothing* against you at all, and let me say that again... *nothing!*"

Through her tears, she looked up at Samuel. "You should have been a pastor," she told him again.

"Mattie, I ran head long into *all* the answers he had been looking for, for seventeen years, and he needed this to *really* get on with his life. I told Mac, and now I am telling you, that there is a phenomenal up side to all this...*if* you will just take a chance, and—"

"You know," Mattie interrupted, "I know one thing that is better already for me, although it still is very painful and embarrassing. I do not have to figure out how to tell him anymore."

"Mattie," Samuel assured her. "Take heart in this. Not only does Mac know everything, but he is so excited about finally being able to see you. Honestly, and I say this without needing to embellish it at all. Genuinely, he cannot wait to see you. One more thing as well, he told me that he has already forgiven you...unequivocally."

"How can he do that?" Mattie just hung her head in shame again. "His life was ruined too, and it was me who did it to him."

"Mattie," Rebecca said softly, "his life is not ruined. Neither is yours, and right here, you and he are at a crossroad. It is like you have two doors available that you can open. One of those doors will let you spend how many more years regretting over what you did not get, and the other door allows you to rejoice over a very possible, I might even say probable, great future."

At that, Samuel silently smiled as he looked at Rebecca for coming up with one of his analogies.

"There is a *cost*, though," Samuel said, expounding on Rebecca's word picture, "for choosing either one of those two doors. The cost of the 'regret' door is continued misery. The cost for choosing the 'rejoicing' door is learning to forgive. Mac has already opened that door for you, Mattie. You have two difficult areas involving forgiveness. You need to forgive yourself, and you and he both need to forgive your mother. The hard part of that last one is that you will have to give up your self-imposed right for revenge. I will get into that another time."

"So," Rebecca told Mattie, "we have a great idea on helping you to forgive yourself. It may take a while, but I believe this is the absolute best idea for you." Rebecca waited for a moment and when she knew that Mattie was really interested, she went on. "We have a very dear friend. Her name is Nancy, and she has been ministering to women of all ages, for years. Women just like you who have fallen into the trap of aborting a child and living with guilt for years. Will you allow me to call her and make an appointment for you? And if you are willing, I will even go with you to meet with her."

Mattie did not hesitate. "I do know I need help," she confessed, "so, yes, go ahead and make that appointment for me, and yes again about you coming with me, thanks."

"I will let you know," Rebecca said. "Most likely early this next week."

"All this sounds too good to be true," Mattie said, "and you know what they say about something sounding too good to be true? So what am I supposed to do now? I mean about Larry?" She held up her hands in an 'I am still lost' gesture.

"Well, I will be in constant contact with Mac, but I will not put words in your mouth. He really wants to see you, but he is also very understanding. He will wait for you to make the move. When you are ready, you let me know, and I will set it up. Maybe right here in my office if that is comfortable for you, but I would ask that you not wait long. I say that for your sake as well as for his."

"Forgive me, but I still do not think that I can come to church," Mattie told them. "I really am not ready to see him."

"I understand, and I am sure he understands also."

They invited Mattie out for dinner, but she declined. "I have my very unthankful, ah," she paused, "my precious mother to make dinner for." Mattie looked at them with an 'I'm loving her anyway' fake smile across her face.

"Good job," Samuel told her. "Keep it up."

CHAPTER 23

Two Reasons

"**H**OW ABOUT A HOT CUP of coffee?" Rebecca asked.

"You got it," Samuel said, smiling. "How long has it been where we could just hang out, just the two of us, for a while not needing to *fix* someone or something? Thanks."

Life for Samuel and Rebecca seemed to fall into a pleasant kind of a lull compared to all the angst they had been facing daily for some time. They would wake up each morning not having anything out of the ordinary on their plates that *needed* conquering before noon. Of course, Mac and Mattie were still in their prayers, and Mac seemed to be in such a joyous mood having found out that his Annie was alive and well. He was living on the hope that she would soon want to meet with him. Samuel needed to encourage him to be patient, but it needed to be Mattie's call as to when, and he understood that. After about a week, though, and Mattie had not mentioned setting up a meeting with Mac, Samuel began to wonder what she must be going through. She had started her counseling with Nancy at the Crisis Pregnancy Center, so he thought that might have something to do with her being uncertain. He had his radar on full blast though, ready to encourage her to meet this man who would still be the love of her life.

Patricia and Randy were also heavy on their minds and hearts, and they prayed constantly for them. Rebecca would almost daily have Pat on the phone to reassure her, "Nothing is considered impossible with God," and to "keep the faith."

Time was slipping by for Jeremy, but Samuel appeared to be the only one who was *really* keeping a light on for him, figuratively speaking. Samuel thought that since Jeremy had all but destroyed so many of his opportunities, it was only a matter of time that he would call or just come home. "I believe," Samuel assured Rebecca, "that the longer Jeremy stays away, the deeper the hole he will be in. Thus, the more complete his recovery will be *when* it starts, not *if* it starts."

"He has never been out of touch this long ever before," Rebecca said sadly. "I am worried that something has happened to him, or that he will choose to never come back."

"We can only pray and hope," Samuel told her. "There is no way that he could not see the genuine love and patience that we had shown him when he was here the first time, and I believe he knows that we will take him in again if he asks. It is his unforgiveness and pride that keeps him away. It is normal for someone who has been hurt as seriously as he has been to close the forgiveness door and to keep the revenge door wide open. That is what is keeping him from even listening to anything about forgiving his father. I am praying that he does that soon. You are always telling Pat to keep the faith for him, and we need to do the same."

They finished their coffee, and he got up to head for the office. Samuel still had a church to lead with board meetings, outreach ministries, men's and women's group meetings, prayer groups to lead, and sermons to write. All that, however, was more like a regular 'in the groove' type of living than anything that would create more drama.

When he walked into the office, he saw that Mattie was busy "yakking" on the phone. He did not hear what was being said, but he did stop dead in his tracks. *Mattie?* he thought. *She has* never *done that before. She only ever used the church phone for business. Also, her attitude and tone had* always *been strictly business, but here she is grinning and laughing, and apparently talking to…a friend? Oh, Mattie, good for you. You have really changed in just one week.* Of course, he had not uttered a single word for her to hear, but when she noticed him, she started to close out her conversation. Samuel caught her attention and waved at her to not worry about it, as he walked toward his office door. But she did hang up, stood up, and asked if she could come into his office and talk with him.

"Sure, Mattie, come on in." He opened the door to let her in, as he swung the door wide open. That was his practice any time he had a single female who needed to visit with *the pastor*. "What's up?" he asked her.

"Do you need to ask?" she questioned rhetorically as she sat down without him inviting her to sit.

Mattie was visibly different, and he had to say something. "Let me just say this. You, Mattie, are not the same Mattie I have ever known, and it looks good on you. I want to assume that you have made some tremendous progress with Nancy?"

"That, Pastor Sam, is an understatement. It is like I *knew* all those things about how to forgive myself, but there was always this 'yeah but' that was forever getting in the way. But it was during my last session with Nancy where it all made sense for the first time. She said that *knowing* and *believing* that you can be forgiven are two different things. I was stuck on how in the world could anyone forgive me for what I had done, especially Larry. I simply lived in a constant state of guilt and shame, and I just knew that I could not be forgiven for what I had done, so how was I ever going to forgive myself? There was one thing that I first had to come to grips with before that was going to happen. I had to face the fact that, although Mom did coerce me into it, I still was the one who simply laid down and let it happen to me. I came up with many excuses then, and ever since, to help alleviate some of my guilt. But when I finally confessed that it was *me* who was the sinner in God's eyes and came clean with my full confession, I could clearly see how he would forgive me. So I figured that if God would truly forgive me, permanently, and he did, why could I not forgive myself.

"And that is not to say Mom is innocent, but it is to say that I *am*...correction," she said, "*was* guilty. I feel so great today because Nancy helped me to accept my sin as mine, and with that, she led me into confessing and believing that God has totally forgiven me of that sin. I know I will get better now because I learned how to forgive myself, and in the same way that God has already forgiven me. Nancy told me also that God has removed even the guilt of my sin, so I can finally be set free. And again, I say, I *knew* all these things, but I just would not *believe* them on the level that counted for me. I could not forgive myself because I kept saying to myself, 'I do not deserve to be forgiven, why should God forgive me?' In essence, I really did not trust God to do what he said he would do. Oh…for others, yes, but not for me. I am forgiven, and I do forgive myself. Is that good stuff or what?"

"Mattie, you have crossed over a bridge that appears to be so difficult for so many to cross over. Not only needing to forgive themselves, but forgiving others in their lives as well, and to do that, in the same way God has forgiven them. Before this is done, you may be called on to help a lot of other women over that same bridge. I am always interested in your kind of testimony. It shows me that there are many sitting right here in our sanctuary, Sunday after Sunday who, like you, need exactly what you needed. Yes, my wonderful newly set free Mattie, you may well be used to help many others."

"I certainly am not ready yet, but Nancy invited me to continue having sessions with her for the purpose of learning to become an advocate like she is. Like you just said, to help other women. I am seriously thinking about that."

"I cannot wait to tell Rebecca," Samuel said. "Would you mind if I did share this with her?"

"Certainly, please tell her everything."

"You know, Mattie, I just had a thought. Wouldn't it be a blessing to her if you came over for dinner with us, and you could tell her yourself? I think that that would bless the socks off her."

"Sure, you just tell me when."

"Well, I will need to clear it with Becca, but I was thinking maybe next Sunday? You know, after church?"

Mattie fell as silent as a stone and just stared at her pastor. She did not say a word for way too long a time, but then finally smiled at him, and said, "I am not stupid, Pastor Sam."

"Whaaaat?" he kind of sang out the single word, feigning ignorance, but had a grin on his face from ear to ear.

"You meet with Larry on Sundays after church. You want to invite him to dinner with me so that the two of us will finally meet?"

Samuel leaned forward in his office chair and confessed. "Yeah, I was thinking that, but on a serious note, I will respect your decision to set that up whenever you are ready. But dinner at our house is still on, if it is okay with Becca, next Sunday. And no, I will not surprise you by asking your Mac, ah, your Larry to come."

"My Larry," she said. "I like that. Maybe he will be again."

Mattie looked at her pastor and sheepishly confessed, "I guess I should be ready to meet him, but I am scared to death. You want to know what is holding me back from agreeing to meet him?"

"Only if you want to tell me," he assured her.

"There are two things that are blockades for me. The first one is that what if he sees me, and he does not want to start up with me again? What if he sees me and thinks that I am not worth the bother? I would not blame him at all, but that would hurt. The second thing is, what if after I see him, I do not want him again? That would hurt also. So I have been just sitting on the sidelines trying to gain the courage to get up and dance." She looked at Samuel with a question mark written all over her face. It basically spelled, "Help!"

"Mattie, you gave me two reasons that are keeping you undecided. That limbo state of indecisiveness you are caught in is a killer. You are on the fence where one side leads you to not seeing him soon, and the other side of the fence leads you to not seeing him at all. In other words, you are bogged down on two reasons why you cannot or should not see him. Now I can come up with a dozen reasons why you should meet with him, and you should do that soon, but let me give you just two. First, you know it is the right thing to do. It is not your fault that you were taken away from him all those years ago, but it surely is not his fault either. He has been waiting for you for all these years, you know, because I told you that he was. The second reason is that I truly believe that he loved you more than life itself back then, and it is possible that he still does.

But even if when you meet, he decides to continue his life a confirmed bachelor, or he finally decides that you are not the one and seeks someone else, he has been gifted by you to finally be set free to choose. And...the same thing for you. You have not been waiting for him all these years, but you now have the opportunity to be set free yourself to choose your direction. But that will only happen after you meet with him and find out for sure."

Mattie smiled at her pastor, nodded her affirmation, and then told him once again, "You should have been a pastor, Pastor Sam. I got it, and I thank you. You say we should meet next Sunday?"

"Good decision, Mattie," Samuel said and smiled back at her knowingly.

"Oh, you are so bad, Pastor, and she smiled back at him. "You had this planned, didn't you? Well, okay, but I will make no bones about it, I am scared to death." With that, she got up and went back to her desk.

Samuel quietly closed the door. When he called Rebecca, she confirmed that dinner on Sunday would be just fine, but when he told her about Mattie agreeing to have Mac join them, he had to pull the phone away from his ear for the gleeful screech that came from her side of their conversation.

"You going to call Mac now?" she asked.

"Yeah, I thought I would. I am sure that Mattie has no idea how much he will be looking forward to seeing her. Talk to you later."

Samuel dialed Mac's number, and it rang several times before he picked up. "Sup, Pastor Sam? You got good news for me, or…or what?"

"Good news, Mac. Mattie agreed to meet. We have asked her over for dinner next Sunday after church. She knows that I am asking you to come, so she will not be surprised. She is ready to see you."

Mac very shyly asked, "What am I going to say to her? The last time I saw her was seventeen years ago. You sure she wants to see me?"

"Mac, I am positive, but she is nervous about finally meeting you. I know you are nervous also."

"I did not say that I was nervous," Mac protested. "Did you hear me say that I was nervous? Hahaha," he faked a laugh. "No, I am not nervous. Heck, I am an MVP state champion, remember? No way, I am not even a little nervous, Pastor Sam," and he paused for a moment and then whispered into the phone, "I am scared to death."

Hmmm, Samuel thought. *That is exactly what Mattie said. This is going to be interesting. Good, but interesting.* But to Mac, he only reassured him, "It will all work out very well, Mac, trust me," and they disconnected.

"Wow, who but God?" Samuel said to himself out loud. He paused to give thanks to God.

CHAPTER 24

It Is about Time

TIME SPAT SUNDAY OUT WAY too quickly for Samuel and Rebecca, where as it felt like a month of Sundays to arrive for Mac and for Mattie. While nervousness and fear traded dominant positions in Mattie's mind, it was a cross between joy and anxiety for Mac. After church, Samuel and Rebecca went home to prepare their meal and ready themselves for what Mac dubbed, "our long-awaited reunion." It was arranged that they each just show up around one.

Time is a killer, when you are caught watching the clock, but watching the clock is a human trait. Especially when you are forced to wait for something you just cannot wait for. No matter what thoughts were running through Rebecca's mind, the clock could not escape her wanting eyes. "Should be here by now, shouldn't they?" she could not help asking herself.

Samuel looked up from the paper he was reading, "Twelve for-ty-eight," he announced. "Not yet, but I will bet if you wait another minute, you will ask again," he said sarcastically as he let an almost inaudible chuckle slip from his sense of humor.

She was not amused but kept on pacing back and forth. Samuel put his paper down and found contentment in watching Rebecca pace and watch the clock.

Finally, the doorbell rang, and it was Mattie. Rebecca let her in, and Samuel was just a little in awe of her. He had never seen her in a fashionable dress with makeup on. Mattie was certainly not overdone, but it showed that she had put her Sunday best on for her Larry. Silently, he thought, *Mac will certainly be impressed.*

"Am I early?" she asked. "I mean I did not want to look anxious or anything, but, ah, well, here I am. I guess that Larry is not here yet."

"No," Rebecca assured her that she was not early. "Come on in and sit down." She motioned to one of the chairs.

She walked in but did not sit. "Think I'll just stand here for a moment," Mattie commented, and she chuckled nervously. "Where's the back door if I need it?"

"Mattie, you'll be fine," Rebecca assured her. "Really, you will be just fine. Please have a seat. When he gets here, you can stand up again if you wish."

"Seriously, I am as nervous as one can be. Not only for not seeing him in all these years," she told them, "but mainly because of the circumstances around our separation and about our child. Not only did he not have anything to do with any of that, but he was just dumped without any explanation."

"I told you, Mattie," Samuel assured her, "that he was doing well with all this. He and I have talked about everything many times this last week. Nearly all his thoughts are wrapped around the joy of knowing that you are well. Do not forget that he is nervous too, but more than anything, he is just glad that you are willing to meet with him."

"Can you just pray with me?"

"Sure, we can." Rebecca wrapped her arm around her while Samuel politely just put a hand on Mattie's shoulder. Rebecca prayed for peace, acceptance, and understanding for her and for Mac. Her prayer had barely ended, though, and the doorbell rang the second time. Mattie just turned to face the door and seemed to be frozen into a solid statue with a smile on her face. As Samuel walked slowly to the door, he motioned back at Mattie to calm down, and Rebecca squeezed her shoulders as if to say, *It'll be okay.*

Mac stood at the open door looking like a teenager on his first date needing permission from his date's father. It was not until

Samuel made a formal invitation, "Won't you come in," that Mac made the move to enter.

Mac stepped into their living room and stopped at the sight of his precious Annie. It was at that moment, though, when his eyes met hers, that Mac seemed to project the most calm and manly confidence that had to have been a magnet for Mattie. He walked slowly toward her as he presented a beautiful bouquet of coral-colored roses to her. "I remember you telling me that you like the coral more than the red," he announced and paused, waiting for her to accept the flowers. "I have missed you, Annie, so much."

Mattie could not reach out to take the roses from him. Both her hands had covered all but her wide-open eyes on her face. She was looking up into his eyes and could not move. Tears were rolling over the top of her fingers as she was as still and as silent as could be. Rebecca moved in rapidly to receive the roses. "Here, I'll get a vase for those," but before she could, Mattie did reach out to accept the bouquet from him without taking her eyes off his. "Larry," was all she was able to say, then she looked down at the roses. "You did remember. Thanks." Rebecca did run to the kitchen and came back with an appropriate vase, and Mattie handed the flowers to her. "Oh, Larry, I am so sorry. I am so, so sorry."

Mac slowly reached out his arms to give her a hug but waited for her to receive him. She instantly dove into his arms and squeezed him harder than any running back he ever had to tackle in the old days. She did not let go for a long time. Finally, he broke their embrace and offered to sit and talk. "Larry?" he started off. "That is interesting. No one hardly ever used my first name. Mom and you, but everyone else always called me Mac."

"I like your first name," she told him. Of course, this first meeting was going to start off awkward, like two interested teenagers meeting for the first time. This, however, was even harder for each of them because of all that had transpired. "So how have you been?" she asked, "and how's the bar doing—"

"Oh, well, it is, ah doing fine. I still, well, run the bar, and, well, how about you?"

So Rebecca intervened by asking Mac, "Why don't you tell Mattie, I mean Annie, about the first time you ran into us? What was it, three maybe four in the morning?"

"Close," he said, "and I wish I had a photograph of your face when you turned around and saw me holding my flashlight on you."

"I don't mind telling you, ah, Annie," Rebecca told her, "that this hunk of a man standing there in the dark that night nearly scared the life out of me, but," and she stopped talking and looked at Mac, "you were found out, weren't you?"

"Yes, I was, and I'll tell you what, Annie, that meeting was the start of the second-best thing that has ever happened to me."

"So don't keep the lady waiting, Mac," Rebecca said, "tell her the story."

"Well, I was coming down from my apartment to do a double-check on things, and I saw these two, ah, vagrants—"

"Vagrants," Samuel interrupted, laughing. "Vagrants?"

"No, just joking. I could tell that they were not any trouble the way that they were dressed, and the way they were acting, but I had to treat the situation as if they were. Anyway, there they were..." And Mac went on to tell the whole story to Annie, and when he finished, she asked him.

"You said that that meeting with them was the beginning of the second-best thing that had happened to you. What did that meeting have to do with anything?"

Mac looked at his Annie and told her. "That night, although I had no idea what was going to happen, was the start that led me back to you."

She lowered her head, showing off her shy side. A side that Samuel had until recently never seen. "And what was the first-best thing that ever happened to you?" Mattie went on, "if you don't mind me asking."

"Well, Annie," Mac said with the seriousness of a judge. "The best thing that has ever happened to me was that touchdown I kept from scoring against us, so we could win State." He was almost able to contain his laughter but did not. Samuel slapped him on the back jokingly.

"Seriously, Annie, the best thing that has ever happened to me, outside of getting to know how to start following Christ, is meeting you for the first time." Then Mac added in a comical way, "You know?" he said, looking right into Annie's eyes, "You had me from hello, and you know it."

Mattie reciprocated in kind with words of her own, and with that, the ice was broken, as they say. The two of them just began to chatter like they had not missed a beat in all those years. Rebecca motioned for Samuel to follow her into the kitchen. When they were out of sight of Mac and Annie, Samuel did a silent *yes* bump with his fist, like a rookie football player might after scoring his first touchdown.

Rebecca began her final preparations for dinner, and after a short while, Samuel peeked his head around the corner to check out the two new lovebirds, and it appeared like they were going strong. Rebecca even felt guilty when she had to call them twice to the dinner table. "Dinner's on."

After dinner and the catching up was as far as they thought that they would go on this first meeting, Rebecca asked them both. "Your names!" she said. "First you, Mac. I want to assume that we all, maybe even you, ah...what, Mattie, will find it appropriate to continue to call you Mac?"

"No...Mattie argued. "Sorry, but Larry to me is Larry, thank you very much."

"Mac is fine though," Mac said, "for everyone else. I prefer it, and except for Annie, I am not sure anyone else on earth knows my first name, or if they do, they will not care. No, Mac is fine."

Rebecca just looked at Mattie for a moment. "You, on the other hand, are going to be a difficult case, aren't you, ah Mattie, or Anita, aka Annie."

"Yes, I know. Everyone on earth except for my mom, Larry, and his family, know me as Mattie." She offered up a frown just as she mentioned his family. She could not help but notice that Mac looked just a little hurt. She had no knowledge that his brother Buck had been shot to death, or that his mother was gone. Everyone at the table knew but her. Mac covered it up with a genuine smile and a "tell you later" comment and went on like nothing had happened.

"I will always call you my Annie," Mac stated, looking at her.

"Mac, Rebecca, and I came to an understanding on your name if you like it," Samuel butted in. "We agreed that you are Mattie to us at church and Annie for Mac. I think that if anyone must ask, or just needs to know, we will simply tell them that Annie has always used her middle nickname Mattie at church. Is that okay with you, ah, Mattie?" she agreed and they all applauded, and that settled that.

They all talked for some time after Rebecca and Mattie had cleared the table and washed the dishes. They said their goodbyes, and Mac and Mattie walked out together. Samuel locked the front door and invited his Becca back into the kitchen for another cup of coffee.

"What a wonderful day this turned out to be," Samuel said nonchalantly as Rebecca poured the coffee.

"It looks like the two of them are out of the woods and headed for a new and wonderful beginning. Isn't that a miracle?" Rebecca said in amazement. "Wow, seventeen years after each of them, not knowing what happened to the other, finally getting back together? Who but God could do that?"

Samuel did not respond, and after a few minutes, Rebecca felt like something was wrong. "What?" she asked. "What are you thinking?"

"I'll agree," he told her. "Certainly, they are out of the woods, as far as their relationship with each other is concerned, but—"

"But what?" she questioned.

"Becca, until Mattie forgives her mother, and I mean more than with only words, she is not close to being out of the woods all together. Same with Mac. Until he truly forgives Mattie's mother, he is not totally out of the woods because he is about to face some hardwood trees he has not yet had to face. Right now, I mean today, each of them is on cloud nine. Mattie for the first time since she left Mac, all those years ago, has experienced a real breath of fresh air. Her Larry is back, he has forgiven her, she has forgiven herself, so how much better can it get? Right? Well, Mattie told me that her mother has not changed, so Mattie will need to confront her mother sooner than later. How do you think that will go?" Samuel sat, thinking for a moment and then, "How about this?" *'Hey, Mom, you remember that boy I was in love with and who I got pregnant with? You know that Larry Macpherson guy? The boy whose family owned that bar, Bobo's? That boy you made sure would be taken out of my life forever and subsequently coerced me into aborting his child? Well, guess what, Mom, he is back, and we are getting together again.'* Oh, and when Mattie does confront her mother, she will likely respond with something like, *What…that evil boy who ruined your life…and mine. Are you kidding me…he is back? Well, we will just see about that!'*"

"Boy you sure can paint a story," she told Samuel.

"That is why I think that neither one of them is completely out of the woods," Samuel continued. "They still have some of those hardwood trees to dodge. That picture I just painted for you is probably the most likely scenario. If her mother pitches her normal 'I am going to make life impossible for you and for him' again, Mac and Mattie will need us more than ever. I have no fear that they will survive, but it will be difficult, at best, and that is why I want to make a preemptive strike on their behalf. Teaching them to genuinely forgive Mattie's mother will ultimately be all the protection they will need. If they can get there, they will not only survive that kind of evil attack, but it will enable them to grow in their relationship. That one thing will set up a foundation for them that cannot be destroyed. They will experience more honesty, peace, love, and endurance than either of them could ever hope for. *Your* testimony of forgiveness," he told Rebecca, "will be a bright light and an enormous aide for Mattie. You have totally forgiven your father in every way. That, and her new association with Nancy, can be all she needs to finally break through her last unforgiveness barrier she has been hiding behind and permanently forgive her mother. Mac and I have gained a mutual respect, and I think that is all that is needed to see him walk away from those last few hardwoods and permanently forgive Mattie's mother also. Especially when he sees Mattie succeeding."

They spent the next several hours taking care of some minor things that were needed around the house and then settling in for a movie. They were both exhausted and decided to call it a night. "To the bed and beyond," Samuel jokingly boasted as he challenged the stairs to their bedroom.

CHAPTER 25

Evidence

S AMUEL SAT IN HIS OFFICE laboring over his upcoming sermon. Wednesdays were his close everything else out and 'work on my sermon' day. Often, he would struggle as he studied to put together the most appropriate Scriptures for his teach. It always worked out, but today he just could not produce anything that did not seem out of place in one or more areas. After sitting for a lengthy period, leaning on his altered and realtered notes, he closed his notebook in frustration on all he had tried to write. He turned his office chair around to look out of his large bay window and was instantly taken back at the sight of his late spring/early summer garden as most of it was in full bloom. "What an absolute beauty that is," he declared. "Look at all the colors, sizes, shapes, and styles of growing things that God has made. And all that I am looking at represents only a minute fraction of all that there is in all the earth. You truly are a magnificent God," he proclaimed silently to himself. Suddenly, his sermon came to him. "Look at all the people of the earth. The different colors, sizes, shapes, and styles that God has created. Even identical twins have unique differences, and just like that, he thought he knew what his sermon was to be. It would take a while to put it all together, but he had the subject matter down pat. "Thank you, Lord," he said out loud.

Samuel got up and headed for the coffeepot in the outer office. When he opened his door, he saw that Mattie was already pouring a cup. She turned around and offered it, "Here you go, Pastor Sam, just for you."

He received the gift with gratitude, but then asked, "How on earth did you know I wanted a cup of coffee?"

"I didn't. I poured that cup for me, but when you came out of your door, I suspected that that is what you were looking for, so enjoy. I will get another." Mattie stood there staring at Samuel with an unusual look on her face and did not turn around to get herself another cup.

"Thanks," he said again, as he turned to head back into his office, then stopped and turned back around. "Ah, is something wrong?"

"No," she said with a grin on her face. "Something wrong with you?"

"Noooooo? Should there be?"

"No, just asking." She was waving her hand in the air like she was batting a fly.

"Okay, I'll just go back to work now," he told her. "You sure nothing is wrong?"

"I am positive," she said in a bouncy type of voice with a grin on her face that made Samuel think that she was hiding something from him, so he paused momentarily before going back into his office. *Hmmm, the coffee maker, maybe,* he thought. "Did she, what, make some different kind of coffee?" But then he smiled back at her again and waved as if to say, *See you later,* and disappeared into his office.

"Boy," Samuel said quietly, "Mac, you sure did alter my supremely straight up perfect secretary. Good job, though." He sat back down in his chair, wanting to build his sermon, but began to ponder, instead, on all the unusual events that had taken place over the last year. "And some months?" he added. "Wow, how long *has* it been?" He could not remember how long it had been since anyone had heard a peep about Jeremy. "When are you going to come home, son?" he asked himself inadvertently calling him "son" because Jeremy was his prodigal. Samuel just stopped to pray for him again. Winter had come and gone since that awful night that Jeremy had just stormed out with so much anger.

There were a multitude of other almost impossible to believe events that had taken place as well. "But nothing shall be called impossible with you, God," he said out loud. He took a sip of his coffee as he remembered that first visit he had with Mac. How he ultimately 'was found out' for being a great generous gentle giant, and the long story he told about the love of his life. "Wow," Samuel said, wagging his head from side to side as he replayed the whole story of Mattie coming clean with her story and the love of her life. He knew that both Mac and Mattie had been working on forgiving her mother, and probably were already there. He took another sip of his coffee and was totally enjoying his different kind of Wednesday. He chuckled at the memory of what Mac had named 'our long-awaited reunion' dinner, where Mattie and Mac finally got back together. He smiled recalling how the two of them began a wonderful relationship. "That was, what…" He could not recall how long ago that had been. At that thought, though, Samuel froze in his seat. "Oh no, you blind and ignorant man," he called himself. He snapped out of his chair and ran to the door, and when he pulled it open, Mattie was sitting at her desk with that same unusual grin on her face.

"You got it, didn't you?" she said. "Sometimes even you, Pastor Sam, are a little slow."

"It hit me like a brick," he said, "but not while you were waving your hand around frantically trying to get me to see the ring. Yeah, Mattie, I got it. Let me see it, and congratulations."

She lifted her left hand to reveal her engagement ring. "It is the same one he gave me seventeen years ago."

"So happy for the both of you, Mattie. That must have just happened."

"Last night, and thanks to you and Rebecca for all you have done."

Samuel could hear his cell phone ringing in his office, so he raised a finger to Mattie as if to say hold that thought and raced in to grab his call before they hung up. He got to his phone in time, picked it up, and walked back to close his office door. "Becca," he said excitedly, "you will never guess what I just found out."

"Mac proposed to Mattie," she stated. "Yeah, I know."

"How did you find out so quickly?"

"Mac called here because he figured that Mattie would tell you. I thought that he would have proposed a long time ago. What was he waiting for? They have been seeing each other for over five months."

"Doesn't matter, but I think it was because they both had to work through her mother's threats and actions. Anyway, here they are."

"She sure has been a thorn in Mattie's side all these months, and from the things you have told me, that just about tore Mac up. I think they are doing pretty good now, though, don't you?"

"Yeah, they are," he assured Rebecca, "but I have to go. I will call you later."

"See you," she said and hung up.

He went back out to talk with Mattie. "Have you talked about a date yet?"

"No," she said. "We still have a huge load to carry with Mom. She is so obstinate and controlling. She just refuses to give in. She still thinks that she can thwart our whole relationship, but I have told her maybe a dozen times, *"We* are *getting married."* I told her last night again, and boy did she hit the roof…again. Every kind of accusation, condemnation, and threat you could think of just erupted out of my mother's mouth."

"Interestingly," Samuel told her. "Nothing in what you just told me indicated that you are angry at her."

"I am not. I am hurt to be sure, but that is what Mac and I are dealing with. We do not know how it will all turn out, but we are not angry at her at all.

"You and Mac are not condemning her for anything?"

"No, it is like you taught us. I think that we have truly forgiven her. We hold no malice toward her for anything. We have waited this long to get back together, so we felt a little longer would not make much difference to us if that will help her. We are going to wait just a little longer, and if she insists on not coming around, we will get married anyway."

"You both are on the right path. Good for you, Mattie. Therein lies the evidence of true forgiveness," he said out loud.

Samuel returned to his office, but before he could dive into his work, his thoughts invaded his reason and brought him, again, to asking the hard question about his brother-in-law. "Where are you, Jeremy?"

CHAPTER 26

Does Prayer Really Work?

I N THE DAYS THAT FOLLOWED, Samuel prayed continually for his prodigal, Jeremy. Of course, he also prayed for the upcoming marriage of Mac and Mattie, as well as for Mattie's mother, but it was Jeremy who occupied most of Samuel's prayers.

One time, as he was praying for Jeremy, he remembered a story he heard about a western town that had been experiencing a very long-lasting drought. He was not sure if it was a true story, or just one that was made up by someone, but it still had an impact. The story was told where one Sunday morning the pastor of a local church in the area announced that they were all going to gather at the church that evening and carpool out of town into the desert and collectively pray for rain. All but a few of their congregation showed up, and they all drove out of town and began to pray for God to grace the area with his lifesaving rain. The odd side of this story was that one little boy showed up with an umbrella. He came prepared for God to answer their prayer. He believed that if they asked, God would do it, and he did not want to get wet. "Ask and you shall indeed receive," Samuel said out loud, and he began to pray for Jeremy that same way. "Lord," he would confidently say, "I am trusting you to bring him back, and I thank you that Jeremy will be given another chance to see, believe, and live by faith in You." The following day, he went to his friend who had given Jeremy a job in the first place and convinced him to allow Jeremy to have his job back when he did return.

"You know," he told Samuel. "If he does make a legitimate turnaround and is willing to work, I'll give him another chance."

Samuel also went out and purchased some new clothing he felt was Jeremy's size.

"Wow," Rebecca told him. "That certainly is proactive. You believe that he is coming back then?"

"I do," Samuel announced confidently, "I will hold him accountable just like I told you that I would, but let me tell you a story about an umbrella."

"He has been gone so long now," she said, "and he has not tried to contact Pat or anyone for what over half a year? I must confess that I am feeling like he just decided to say goodbye to all of us and simply moved on…or worse. I keep praying for him, but…" and her sentence just trailed off into silence.

Samuel looked at her and smiled. "I don't know how or when, but I am trusting God for Jeremy."

They seemed to have that conversation often, and it seemed to always end with "just trust God," being his last words to Rebecca before turning off the lights when they went to bed.

The days turned into weeks, and the weeks turned into another month. It appeared that everyone who knew Jeremy carried a kind of "hope," but it was Samuel who seemed to keep the light on for him. Mac would ask about him, Mattie would ask about him, Pat would ask about him, and even members of the church board often asked about him. "No one here wants to give up on your Jeremy," one of the elders told him. "We are standing with you in prayer for Jeremy," but Samuel knew that their hope was turning to doubt.

"That's okay," he told Rebecca. "I know it is difficult to keep the faith when you cannot see anything happening. But therein lies the real meaning of faith. As I told everyone, I am trusting God for Jeremy. That does not mean I am going to get to see when, how, or even what God is going to do with Jeremy. It only means that I am going to be faithful to trust in God for him."

After one late-night vigil for his Jeremy, Samuel collapsed on his side of the bed, falling to sleep very shortly after he laid down. He had no idea how long he had been asleep when he was wakened by a noise he did not recognize. He lifted his head off his pillow to get a better understanding of what he heard, and he waited. "There it is again," he said out loud.

"There, *what* is again?" Rebecca said half awake.

"Do not know yet, but it is coming from downstairs. I'll be back," he told her and rushed to put his robe on and scuffle off down the steps. He glanced at their clock as he walked out of their bedroom and saw that it was well after two in the morning. He flipped a light on when he reached the bottom landing, and heard the noise again. It was a light rap on their front door. He knew before he opened it that Jeremy was the one knocking. He swung the door open and quickly flipped the screen door open to show him that he did not have to ask to come in.

"Jeremy," Samuel said in the most welcoming way. "Come on in please!"

Jeremy hesitated and shyly said, "Sorry…I literally have nowhere else to go."

"You are welcome here. Come on in," he told Jeremy again. "Let's go to the kitchen. Becca is asleep, so we can talk quietly there. You hungry? I will fix you something to eat."

"I have not eaten in a while," he said, but then lowered his head, "but I don't want to bother you."

"How about a couple of eggs, and toast. I can make you some fried potatoes, and I might even have some bacon out there. How does that sound?"

"Whew…that would be a feast, but really, anything," Jeremy said. "Look, I would not come here if I had anywhere else to go. You and Becca have given me so much, I am embarrassed to even knock on your door."

"Come on, Jeremy, let me get you something to eat." He led him into the kitchen. He had Jeremy sit at the table and began to fix his meal. "When you are done eating, you know where your room is.

You can clean up in there. There is some shampoo in your bathroom, and I got you some shaving gear. Thought you would need that."

Samuel began to make Jeremy's bacon and eggs while continuing to talk with him kind of over his shoulder. He was not paying real close attention to Jeremy until he heard no response at all, so he turned to see Jeremy's head down cupped with both his hands, and he was weeping. "It is okay, Jeremy. Welcome home, brother," Samuel said softly to him, and at that, Jeremy really lost it.

After he could speak, he quietly asked. "So you are just going to take me back like nothing has happened? I remember how I treated you..."

"And me," Rebecca said and startled them both to attention. "But, Jeremy," she went on to say as she walked across the kitchen floor and knelt beside him. "We love you. Real love, Jeremy, and that will never end." She looked into his eyes, and very slowly and quietly, mouthed the words, "There is one more thing...We forgive you also." She kept his gaze for a moment and then stood up, asking, "Mind if I join you two? I smelled the bacon, and I came down to investigate."

Jeremy could not say a word. He just sat there in awe of his sister and her wonderful husband and shook his head in gratitude from side to side.

Samuel went back to his stove work, but marveled mildly at this seemingly new humility that was oozing uncontrollably out of Jeremy. *Is that genuine?* he thought.

Rebecca sat beside Jeremy and lightly rubbed his forearm the same way she did, he remembered, when he woke up in the hospital over a year before, totally oblivious to what had happened.

Finally, when he had finished his eggs and bacon, and he was able to pull himself together, he spoke. "I don't expect you to take me back in, but..."

"We will take you back in!" Samuel and Rebecca said simultaneously, and they looked at each other and smiled. Rebecca looked back at Jeremy, "We want to take you back in," she encouraged Jeremy.

"Well, I expect you will have some new rules for me, right?"

"Jeremy, our love and forgiveness for you is real, but yes, there are some important issues all three of us need to deal with," Samuel told him. "But all I want from you tonight is for you to know you are welcome here. You get cleaned up and have a good night's sleep. We will talk tomorrow.

CHAPTER 27

Humble Pie ala Grace

JEREMY'S GRATITUDE WAS PEAKED, AS he tried to think where he would have spent the night if Samuel had not opened his door. Although he was no stranger to extremely uncomfortable sleeping conditions, he was growing more and more unable to accept them. He literally had used up his welcome at all the known habitats. Although he was embarrassed to come here, he was even more embarrassed to lean on Pat's generosity. He figured, correctly also, that she was ill-equipped to help him anyway, not to mention what his son would think of him. So here he was, being accepted with grace...again. He knew he could never justify getting his room back, having a clean warm bed..."and a shower," he said as he walked into the bathroom. He really was an "odor walking" when Samuel opened the door to let him in. Neither him or Rebecca, though, made any comment about how he smelled, but he seriously did need a shower. He took his time cleaning up and shaving. He found the new clothing Samuel had told him about. There was one drawer with new socks and underwear, and another drawer with some T-shirts and jeans. In the closet, he found a jacket and a new pair of shoes. "How did you know, you old fox, that I was going to come back?" he asked as he leaned down to pick up the shoes and check the size. "Wow...I will never be able to pay you back." Then he thought that there had to be something wrong with his half sister and her pastor husband to do all this for him...again. That thought, though, occupied his brain for a meager moment when he corrected himself. "No...the only thing wrong with them is me, and there is a bundle of somethings wrong with me."

He climbed in between the clean sheets and marveled at how long it had been since he had had any more than a cot to slide into. It was after five in the morning, and it did not take him long to say adios to his consciousness.

It was almost noon when he found his way into the kitchen sporting his new shoes and clothing.

"How you doing, Jeremy?" Rebecca turned from the stove to welcome him.

"I feel clean and fresh and rested for the first time since I was here last year. You know," he said, looking down, "I cannot thank you and Samuel enough." She could not help but notice that he was not only demonstrating a grateful heart but a proper mature humble manner as well.

"You have changed, Jeremy, I think, and I like it."

"Well, if I have, it is mostly due to you and Samuel." Then he paused before saying, "And some really hard knocks."

"Samuel had to go into the office but is planning on taking half the day off. Your timing is perfect. Lunch is ready, so we are just waiting for him. She brought him a cup of coffee and sat down beside him. "We are hoping that you will fill us in on where you have been and all that has happened with you in these last several months. You must have had some real challenges."

"Yeah," he said, "that would be an understatement, thus the hard knocks."

"The upside of hard knocks," she told him, "is that although they are painful, there is no better or more permanent educator."

"I have been an idiot, Rebecca, and selfish. I have been doing a lot of thinking. I have missed so many things."

All Rebecca did was nod and smile, but in the back of her mind, she was pondering, *Wonder what's going to happen next?*

Jeremy suddenly seemed to have nothing to say, so she got up to get him another cup of coffee. When she sat back down, she asked him, "You remember some of the things Samuel was trying to teach you about God, the Bible, and your life?"

"Yeah, I do, well some. I remember feeling like you were trying to shove your religion down my throat."

"You still feel that way?" she asked him.

"No," he said instantly. "Honestly, Rebecca, I do not. I know that is exactly how I felt then, and although I still do not understand more than I do understand, something has happened to me in this last year. I have stumbled over all the same rocks for so long that it has made me, well, for lack of a better way to put it, want to shut up and listen, instead of stand up and fight. No," he said again, "I need help, and I know it. When I was here before, I really did believe all of what you and Samuel told me about Jesus. The rest of what Samuel was trying to teach me, I think, I just stuffed in my 'out of sight, out of bounds' bucket. Especially the forgiving part. I know I need God to forgive me for all I have done, but me forgiving Dad? That was one tall order. I still have trouble seeing how anyone could forgive him, but I am willing to listen. I really am."

"Good," Samuel said loudly as he walked up behind them, and they both jumped. Jeremy shot up from his seat with his hand over his heart.

"Wow…is there a doctor in the house?" he said comically. "First, it was you," and he pointed to Rebecca, "last night, and now it's you this morning, Sam. Wow!" he said again.

"Sorry," Samuel said through his uncontrolled laughter as he patted Jeremy on the shoulder. "You okay?"

"Yeah, I'll live," he said and smiled back at Samuel as he sat back down.

"It is so good to see you, Jeremy, and I am so glad you came back home."

Jeremy did not miss the 'came back home' statement, and he could not help but feel shame again for the way he had treated them. Samuel pulled up a chair and Rebecca served lunch.

As they ate, Jeremy began to recount some of the things he had gone through. As he shared his stories, Samuel and Rebecca both could see a definite change in Jeremy's temperament. Even though he told them repeatedly that he was ashamed for so many things, he still seemed to have no problem being honest. He told them about some of the awful things he had gotten himself into, but as he did, he was not blaming anyone else for his situation. Previously, that would have been one of his main identifying characteristics. Also, it appeared that he was genuinely sorry for all he had done and was not producing any excuses to cover his chosen path.

"You really have changed, Jeremy," Rebecca told him again.

"Here is another interesting twist," he went on to explain. "I have lived on the edge of starvation, carrying a backpack full of regret and even hatred, ever since I left home when I was seventeen, maybe even before that. I have always been able, though, to find something to eat and some place to sleep, but not in these last six or seven months. It was like someone just pulled the rug out from under my feet." He fell silent and hung his wagging head as if in disbelief at the memory. "Something changed," he went on. "I literally could not find a way to make things work out. Not to mention that winter was slamming the door on me for any way to stay warm. Even the Rescue Mission closed their doors on me, except to get a meal occasionally."

"So what did you do?" Samuel asked.

"That is when I chose to hitchhike down South. I reasoned that I would at least be able to stay warm. I was at the Rescue Mission downtown one night standing in line for a meal. It was already cold out but was going to get even colder before dawn. I had nowhere to go, and I did not have any cold weather gear. I talked to this guy standing next to me, who told me that he always went South to escape the cold. Well, I spent the night under that bridge over there on Adams Street and froze. The next day, I figured that since I had nothing else I *could* do to stay warm, I would just give that a try. It took me a couple of weeks to end up far enough south for their winters to be warm enough to live without the need of a winter coat. I still had no place to go, and I was hungry, so I looked up the Rescue Mission there. They were willing to help me some, but did you know that some of the different missions around the country talk to each other? They had me figured out within a couple of days. The only difference between there and here was the temperature. I still could not find work anywhere, so you know what you do when you have nothing, and I mean nothing, and you cannot get anything, and you are hungry?"

"You steal it," Samuel said.

"I am not proud that I did that, but yes. All I stole was some food, though, and only a couple of times. I went hungry, more often than not. But…I did get hooked up with this guy, again at the Mission, who had this 'foolproof' way to get a lot of money quick, and—"

"Famous last words," Rebecca said, interrupting.

"You got that right, but there I was. He knew of these rich people, he said, who were going to be gone for the weekend, and they were supposed to have a lot of cash in their house."

"You got caught, didn't you?" Samuel concluded.

"He got caught. I backed out before he even attempted the robbery. I did not even know where it was supposed to take place. All I know is that the police came and arrested me for being a party to the crime. I guess when that guy got caught in the act, he told them that I had helped him but that I had gotten away. I still do not know why he did that, except maybe he felt that had I helped him, he would not have been caught at all. I spent two weeks in jail before coming up in front of the judge. Finally, this, ah 'friend' of mine confessed that he was the one who planned it and executed it alone. They told me that since I knew about it but did not call the police, I was an accomplice. I was still guilty, they told me, even though I had nothing what so ever to do with it. It was that guy's third arrest for the same thing, so they threw the book at him. I think he went off to state prison. Me? Well, they gave me three months in jail and a very stiff warning to go back home and do not come back. I guess they had some kind of fund, maybe it was from the Rescue Mission, but they gave me a bus ticket, drove me to the bus station, and an officer waited there with me to make sure I got on the bus, and I was off. That got me downtown here about one in the morning, and I finally got a ride here last night, well, this morning. I am so sorry, but I really had nowhere else to go." He sat back in his chair with his head hanging down again, but his eyes were looking up at Samuel.

"I can see that something has changed in you Jeremy," Samuel said, "but you need to know—"

"Oh, don't worry. If you do not want me to stay here," Jeremy quickly interrupted, "I completely understand. Seriously, it is okay. I thank you so much for the clothing, the warm bed and all, but I do not want to be in the way any longer. If you will let me stay here just until I can work something out, and I promise I will not take a long time, that would be great. Please believe me, though, when I say that I really do want to get my life together this time, well maybe for the first time."

"It's okay, Jeremy, you look like you are ready to listen to some sound advice, now. Is that what I am hearing?"

"Yeah, I think I am," he said softly. "I am ashamed of what I have done in my life, but where I used to get angry, I mean out of bounds angry, I am only ashamed now. I am especially ashamed because you helped me see what a good life I could have had the last time I was here, and I just threw it all away. So even if you do not want me to stay here again, I still am only blaming myself, and I am asking you to forgive me."

"That is pretty profound stuff, that," Samuel told him, "compared to what I heard from the Jeremy I knew last year. Becca and I have already decided and, in fact, have prayed and were hoping to get you back. That is why I already had some new clothes waiting for you." Samuel hesitated, thinking, before going on with what he wanted Jeremy to hear. "Jeremy," he said, "you sound like you have been open and honest with us, so I will do the same. We really do want you to stay with us, but that will come at a cost to you this time."

Jeremy opened his mouth to say something, but Rebecca cut him off. "Please listen," she told him.

"I am not sure how you are going to take this," Samuel went on to say, "but I am hoping that you will not only accept this, but will understand and agree with its wisdom. And before I tell you what it is, you need to know that this is only for your benefit, not ours."

"You don't have to convince me of that," Jeremy confirmed. "You both have had my best interest at heart from the start."

"Okay, let me start with this. Do you want to stay here with us, knowing now, more than ever, what we are like, and knowing at least some of what we will be asking of you?"

Jeremy did not waste a moment to think about the question. "Yes, I would want to stay here, but like I said, I really am over making life hard for you. If me staying here will cause you more anguish, I will leave. On the other hand, if you do allow me to live here, I will do anything you ask because I know that whatever you ask of me will be for my benefit."

"Before we open up our home to you again," Samuel said in kindness and love, "you will need to mean it when you say, 'I will do anything you ask,' without any reservations. I do not want to come across like some dictator, but to be honest, you have a *not so wonderful* track record."

"I know I do, and I do understand. I will do my best—"

"Your best," Samuel interrupted, "is usually all that anyone should ask, but it is your best that has been up for interpretation for years. I know your character, Jeremy. When you 'want' to succeed at something, you will. Look at how well you performed at your job. No, I certainly will accept your best, as long as you accept *my* interpretation of what *I* think your best can really be."

Jeremy looked at Rebecca and smiled. "How does he come up with all this stuff? It is like he can read my mind."

"Yeah," she agreed and smiled back at him. "Scary, isn't it?"

He looked back at Samuel. "I would have objected at just about everything you just said the last time I was here, but I get it. You are right, and I will listen."

"I need you to make some thought-out commitments, Jeremy," Samuel announced. "If you agree to those conditions, you are not only welcome here, but we are so overjoyed to have you stay here with us again. The things I will ask that you commit to, I honestly believe are all you need to finally unload your backpack full of regrets and hatred. Jeremy, you can do this, and when you do, it will propel you into a productive happy life."

Samuel spent the next hour and a half pot of coffee laying out what he wanted and expected Jeremy to commit to. Everything from continuing their nightly "man-to-man" Bible studies to going to church, finishing his GED classes, but most importantly, agreeing to simply 'do it' whatever *it* is when he did not understand or even agree. "At least for some time," Samuel told him. "Until you are able to see that backpack of yours getting more and more empty."

"It already is a little lighter," he told Samuel. "I had a lot of time to think while I was locked up. I started to wonder why I thought I was this loser I always told myself I was. I began to question if I really was a loser, or if I only used that as an excuse for failing. I did not get far figuring that out, but the biggest issue that has kept that backpack of mine closed was me not accepting responsibility for my own actions. Not without finding someone or something else to blame for my misery anyway. Running that through my best attempt at reality humbled me into acknowledging my need for help." Jeremy sat still in his chair looking from Samuel to Rebecca, but with a confidence they had never yet seen in him, he quietly stated, "I will commit to all of this."

Rebecca scooted her chair over closer to Jeremy and again laid her hand on his forearm. "What this all has to do with is seeing you finally set free from your guilt feelings, your inferiority complexes, your fear of not being loved, and so on. My heart and Sam's heart have only one motivation. That is to love you into truth and see you grow."

"I know that," Jeremy said. "I am only stuck on how well I know myself. I am being truthful when I say I am willing to work at all this, but I am worried a little because I know that I mess up a lot. I guess I am asking for you to be patient with me. Even after I got out of jail, there were several times that my old attitude popped out like someone just slammed a hammer down on my thumb. It seems like I cannot control my—"

"Let me confirm that for you," Samuel announced. You *will* have times when you will fall back into your old, ah, undesirable self. Often, maybe. But…that is to be expected. It is like falling over, again and again, as one learns to walk, but getting up is the key here to your success, and we," he told Jeremy with kindness and love again, "will not give up on you."

"I cannot thank you both enough," Jeremy said with a frown on his face, "but there is something else while I am baring my heart. I have been thinking a lot about how I can become a father to Randy. One who he can be proud of. Do you think that is a possibility, seeing that he is as old as he is now? Oh, and Pat too...do you think?"

"No, Jeremy, I do not *think* that is a possibility," Rebecca told him. "I *know* it is a possibility, and most likely, a probability. You can do that. Give it time though. Do not expect too much too quickly. And with that, there is one more thing."

"There seems to always be one more thing," Jeremy told them. "I am ready, what is it?"

Rebecca looked at Samuel, smiling. "Go on, tell him. It will make his day."

"Well," Samuel announced. "You ready? I got your old job back. They said that they would take you back as long as you agree, like before, to get your GED. And that you become and stay the good employee you were before."

Jeremy was totally overwhelmed. "No!" he exclaimed. "You are not joking, are you?"

"No, not joking, Jeremy."

"Not that I am complaining, but how could you work that out?"

"Simple," Samuel told him. "Your employer, being an elder of our church, holds as part of his ministry a greater importance in seeing people overcome whatever they are facing than making money. He, like us, wants to see you succeed, but it is not just a gift. Truth is, Jeremy, you did prove yourself when you worked for him before. One of the biggest reasons he is willing to reinstate you is because of that. He did not know when, or even if, you were coming back, so you need to call him tomorrow to arrange when he wants you to start."

"Is there anything else I need to know?" Jeremy asked his benefactors.

"Only one thing that I can think of," Rebecca said, looking first at Samuel and then at Jeremy.

"What would that be?" Samuel looked genuinely puzzled, thinking he had covered everything they had previously talked about.

"Dinner," she said. "Jeremy what would you like for dinner?"

"Thanking you is too small a statement, but thank you so much again, and I know your cooking," he said to Rebecca, "so whatever you want, that is what I want."

Samuel and Rebecca escaped to their room. "I think I'll take a nap," he announced.

When he and Rebecca were alone, "What is that old adage?" she asked. "All's well that ends well?"

"Jeremy is not healed yet, Becca. He has a long row to hoe, and you know what his real test will be, don't you?"

"Yeah, I do. It will be when the rubber meets the road again. When he will be expected to truly forgive our dad."

"I am sure, even though he thinks he is, that he still is not ready to put that fire out. I will admit, though, that I am more encouraged than ever from his actions today. My gracious, I think that God has been doing a work on him. I think he may have really turned a corner."

They prayed for Jeremy again, and then Samuel asked if he could make dinner.

"Sure, but it's got to be more than opening a can of beans," she said jokingly.

"I was thinking of putting some burgers on the grill."

"Sounds good to me. Bet Jeremy will love that too."

Samuel and Becca laid down and spent the next couple of hours attempting to nap, but silently could not stop thinking about all that they had just seen in Jeremy.

"You are so good, God," Rebecca said out loud. "You are so good. Thanks for my brother."

They all ended this unbelievable day having a fantastic cookout, like any 'normal' family might.

CHAPTER 28

The Last New Beginning, Again?

T HE FIRST WEEK OF HIS return proved to Samuel and Rebecca that Jeremy meant what he said. He contacted Pat almost right away. He even asked for her forgiveness. He had no idea what was going to happen there, but he sure was intent on making "things" right for her and Randy and told her so. Pat quietly told him that that would be wonderful but could not stop crying. He remembered thinking, *She still loves me*, although he could not conjure up a single reason why she would.

He also called his gracious employer, apologizing and thanking him simultaneously for his job again. He was told that he could start the beginning of the next pay period. Jeremy's transition back to *normal* seemed to be flawless, but the first knock-your-socks-off discovery was meeting Mac his first Saturday morning back, as he walked nonchalantly into the kitchen to get his coffee. The look of shock on his face would never be duplicated...*ever*, as he saw that Mac was eating breakfast with Samuel and Becca like they were the best of friends. He stopped dead in his tracks and just stared at this huge proprietor of Bobo's, who he always feared. The last time he remembered seeing him was almost a week before he ended up being picked up out behind this totally unpredictable huge man's low-life bar, and that had to be over a year before.

"Whaaaaa!" was all that came out of his mouth, but to his additional 'off the charts' surprise, Mac stood and offered his hand for Jeremy to shake. He had a welcoming smile on his face that was so uncharacteristic for him that Jeremy just stepped back, not knowing what to do.

"Hey, Jeremy," Mac announced in a most charming manner, "I do not bite. Come on over here and get to know me. Have a cup of coffee with us, and I will tell you a story that you may find difficult to believe, but I assure you it is true." Mac sat back down.

Jeremy did not move, so Rebecca, with an uncontrollable grin on her face, stood and walked around to take Jeremy by the arm and physically lead him to the table. A place had already been set for him, but when he sat down, to say that he was awestruck would be an enormous understatement. He had no words at all.

Mac gently placed his huge paw across Jeremy's hand and told him, "I am not the man you remember and in time, a short time I am sure, you will see that. Be at peace. I *can* become one of your best friends."

Jeremy just sat there and could not take his eyes off Mac for a while. Finally, he said sheepishly, "Can I have a cup of coffee?"

"Sure," Rebecca told him, and she got up to get him a cup. "Do you want some breakfast? We saved you some because I did not want to wake you before when we started."

"No, but thank you," he said to her over his shoulder, still not taking his eyes off Mac. "How, I mean, when, or should I say…" His words just fell short of making any sense at all.

Mac let out a belly laugh, and when he had finished, he told Jeremy. "It has been, well, I guess the better part of a year ago now when I was that hard-core bar owner you remember. I know that there is a multitude of things that you need to find out about me, but the first thing is this. I have, since you knew me last, given my life to Christ, and I am studying and learning how to live my life for him. I know what a long shot that is for you to grasp, but it is the first thing that you need to know about me now. If you like, I would love to just sit and rap with you, not only about my alteration, but about a lot of things you never knew."

Again, Jeremy had nothing to say, but confusion filled his facial expression. He just could not believe that this huge man, previously known as a no-nonsense booze pusher could make that kind of change without some ulterior motive packed in behind what he was being asked to believe. Silently, he suspected that maybe his bar was failing, and that he was grabbing at straws to escape bankruptcy or something.

Samuel and Rebecca were still as statues, waiting for Jeremy to say something, while shifting their gaze between Mac and Jeremy. Mac was looking straight at Jeremy who was looking straight at Mac, but not a single peep came from Jeremy.

"Not like you," Mac finally announced, "having nothing to say. I remember you as not being able to shut up, well when you got on one of your tangents."

"What!" Jeremy finally fired back at Mac, "now that you are a Christian, what happens to Bobo's? Are you still going to go in there every night and continue to pump booze into us low-life idiot types who never did know how to stand up straight?" Jeremy suddenly remembered what he had told Samuel and Rebecca about him not being able to control his mouth. Simultaneously, a story Samuel taught him, earlier, also came to mind. A story about how your mouth was like a rudder to a huge ship. He instantly regretted saying what just came out of his mouth, but it was too late.

The whole table fell deathly silent. Mac's look of joy left his face, and not only Jeremy collected all his old fear he possessed for this mountain of a man, but so did Samuel and Rebecca. Samuel started to say something, but Mac held up his hand to stop him from saying anything. He looked directly into Jeremy's eyes. He glared at him long enough with that perfected 'the next thing I am going to do is get up in just a moment and kill you' look that Jeremy almost shrunk beneath the table. And for the second time in as many minutes, he regretted saying anything at all. *There I go again*, he thought, *open mouth insert foot, and this time clear up to my knee cap*, he added to his imaging. He literally froze waiting for Mac to do his worst. Rebecca did not see it, but Samuel finally did. Mac had what Samuel had learned to identify as the look of an actor on his face. Samuel lowered his gaze slightly, so as not to give Mac away, and cupped his mouth to hide his smile. He knew Mac was putting on a show for Jeremy.

"Jeremy?" Mac said in his customary "look out for what's coming next" attitude. Jeremy froze waiting for the pounding he figured was about to happen, but Mac's voice softened like he had just been issued a halo. He reached out to gently pat his new unbelieving friend on the shoulder with a smile on his face that could melt the heart of the meanest man alive. Jeremy flinched hard at his touch, expecting the worst, but Mac smiled again at him. He slowly told Jeremy, "I cannot pump booze into anyone anymore. I tell you, I am a changed man, and I am in the process of selling the bar. In the meantime, I have closed it permanently and went to work for a company with a real job as a buyer. I'll tell you all about that sometime, but I acquired a business degree some years ago, and it is paying off." He ended with, "Trust me, Jeremy, when I tell you that I am believing that you and I can become the best of friends." Mac let his act out of the bag when he not only smiled yet again for Jeremy, but also laughed loudly as he gently slapped Jeremy on the shoulder.

Jeremy loosened the death grip he unknowingly had on his coffee cup and told Mac. "That may take some time, but I gotta tell you, you scared the snot out of me just now." He relaxed, and after a moment to recapture his normal breathing, he added, "But you know, I am learning too that I have a big mouth, and I want to learn how to become a Christian as well. Sorry for my words. Can you forgive me?" he asked Mac.

Rebecca shot an uncensored look of shock of her own at Samuel when Jeremy made his "can you forgive me" request. "Wow," she mouthed without making a sound to her husband who was cool as a cucumber.

"Not only is that not a problem," Mac told Jeremy, "but I forgave you before you asked me to."

Finally, Jeremy looked at all three of them and quietly yet humbly issued one single but sincere word, "Thanks."

Mac stayed for another half hour or so, talking to Samuel and Rebecca about his Annie, their upcoming wedding, and his struggle he had had learning to forgive her mother. "You always told me, Pastor Sam, how forgiving her, even if she did not deserve it, would set me and Annie free. Boy, were you right on that one." They had to take a moment and bring Jeremy up to speed on who Annie was and a little about how they met. However, since telling the whole story could have escalated into next Tuesday, they told Jeremy that he would have to be content on the short version for the time being. As a result, though, there were times when he was simply left out of the loop. That was when he opted to eat breakfast. So while Mac and Samuel continued to talk, Rebecca got up and brought him a plate. All the while he was eating and listening, Jeremy could not stop thinking of Mac's unexpected turnaround. Those words he spoke kept echoing in his brain: *I have, since you knew me last, given my life to Christ, and I am studying and learning how to live my life for him.*

Finally, Mac saw that it was time for him to leave. "Gotta go," he said, and he thanked Rebecca for breakfast as he stood. He turned to Jeremy and tossed an open invitation at him. "Whenever you want to, I will make myself available to get together with you, and we can work at us becoming good friends." He reached his enormous hand out the second time for Jeremy to shake, and this time, he did shake hands with Mac, but the only thing Jeremy had to say was, "Good gracious…that is the biggest hand I have ever seen." Mac waved his goodbye to him and was off.

After Mac left, Samuel asked if Jeremy would like to accompany him into his office. "Jeremy, I tell you again, I see a wonderful change in you."

"Oh, you mean with my loaded cannon of a mouth? I am so sorry. It just popped out like a bullet from a gun."

"You are doing great. You came back and apologized and ended up none the worse in the process. Once again, though, I will tell you. What just happened to you this morning is likely to happen again and again. Like I told you though, it is not how many times you fall down that counts, it is how many times you get up that wins the race. There is a lot that you can learn from your first bump in the road here this morning," Samuel encouraged Jeremy, "and I have confidence that you will." Jeremy nodded in agreement, so Samuel smiled at him, reached out and took his hand, bowed his head, and prayed.

"Did you get that?" Rebecca spit out her whispered excitement to Samuel as they readied for bed later that night. "Did you hear him say that?" she said again. "He asked for Mac's forgiveness. Not only that, but Pat told me on the phone that when he called her, he asked for her forgiveness also." Rebecca could not contain herself, so Samuel just stood there with his arms crossed staring at her and waited for her to finish. "I told you," she boasted, "that all we needed to do was just trust God for him, and bingo, here we are." She turned to face Samuel, reached up with both her hands on either side of his face, and gently pinched his cheeks. She pulled her face up close to his, looked him straight in the eyes, and proudly announced, "I told you so," and chuckled. "Huh, didn't I tell you?"

"Yeah, you told me, Becca. Thanks for keeping me humble." They both laughed.

"Do you remember that sermon I put together some time ago?" he asked her, changing the topic. "You know, that one I wrote at the office? That one that I titled 'Where Does the Love of God Go?'"

"Sure, I do, and boy would that make a great sermon for Jeremy to hear tomorrow."

"Yes, it would, and of course, that is why I brought it up. I had a sermon ready, but I think I will swap it out for that one. I too think it will impact our Jeremy."

CHAPTER 29

What the Difference Is

S UNDAY AFTERNOON FOUND JEREMY ALONE in his room contemplating all that had happened his first week back with Samuel and Rebecca. They had eaten lunch just after they got home from church, and then he quietly escaped to his room. He knew that Rebecca would not call him to dinner for several hours, so he decided to just slow down and think. "Everything is set up pretty good," he pondered, "and I know I do not deserve any of this." He chuckled at the memory of meeting Mac the day before. "What a surprise that was! I cannot believe my good fortune…again." He had even been gifted with his job back. "Yeah, everything is working out well." Then his ponderings shifted to the commitment he had promised Samuel and Rebecca. He had every intention to keep it, but something was different this time. He sat up in his bed thinking out loud again. "What *is* different?" but then it came to him. "What the difference is this time is that I really want to keep it, whereas before I only agreed to their requests because I felt I had to, but I will not fail again," he spoke to the walls of his bedroom. "I WILL NOT!" and as he said that louder, he realized that he was making his own promise to succeed.

Then his thoughts shifted to the sermon he heard that morning on the love of God. "It sounded like that was designed just for me. So…*where* does *the love of God go*?" he asked himself as he laid back down and remembered how penetrating Pastor Sam's words were. "Wow," he said, "Which one *am* I? The one who says he believes but doesn't, or the one who says he believes and really does but does not act like it or won't take the next step?" It didn't take much thought though for him to answer that question.

Jeremy really did believe that there was a God, and that his Son Jesus did die on the cross, as the Bible said he did, for his sins. "But where did that leave me back then?" he wondered. He also remembered all his sister and brother-in-law had done for him then to show love "that I have never known before," he admitted. Now, alone in his room, he was trying to make sense of everything as he was reminiscing all those past days. He visibly cringed at how, *in the end*, he just tossed it all away. His mind was swimming with questions, but one kept surfacing, demanding his attention. "What did that faith of mine really mean to me back then?" He could not get that one question out of his mind, but then he began to refine the question, "What about my belief in God?" he quizzed. "If, in truth, I did believe back then, why didn't anything change? Why did I just dump it all out the window in one huffy act of anger? Boy, pride is a killer, isn't it?" he said out loud. "Yeah, my pride sent it all packing, didn't it? I just stomped out of here with a chip on my shoulder as big as an oak tree, selfishly closing the door on all the great things that were being done for me. How does that translate to '*I believe in God*...'" He sat back up in bed again, completely covered with regret. After a long while, he leaned back down on his bed, consumed in guilt and shame. It bent his mind like a plague for all those memories. It kept his ability to think about anything else adjourned.

He had no idea how long he just laid there jailed to those thoughts. "So what will make the difference this time?" he blurted out, as he sat back up again stiffly, then he smiled at himself. "Look at me, sitting up, laying down, but what in the world *will* make the difference this time?" At first, he had no answer for himself at all, but he began to investigate in depth all of what happened the last time that made him throw it all away. "There must be some logical answer to that. I mean, what? My father? Yeah, there's that. Boy, he was, ah probably *is* the biggest part of my hurt, but honesty and truth must surface here somewhere on that...on him. How long can I lean on that for an excuse for continuing to ruin my life and others, and where does my faith in God, in Jesus, or the Bible come into play with my father? I am going to be thirty-three soon, and I have spent my entire life begging trouble, and so often, I just seemed to fall apart right at the finish line. WHAT?" he demanded.

Then something hit his thoughts, like a brick to his forehead. "What would make *the* difference this time over the last time?" he said for the third time, but this time it was not the same kind of question. His excitement peaked as that thought came to him more like the beginning of an answer. "Mac...wow, Mac." He began to recap some things that Mac had said about himself not being the same man as he was. "Well, what made the difference in *his* life?" Jeremy stood up this time with his curiosity in full vigor. "I am a believer just like him," he said, but then he remembered the rest of what Mac had said. *I have given my life to Christ, and I am studying and learning how to live my life for him.*' Jeremy's whole being stood still like time itself had stopped. His room was so quiet that he could hear his heart beating. Finally, "That's it!" he said. "There's *the* difference," he announced to his silent bedroom. "That is it," Jeremy continued, allowing himself to reason differently than he had previously. "I believed, well, I think even before I came here the first time." He remembered his mom, as bad off as she was, tell him some things that led him to believe that Jesus was real, but he never went any further. "But isn't that like so many of us, ah, *Christians,*" he said, and he used that word in a less than admirable way. He remembered talking to so many men when he was at the Rescue Mission, and almost all of them professed to believe in Jesus. "But nothing ever changed in *their* lives," he said out loud. "Nothing ever changed in *my* life either." He went on to basically preach to himself. "I think I always believed that there was a God, and since Samuel explained salvation to me when I was living here before, I believed that Jesus did die on the cross to cover my sins, but that was as far as I ever got. Now, looking at all this, I am starting to shift gears in all my thinking. I think I've got it. '*Where* does *the love of God go?*' Indeed. I am not a nonbeliever, but until, well, maybe right now, I was a believer who never investigated what it really meant to become a believer *and a follower* of Jesus and his teachings. Why is it so hard for anyone to cross that barrier? The barrier that keeps even real believers from becoming followers. Wow!" Jeremy said. "It is all right there, isn't it? It is all right in front of us in the Bible. Easy to read, easy to understand, but…" He stopped to think again. "That is why Samuel still wants to spend time every night teaching me. But who put that barrier there in the first place? What am I supposed to look for now, and is there something I can do to make sure I do not end up failing again? And…" the thought just hit him. "What about Pat and my son Randy? I have really busted up their lives. What can I do about them? Wow, is there something that can keep me from succeeding or keep me from failing? How do I keep from falling back into that hole I have been living in for, well, all my life?" Jeremy dropped to his knees uncontrollably beside his bed and prayed. "God, I do not really know how to pray, but I need help. I do believe in your Son Jesus, and I am asking you to open my eyes to all You want me to know." Jeremy got back up into his bed and thought how important Samuel and Rebecca would be in teaching him all the things he did not know and understand.

Dinner that night was noticeably different. Jeremy's demeanor was clearly joyous, and for the second time, they noticed a mature kind of confidence. He did not have much to say, except for going a little overboard complimenting Rebecca's great cooking. He looked like he had an enormous announcement to make but did not know how to approach the microphone.

"So," Samuel finally asked. "What's up? You look like something is, ah, well, something is different, at least you seem to appear like something is different."

"Yeah, there is a lot different," Jeremy finally opened up. "Something really good."

"Care to share?" Rebecca asked.

"Love to," he told them. "When I can put it all together, that is. Maybe we can all get together tonight instead of just you and me, Samuel. I would love to tell you also, Rebecca, what I think I have discovered."

"I cannot wait to hear this," she told her brother. "Good stuff you say?"

"Really good stuff. Well, I think it is," he told them.

They finished their meal, and even before Rebecca cleared the table, they all went into the living room. Samuel and Rebecca were on pins and needles waiting for Jeremy to tell them what it was that he thought was "really good stuff."

"Isn't it interesting," Jeremy began, "how you can stand in a darkened room with your hand on the light switch, and do two ridiculous things? First thing is that you know you can turn the light on so you can see where you are going, but you don't. The second ridiculous thing you do is complain about how dark the room is."

Samuel smiled at Jeremy. He knew exactly what had happened to him but waited for him to tell his story. "Been there / done that," he told Jeremy. "Go on. I am anxious to hear how you finally figured out your need to flip the switch."

"Now that is an interesting choice of words you just used," he told Samuel, and he repeated them. "How I finally figured out my *need* to flip the switch." You deliberately chose to zero in on me identifying my *need* to turn on the light, not just that I did turn it on. It was a *need*, and I think it just came to me. Well, that is my, ah 'good stuff' I wanted to share, and I think it was God who showed me my *need* to flip the switch. Or should I say, it was God who turned on the light?"

"The key here," Samuel proclaimed, "is that *the* light that was turned on is a gift, and it sounds like that light is now in you?" Samuel posed that last statement to Jeremy as if it were a question.

"What I don't know at this stage is so much more than I do know," Jeremy said, "but if having God's light in me makes me want to learn more, then I would have to say…yes…absolutely."

Rebecca stood and did a wiggle the way only a woman could do, and shouted, "Hallelujah!" but Samuel fell totally silent. Rebecca slapped him on the shoulder the way only a woman can do and get away with it. "Huh? That is fantastic, isn't it?" But her excitement and question seemed to hold a lot less power on Samuel. He did not respond the way she expected him to. "What?" she said as she sat back down.

Samuel smiled at Rebecca and reached over and patted her hand but leaned into Jeremy's personal space to have a serious meeting of the minds with him. "Jeremy," Samuel began, "I am extremely over-joyed at your revelation. I truly am, and I do believe you, but I know why you could not flip that switch the last time you were here...and you were close. I also know that there still is a possibility for you to go back to that light switch and try to turn it off again."

"I know," he said. "I spent the last couple of hours in my room pushing that scenario through my mind. I asked myself several times, in several different ways, 'What happened last time?' and 'What will make the difference this time?' I think what made the difference between the last time I was here and this time was remembering what Mac told me about his life changing. How he 'gave' his life to Christ and how he is studying to learn how to 'live' his life for him. I clearly see the difference between the way I viewed things, everything, the last time I was here, and the way I want to learn how to view things now."

"Jeremy, although I have so much compassion and understand-ing for you, it is imperative that you come to grips with your most unsettled side of things."

"I get it," Jeremy said, looking at Samuel with an understanding of what he was leading up to.

"You know exactly what I am going to say next, don't you, Jeremy?"

"I do," Jeremy said, "and now that you have bridged the topic, I understand why you did. That was what messed me up the last time I was here, wasn't it? It was when you tried to help me understand the importance of me forgiving my father."

"It is absolutely necessary," Samuel told him. "That light you just spoke of is real, but the real trick in letting it make a difference in your life on a permanent basis is learning to forgive. You have already learned what the consequences are for unforgiveness. Learning to forgive is a process, and it will change your life each day of your life much the same as you learning your need to flip that light switch on. Forgiving your father, you will find out, is going to be easier than you think. Once you decide to submit, or better put, commit, to all the biblical teachings available to you, it will lead you into a whole different lifestyle. One where you will want to and be able to forgive anyone anything _before_ they even ask for forgiveness."

"Okay," Jeremy said, "I clearly see the necessity for me to forgive my father. Honestly, I really do. Isn't it interesting, though, how the first thing, and the hardest thing I have to do right now in this new beginning of mine is exactly the same hardest thing that I failed at before. I will confess, though, that I am tempted to run, like I did last time. I will not, I promise, but I would love to know why that is."

"I will be prepared to help you understand that, Jeremy, and more when we get started tomorrow night," Samuel told his new disciple.

Jeremy looked at Rebecca and asked if she knew how to bake a really good apple pie.

"Sure, I do, but why do you ask?"

"When you see that I am truly overcoming my unforgiveness or that I have genuinely started to forgive Dad the way I know God has forgiven me, would you bake me that apple pie as a reward?"

Rebecca jumped from her chair and again was ecstatic over her brother. "Hallelujah!" she shouted again. "I will bake you that pie tomorrow."

"Now... I can agree with Rebecca and harmonize with her Hallelujah," Samuel announced. "Jeremy, you truly have crossed a huge bridge in your life. Congratulations."

No one went to bed early, and rejoicing was not even a good enough word to end all three of their nights. Samuel did give Jeremy one final warning, though. He opened the Bible to 1 Peter 5:8 and read out loud to him. "Be vigilant for your adversary the devil roams around like a roaring lion seeking whom he may devour." He spent only a minute explaining that to Jeremy but told him that when they meet the next night, he would get into that in depth.

CHAPTER 30

Wounded and Healed or Wounded and Defeated

A RACE IS RUN FOR TWO *reasons. It is obvious that one of those reasons is to be the first one to complete the course. The second reason is not so obvious, but everyone who ends up finishing is a winner. You can come in last behind everyone and still be a proud winner for simply staying the course and completing the task. But there is only one loser. That would be the one who knowingly, deliberately, without good cause, drops out anywhere prior to crossing the finish line…and the words* "good cause" *are seriously up for interpretation.*

So…how did *these* precious souls run *their* race?

JEREMY

The very night after Jeremy finally came to grips with the largest of his spiritual needs, which was to forgive his father, he could not wait to get back to work and prove himself. He only had a few days left before his second "first" day on the job. He had made up his mind to seriously work at becoming Mac's friend, and he also wanted to become a for-real-deal father to Randy. "Is it possible?" he asked himself several times, "that I could also become a trusted husband for Pat as well?" But then he reasoned, "Not sure she will ever want me back, and I wouldn't blame her either, but..." Jeremy was not the same man who had believed wholeheartedly that he was totally worthless the year before. Jeremy really had crossed over from thinking only about the hurt that had been inflicted on him and started thinking on how to help those whom he had wounded. That one slice of maturity is the single most recognizable proof that his complete healing was on its way. Forgiving others, when they do not deserve forgiveness or ask for it or even if they do not recognize that they need it is the only healing salve that will push that devastating sickness of unforgiveness to the curb. Jeremy was not only knocking on that door, but he had opened it, walked right through it, and was asking for forgiveness for himself for taking so long to forgive others, especially his father.

"It is vital," Samuel taught Jeremy, "that believers need to live out or to practice, to demonstrate and exhibit the salvation they have in Christ. Working that out means a daily exercise in demonstrating and exhibiting their faith. It is not difficult, really, but it does require a developed discipline of living out what it means to be a Christian. Nothing, then, is more of a hindrance to that end than a heart that holds onto unforgiveness."

Jeremy had genuinely forgiven his father. There is no question about that. But he easily could, like the rest of us, allow his thoughts to return to some of the heart-wrenching memories that caused his regret, revenge, and unforgiveness in the first place. That is why he would need time, training, patience, and love to help him develop that daily practiced discipline. That then would allow him to graduate from "novice" to "experienced" in the art of forgiving and living for Christ. Succeeding with that, victory in overcoming any residual pain left from all the severe emotional wounding he had had to endure would have to follow.

Samuel also wasted no time teaching Jeremy about who his enemy really was, and is, and what to do about that. "The sooner you can honestly recognize that it never was your father who ultimately wanted to destroy you, the easier it will be for you to develop your daily battle plan against any leftover pain and regret. God is faithful," he went on to teach Jeremy. "As long as you never forget *his* principles of forgiveness, you will be completely successful at overcoming everything your enemy, as well as your previously unforgiving heart would want to throw at you."

After a few weeks of Bible study, and Samuel teaching him how to pray, Jeremy began praying one specific prayer every night when he was alone. *"Father God, forgive me for wounding my son, Randy, and help him to forgive me, his father, as I have learned to forgive my father…Help me to forgive myself as I forgive others. I pray for my father for him to see his need to seek forgiveness for all he has done against his children and against you, heavenly Father."* He ended up naming his nightly prayer his "Father Forgive," prayer.

Jeremy certainly was healed, and his words and actions demonstrated that he really was. Even his self-loathing and immense inferiority complex had miraculously waned.

MAC, ANNIE, AND ANNIE'S MOTHER, MRS. SANFORD

It was only a couple of months after Jeremy's miraculous return that he did indeed became a good friend to Mac. Mac had even asked him to be his best man in their wedding. That, interestingly, turned out to be the new beginning for Jeremy and Pat. Annie, prompted by Rebecca, had asked that Pat be Annie's maid of honor. Can you see it? Jeremy as Mac's best man, and Pat as Annie's maid of honor? Could there be a better setup?

Mac and Annie's wedding was a very formal affair, meaning tuxedos, flowers everywhere, matching gowns for all the bridesmaids, and the works. Mac, like most men, however, would have been happy enough with a small intimate group of close friends and a smaller ceremony. He could not, however, defend himself against Annie, who told him, "I have waited all these years for you, and I am not going to allow my wedding to end up a simple *'blip'* in history." He also did not try to convince Rebecca and the dozen or so other women from the church to agree to a "hey, what's wrong with a simple walk in the park kind of wedding?" So he conceded, without so much as a whisper of a disagreement. He told Samuel, though, that he felt like the women make all the rules, to which Samuel informed him that this was only the beginning. He slapped his huge young friend on the back and laughed out loud. Mac was not amused. When the day of the wedding came, Mac was behind closed doors with Samuel, Jeremy, and some of the men who agreed to be groomsmen, and all of them kept telling Mac not to be nervous. To that, he kept telling them that he was not nervous, and that he could not wait to marry his Annie.

The ceremony was glorious, mostly because from start to finish, it was a totally Christ-centered celebration of one man and one woman being fused together in holy matrimony. The ceremony went off without a single glitch. Samuel led them each in their vows, and then... "I now pronounce you husband and wife. You may kiss your bride," he said, looking at Mac. Then he turned and introduced Mr. and Mrs. Macpherson to the congregation. At the reception, many had to ask Annie about her name. "I have always gone by Mattie all those years," she told them. "That is my middle name, but my first name is Annie, and that is what you can call me now, but I will answer to Mattie if you forget. It's all good."

Annie's mother did not come to her wedding, and it did hurt, but they knew in advance that she was not going to attend. There were unbelievable times during the months leading up to the wedding when her mom had just ripped at Annie's emotions with accusations, condemnations, and threats. What she could not comprehend, though, was that Annie did not buckle under any of them. Mac and Annie moved into a very nice apartment, near where her mother was now left to live alone. Between Mac's income, which was the most he had ever earned, and hers, they could live comfortably, and still have plenty left over to aide Annie's mother. She perpetually refused their help but always had to accept. About two months into their new life, Annie, who still had some hurtful feelings over her mother's total lack of accepting Mac or their marriage, asked Samuel again for some advice.

"Have you and Mac truly forgiven her for all she has done, and all she is doing? Do you hold any malice against her...at all?" He really emphasized the 'at all.'"

"No," she told him instantly. "Not even a miniscule amount of anger or hatred. We really have forgiven her."

"Does she know that?" Samuel asked.

"I don't know," she answered. "Do you think we should tell her that we forgave her when she thinks that we are the ones who need to beg her forgiveness?"

"Yeah, I think," he told her.

"You know," she said, "you should have been a pastor." She smiled a knowing smile at him.

That next night, giving no warning, Mac and Annie showed up at her mother's house. Annie knocked and told her mother through the door who it was. Her mother yelled at the top of her lungs, "Go away!"

"Mom, we are not going to go away. I love you, and I want you to give me at least five minutes."

"What to do you mean, *We* are not going to go away?" she yelled again. "You brought that rundown football player, booze pushing husband of yours with you, didn't you?"

"Yes, I did, and I am going to unlock your door, and come in, if you won't open it yourself. We need to talk."

"There is nothing to talk about. You ruined my life, and I will never forgive you for that. You chose that low-life bartender over me, and, and I…" She quit talking when her door swung open, and Annie walked in, followed by Mac. She simply froze, eyes wide open in fear at the memory of how large this man really was.

As Mac slowly followed Annie into the house, he made an exaggerated effort to move away from her mother, holding his hands up as if to prove he meant her no harm. Ever so gently, he said, "Please, Mrs. Sanford, I promise you, I mean you no harm whatsoever, and I know that it may be difficult for you to believe, but I also care a lot about you."

She did relax some, believing that he was not there to physically hurt her, but she sat in silence, looking like she was pouting. Seething might be a better word. "Mom," Annie said softly as she sat beside her mother, reaching out her hand to touch her mother's arm. "Please, Mom. I mean it when I say I love you, but Mac and I have something very important to tell you, well and also to ask you." Annie turned her gaze to Mac, who slowly bent, and then kneeled on the carpet several feet from Annie's mother.

"Mrs. Sanford, we know that you blame Annie and me for ruining your life. We also know and acknowledge our sin before God, and all the hurt that has brought to you. For all that we are heartfully sorry, and are asking for your forgiveness."

"Never," she spit the word out, turning her head away, and crossing her arms in disgust. "Just go away."

"There is one more critical thing, Mom," Annie said in kindness. "Mac and I want you to know, and we mean this with no malice." She paused to be sure she had her mother's attention. "We, from our hearts, truly forgive you for everything."

At that, her mother hit the roof. She turned to face Mac and then Annie. "You forgive me? You insolent inconsiderate hardhearted daughter! I have done nothing to be forgiven for. What are you accusing me of? What kind of thing do you think I have done to need your forgiveness?"

Annie was about to open her mouth, but her mother cut her off. "No, skip it, I know what you are going to say, and you are wrong, like you have always been wrong. You know what? Leave, just leave." She crossed her arms again, turned away, and that was the end of that.

Annie slowly got up and stood in silence for a moment. She bent over and kissed her mother on the top of her head and said in almost a whisper, "Mom, I mean it when I say I love you and that I forgive you."

Her mother jerked her head violently away from Annie and did not watch as Mac and Annie quietly walked out her front door.

As the years passed, Annie mostly, but Mac also would try again and again to show love and compassion for her but achieved no positive results. They finally gave up on her the day Mrs. Sanford passed away. She still had a death grip on her intact bitterness. She never softened her unforgiving, hardened heart, clear to her last breath. Annie wept like a child when they put her mother in the ground. The permanent upside to their lives, though, was that Mac and Annie both were certainly healed from the pain of unforgiveness.

Bobo's Bar and Grill: A Metamorphosis

The lifespan of Bobo's Bar and Grill is easy to trace. Mac's grandfather started the business, and Mac's father owned the bar after that. Mac's older brother, Buck, took it over when his father died but was shot to death at a very young age. Mac grew up in and around the bar from his birth, and when Buck died, Mac took it over. There was no one left in the family to take the bar over from Mac when the time came, so Mac was the last owner/operator of Bobo's Bar and Grill. Mac had decided to close the bar and put it up for sale after he had finally given up on ever finding his Annie. Wonders never cease though, do they, because just at that time he was reunited with his Annie, but still wanted to end his reign over Bobo's.

"What is to become of Bobo's Bar and Grill and his adjacent two-story building?" Samuel asked rhetorically. "The building houses Mac's apartment up and two more lesser apartments down, although both of which had not been used in decades and a huge storage area in the basement. Bobo's is a perfect place for a coffeehouse and rescue with eight beds, for souls who cannot survive otherwise." Samuel pitched to his board. "Not to mention all the men and women living in or near that Sixth Street Park who will end up being our target ministry. I am not sure how much Mac wants for his place, but I know that he is serious about selling."

The church made an offer to Mac, and he did not hesitate. "Sold," he said. It was arranged that he could stay in his apartment as long as he needed, knowing that he was going to be married in a few months, and he would use that time when he was not working in his new job, and courting Annie, to start the remodel of "The Sixth Street Coffee Bar and Grill." There was no end of volunteers who jumped at the chance to help, and voila...Talk about "many hands make light work." New life had begun in one of the poorest, lawless, overrun areas of the city. The overall reconstruction, remodel, and subsequent inspection to make it all legal was underway. It was operational by the time Mac and Annie were married and living in their new apartment. It did not take long, however, before Samuel and his group of volunteers found that they did not have enough people to run the coffeehouse daily as planned. They had to settle on weekends only, and sometimes that was hard to cover. The outreach to the area and the park was sparce also, but again, not for lack of funds. It was for lack of volunteers. But the dream that Pastor had had was started and was operational. "This is a fantastic beginning," he told the board. "All we need now is someone to move into Mac's old apartment, and be a live-in manager for the coffee shop. Just keep your eyes and ears open," he told them, "God is faithful." Bobo's Bar and Grill did not need healing, it just needed to be corrected and changed with a brand-new ideal in place, and it was.

PAT AND JEREMY, RANDY, AND PAT'S MOTHER

When Pat was asked to be Annie's maid of honor, she wanted to say no at first. Jeremy was going to be Mac's best man, and of course, that meant that she would, out of necessity, need to interact with Jeremy often. She did not know if she would be comfortable with that. However, she agreed, mostly because of Rebecca's prodding, but also because she had started to see such a change in Jeremy. Jeremy had, as they say, cleaned up pretty good. His work ethic, she was told, was nothing short of immaculate. He would call her often, just to check on her, and he went out of his way to spend time with Randy. At first, that meant visits to her house, but that turned into him taking Randy out on short excursions. He would take Randy to Science Central or the library and hang out with him in his kind of book area. When the weather was good, he would even take him to the park and shoot hoops with him. He began to encourage Randy and, more importantly, started becoming his friend. Then he started picking him up every Saturday and taking him to breakfast or lunch. The real change Pat noticed was not in Jeremy, though. It was in Randy. He began to look forward to seeing his dad and often could not wait. "Dad's coming, see you later, Mom," and he would dash out the door as soon as he saw Jeremy drive up. The real permanent change in Randy, though, started when Jeremy took him "sunset fishing" once. That was what Jeremy called it. Jeremy and Randy sat on a pier that stretched out over the water at sunset, and although they did not catch a single fish, they sat there side by side talking. Randy told his mother later that that was when... "Dad asked me if I would forgive him."

"So," Pat asked, "did you?"

"I think I did," he told her. "I don't feel bad about him anymore." Randy, like so many kids his age, did not really understand all of what had happened, he only knew that he loved to hang out with his dad.

Jeremy never missed bringing money to Pat every payday, and Pat was starting to hope yet again. But Pat silently guarded herself just in case. There was no doubt that she had more than ample reason to feel that way. She had been hurt with her hoping way too often in the past. It did not help either that her mother could not have been more negative against, "this new Jeremy of yours," she called him. "Come on, Pat," she would tell her daughter. "Have you forgotten? He did not even have a job the day you married him and look at all the yelling and hatred he has brought into your and Randy's lives. Oh, and mine, I might add. Have you forgotten?"

"No, Mom, I have not forgotten, but listen... Samuel and Rebecca, and I know you trust them, both tell me that Jeremy really has, this time, made a complete turnaround. It has been months now, and I want to believe them. Look at the wonderful way he has been with Randy."

Her mother crossed her arms and shrugged a kind of "yeah I see that...but..." shrug. She was balancing herself to be counted half in and half out "on that." Overall, though, she stood her solid ground on, "I don't trust him anyway," but for Pat's sake, she did not say any more about this new Jeremy.

Indeed, Jeremy had changed, and time would prove that to Pat's mother. But it was at Annie and Mac's wedding that something started to change in Pat. Even before the ceremony started. Pat could not take her eyes off this man. She remembered the day she met him in that Starbucks, and how he looked like he did not have a solid nickel to his name and no way to get one. She remembered how after just a short time she became attracted to him, and, from then on, could not stop thinking about him. She remembered also that most of his being hurt, and most of his hurting his family was a result of one evil man who seemed to enjoy destroying him. Looking at him now, though, from across the church stage, she could see how that man was not going to succeed at ruining my Jeremy. "Huh," she said quietly, "my Jeremy? Where did that come from?"

She forced herself to take her eyes off him and focus on the wedding. The music, "Here Comes the Bride," began, and everyone stood and turned to honor Annie. Pat turned also to face the bride, as she was being walked down the aisle by the church's head elder. Pat was faithful and professional as maid of honor. She performed perfectly, carrying out her assigned duties that had been rehearsed the day before, but again, she could not control her Jeremy thoughts. What really brought the "I want him back" feeling, was when the wedding ended, and Mac and Annie were walking back up the aisle. She looked up to see that Jeremy had stepped up to her side, lifting his right arm slightly like a real gentleman inviting her to take his arm so that he could escort her out of the church behind the bride and groom. That short walk with her arm wrapped in his took less than half a minute to complete, but in Pat's heart, it seemed to take an hour. She had never seen Jeremy in any kind of suit or sport coat or tie or even dressed up at all. The most she ever remembered him *dressing up* was when he was sporting a new shirt and blue jeans the day they got married in the courthouse. She found out later, although it made no difference anyway, that his new shirt and blue jeans were not new, and that they had been loaned to him, and of course, that is why they were a little baggy. She did not care then or now about all that, "But, baby, look at you now," she thought, looking up into his face, as she felt like she was his queen. He looked good. Clean cut, hair trimmed and combed, standing tall in his tux, but most of all, she saw how he carried himself. It was like he had all the confidence in the world, without the boasting, and he appeared to know exactly what he was doing.

At the reception, they both sat at the bride and groom's table, and when it came time for the best man's speech, Pat watched Jeremy stand and give glory to God for his changed life. He gave honor to Mac saying that a good part of his altered life was due to the friendship Mac had bestowed on him, and how he now considered Mac a Christian brother more than a friend. He toasted the married couple with a glass of iced tea, instead of an alcoholic beverage. Pat knew that her mother, whether she would admit it or not, could not help but be impressed.

"Would you honor me with a dance?" Jeremy asked Pat so politely after the music had started.

"I thought that you would never ask," Pat was thinking, but the only thing that came out of her nervous mouth was, "Sure," and she stood up to take his hand. "I still love him," she kept thinking, "I do…"

Jeremy continued his pursuit to be the best father for Randy that he could be. He told Pat, and on one occasion, Pat's mother, that that was his ongoing goal. "I intend to be the father for him I never had, and one who Randy can be happy to be with and be proud of."

Shortly after the wedding, Jeremy, after being encouraged by Rebecca and Samuel, asked Pat if she would be willing to date him. She agreed, so he asked if he could pick her up on the following Saturday morning. She was a little taken back, as she was thinking more like a dinner date or something like that, but she did not question his choice. "Sure, that would work," she told him. She almost cried when he took her to the same Starbucks where they first met all those years before. As they walked in, she could not help but notice that a couple of the Starbucks employees were staring right at her with a Cheshire-cat grin on their faces. She looked up at Jeremy for support or an explanation, but he did not give her one. He only began to lead her to a table where he wanted them to sit. They were still several feet away when she noticed that a table by the window had two cups of coffee already poured waiting for them. She froze dead in her tracks, but not for the coffee but because she also saw a large red ribbon stretched across the two-top that read, "Bada Boom Bada Bing."

Jeremy was true to his word, and Pat's mother had to acknowledge that Jeremy was exactly who he said he was. Jeremy was almost ready to take his GED final, and was confident he would pass. He found out that he was not so stupid after all. He was encouraged to start night classes to eventually earn a degree. "Could I actually do that?" he asked.

It was not that long after Mac and Annie's wedding, and Jeremy dotting all the right "i's" and crossing all the right "t's" that he finally proposed marriage to Pat. Even Pat's mother was in total agreement with that. She told Jeremy that he had proven himself completely, and that she was more than willing to give her blessing to them both. Randy also was elated and could not wait for his dad and mom to get married.

All that needed to happen for Pat, Randy, and Pat's mother to be healed was for Jeremy to finally let go of the stubbornness that he allowed to control his unforgiving wounded heart. When he became healed by learning to forgive others, mainly his father, in the same way that God's unconditional love through Jesus had forgiven him, they were all able to be healed.

SAMUEL, REBECCA, AND REBECCA'S MOTHER, DELLA

Samuel Kensley had known from an early age that he wanted to be a pastor of a church. His pastor father was one of the most admisred and respected men in the community, not only in his church. Samuel could not think of anything else he wanted to do, so his life was aimed in that direction even before he started high school. He entered university needing to work his way through, as he did not qualify for a scholarship, but that beginning was the best thing that ever happened to him. He learned more about life and the basic psychology of his human counterpart outside the classroom than he did inside. His propensity for caring more about others, especially the homeless, the "down and outers," so many called them, was amplified during his work in the inner city while going to college. He met the love of his life, Rebecca, first while still at home in his senior year at Jefferson High. When he met her, she was one of the saddest girls he had ever known. Samuel's father had trusted him with leading the social side of their youth group, and it was during that time that

Rebecca just showed up one Sunday looking angry and ready to leave before she even sat down. He watched her change some by the time he went off to university, and his first two years were not on campus, so he was able to see her frequently. He became an interim youth leader/pastor his second year of college, and with his father's leading, Rebecca really started to shine. His last two years of university were on campus, so he only saw her on holidays and during spring break. To make a very long story very short, they fell in love, and were married about a year after he had graduated from seminary. Rebecca still struggled with many root issues from her childhood that were generated from her father. However, she finally found love, peace, and a confidence that would never again be broken. She became as much a part of their ministry as Samuel did after his father passed and they made him senior pastor.

Della, Rebecca's mother, also had a serious load of hurts to overcome, but by the grace of God she did overcome. She was even a major part of Rebecca's healing as well. Della remarried a few years after Samuel and Rebecca were married and moved to Sturbridge, Massachusetts. They saw her on holidays, and exchanged visits a couple of times a year. Della was kept in the loop about Jeremy, Pat, and Randy, especially during Jeremy's rescue and subsequent adventures. Rebecca was faithful to share with her mother when and how Jeremy had finally been healed completely from the unconscionable destructive power of their father, Daniel Townsend. Fortunately, for many people, Samuel did not need to be healed, well the way most of the rest of them needed to be healed, but he was used to aid in Rebecca being healed.

DANIEL TOWNSEND

There is no dispute that Daniel Townsend was a beast of an uncaring husband and father. Further, there is no excuse that he could give for his demanding, dysfunctional, and over-the-top destructive ways. The final insult being that he had no difficulty blaming anyone or even everyone for his lack of happiness. A person like that truly cannot be reasoned with, but don't you want to ask some questions?

I do…like, how early in his life did he begin his reign of terror? Who were his parents or grandparents, and where was home for him growing up? Did he have sisters or brothers, aunts and uncles, cousins… family? However, there is one much more important question that tugs at my curiosity, and that question would be, "What had happened to this mean, hard-hearted man in the first place, that would give him credence to think the way he thought or to act out the way that he did? What was it that put the *bitter* in every cup of life he lived, and what took the caring, sweet, kind, patient, loving out of his every day existence?" We do not know if Jeremy's mother ever asked Daniel about his family or background. One would assume that any woman who is about to marry would want to know some of those things. But Della, Rebecca's mother, did. She asked him all those questions, well, except the main question about his anger, hatred, and bitterness. She had no idea when she finally agreed to marry him that he was like that. But therein lies another one of Daniel's devious characteristics. He had the uncanny ability to keep you in the dark. He could tell you what you needed to hear without directly answering your question. He could show you what he knew you wanted to see, without giving up any information he did not want you to see, for him to get what he wanted. Della told everyone at "the meeting" that she did in fact ask him all those questions, and why she did agree to marry him despite not getting great answers.

The meeting was initiated just after Pat and Jeremy got married. In attendance were Samuel and Rebecca, Mac and Annie, Jeremy and Pat, and Della. Randy was initially thought of to invite, but prudence dictated that he should stay home with Pat's mother. Mac and Annie were invited because of how close they had become to the family and because they were such strong prayer warriors. Della's previously planned visit to her daughter Rebecca's house was what sparked the idea that they all get together to have an old-fashioned "pow-wow." What the meeting was all about was to discuss what may be done about their out-of-bounds Daniel Townsend.

So, you may ask, Why should any of these perpetually wounded people have such a concern for this terribly impossible man? It's simple, really. You see, once you care more about someone's eternal destiny than you do about 'my rights' or 'what you did to me,' this kind of action might well be considered inevitable. It had more to do with where Daniel Townsend might end up in eternity, and how long that eternity will last, than it did about rights and wrongs, or earning or deserving. Even though they were completely correct in their judgments of Daniel, it still boiled down to a simple choice. Either they figure out how to extract a pound of flesh out of him that was genuinely due them, thus satisfying their personal sense of fair play. Or they could *forgive him completely* and let God deal with the fair play angle. Everyone sitting around this table had learned how to forgive him completely because each of them had had to take a good long look into their own mirror and admit how much God had forgiven them. They each were over the comparison game of trying to label how much worse his sins were than their own.

Rebecca had fixed a simple meal, served the coffee with dessert after, cleared the table, and Samuel started.

"There is no one on this planet who would have more reason to just walk away from this monster of a man, without even looking back, than Della, Rebecca, and Jeremy. And to do that, hoping that he really would die an unloved miserable, bitter-to-the-end death. Instead," he said, looking on them with compassion, "they are willing to do whatever it takes to be part of God's grace through Christ, to give even this monster of a man a chance while he still holds breath. Even if," Samuel added, "it means being hurt, appallingly, yet again. Their willingness to do that is because despite all Daniel had done to them, they have truly forgiven him entirely. They have learned what the power of God's forgiveness is and what He might do as a result of that." None of them had seen, or even heard anything about Daniel for years, except Jeremy, and that had been about two years past.

"I remember," Jeremy said, "what Dad told me back then. He said that he thought he had only a couple of years left to live, and, here we are. Do we even know that he is still alive?" Jeremy fell silent for only a moment, but then… "You know, I remember that night like it was yesterday and how painful it was. I wanted to die that night, and I would not look forward to facing off with him again now. However, for me to tell him what I feel I must tell him, I think that is exactly what needs to happen. I need to go again and try to talk with him. But here is the upside, I have been totally healed from all those hurts that he had levied on me all those years, and that gives me a special coat of armor. I perceive that when I do see him, or should I say, if I see him, he probably will not have changed, but he will never again be able to issue a death blow to my heart."

"Nor to mine," Rebecca assured Jeremy, "so I want to go with you."

So it was settled after some prayer and discussion that Rebecca and Jeremy would visit Daniel Townsend to tell him that they had forgiven him and try to minister to him at the same time. Samuel suggested that "the rest of us will keep the two of them up in prayer for support, whichever way their encounter goes."

When they got to Daniel's house, Jeremy knocked on his door, and they waited. The porch light came on, and a woman answered the door. She was not the same woman he remembered from the last time he had been there almost two years before. Jeremy introduced himself as Daniel's son and asked if they might come in to see him. Again, they had to wait on the front porch for an answer. After a long time, they simply heard the identifiable inside door lock "click shut," and the porch light just went out.

They waited for about a minute and then... "What do we do now?" Rebecca asked Jeremy.

"Well, it doesn't take a rocket scientist to see that our father does not want to see us, does it?" Jeremy told her.

It was as clear a statement as ever could be made when the light went out that Daniel Townsend was not interested in seeing his son. He had no idea that his daughter was even there.

What was there left to do indeed!

"Let's go home," Jeremy told his sister. "Let's just go home."

CHAPTER 31

The Heartbeat

"WHAT DO YOU THINK?" THE story master asked as he stood. "Did this story that I just told you provide the ending you would have been looking for?" He waited for some kind of a response as he walked closer to the edge of the stage. "Okay, well, before I actually do end my story, and there are two additional main points to share, let me ask you this question. What do you think ended up happening to Daniel Townsend? Or, a better question might be, what was your instant and maybe instinctive thought that you would *want* to hear had happened to him? And, before you allow your Christian training to take over, were you thinking that he does not deserve hope, love, or understanding? I mean, really, look at the way he was his whole life. He does not have any redeeming qualities," the Narrator paused before continuing. "At all," and he paused again, "NONE," he paused yet again… "does he?" The Narrator fell silent again, momentarily, before going on. "You know," he said, looking down at his watch, "I have been up here sharing this story with you, for just about an hour and a half, and it would not be difficult for me to use the next hour and a half cataloging all of what this rotten, evil Daniel Townsend said and did in his life, and that hell is not good enough for him. Do you *want* to hear, and again I am asking that you seek the honesty of your inner being that he did in fact face that horrible unloved death I mentioned? That his ending was bitter beyond comparison for lack of being able to be set free from all his pain? Are you covertly hoping that he will get precisely what is coming to him?" Again, the Narrator just waited for an answer, but this time, he held his silence until the tension in the hall was palpable. "That question," he finally said, "tends to expose some spiritual nerve endings that have been and are being guarded by the human in every one of us, do they not? Revenge and/or regret, and the demand for a pound of flesh as payment, are the norm, sometimes, aren't they? Or at a minimum, we want to see some kind of compensation for all those wicked wrongs he had done, right? Lastly, since he did not repent, ask for forgiveness, or even show any signs of remorse, no kind of love or understanding should even be considered. Is that not fair and just? Do we not *want to think* that that is exactly what God would say? An eye for an eye? Okay," he conceded, "that really is just about par for the course, for every one of us, sometimes anyway, isn't it? But...let me finish my story about our wicked Daniel Townsend."

Jeremy and Rebecca were not allowed entrance that night they went to see him. The woman who turned on the light and answered the door was not the same person Jeremy remembered from the last time he had been there two years prior. The woman answering the door this time was a hospice nurse assigned to Daniel, as he was literally days away from finding out that there really is a hereafter. As Jeremy and Rebecca stood there on the porch, and the light just went out, they could do nothing else but give up and go home. The whole group simply had to give up, consoling themselves that they had done all that could be expected of them. That was not good enough for Jeremy, though. He asked for, and was granted, his next day off work. He and Rebecca went again to see their father. After being refused entrance two additional times and not giving up, Daniel relented out of morose curiosity and let them in. He was told that his son Jeremy wanted to talk with him, but not that anyone else was with him. He found that out only when he saw Rebecca standing beside his son. Daniel was weak, thin, and unable to raise himself up in his hospital bed that had been provided for him. He still had all his mental faculties, though, and there was nothing wrong with his experienced degrading, insulting mouth. He plunged right in, demanding to know who this stranger was, *"What, is she your girlfriend or something?"* and what in the blazes Jeremy wanted now. *"I told you I have nothing to give you."* Then he repeated his disappoint-ment of Jeremy and again attacked his character. Jeremy and Rebecca just listened for the next few minutes, not trying to defend or cor-rect. Their father ended, yet again, with, "You are no son of mine." Even though Jeremy had talked about his special coat of armor, he was pleasantly surprised that it really was there, and that it really did work. He felt no emotional hurt at all from his father, who he now knew was the only wounded person in the room. Jeremy simply told his father that he had completely changed, had given his life to Christ Jesus, and that his life had, by God's grace, been cleaned up. That he was there visiting him to ask for his forgiveness for anything that Daniel held against him. Daniel just scoffed at him. "Dad," Jeremy said kindly, "there is one more critical thing. The biggest rea-son for my visit is to tell you honestly that I forgive you completely for everything." Daniel just laughed at him and appeared that he was ready for another round of insults but was only able to cough out a, "Yeah, sure." He looked like he needed to rest for a moment. They all waited and then Daniel continued. "That just proves you are still looking for excuses for being the loser I always said you were. So... who's this?" he said disrespectfully, looking at Rebecca. She stepped up close to the side of his bed and leaned over to be as close to his face as she felt comfortable enough to be. She looked right into his face with tears gently streaming from her eyes. "Who are you?" Daniel said a second time, "and what's your story?" he demanded. Rebecca could not force the words from her mouth quick enough, before Daniel again demanded that she speak. "Well, what is it?" he said. "Come on, spit it out, I—" but then Rebecca gently reached down and caressed his cheeks with both her hands and said, "I forgive you too, Father."

What one single thing could it be that can turn an angry bitter, hardened heart from telling you to shut up and listen to me into a soft pliable, willing to shut up and listen to you, heart? What one sin-gle word could there be that would cause a lifelong hatred of every-thing good to bend instantly and see love and acceptance? What one single person will be the one who should be the instrument, used by the Holy Spirit of God, to open any hardened heart, for that one to clearly see the need for true repentance? It really is different in every case, and that is why God gets all the glory for a changed life and not any one single person.

So, them just "being there" was the one single thing, and "*father*," was the one single word, and "Rebecca" was the one single person, and their giving God all the glory was what it took for Daniel Townsend to lose all control of his emotions. No one prior to this very moment ever saw Daniel Townsend in any kind of an out-of-control state, but here he was. Why? Well, it really does not matter, but maybe it was some unspeakable guilt that was suddenly unlocked from its perfectly dormant state just at that moment. Maybe that one act of being told he was forgiven took him instantly back to how horrible his father had treated him. Or maybe it was at that moment when she touched him and called him 'father' that he realized that he was looking into the tearful eyes of his estranged daughter, whom he had not seen for over forty years. Maybe it was the memory of her mother Della, who he really did love, thus sparking the memory of how he systematically threw them both out. Either way, his heart was wide open to hear and accept the gospel of Jesus Christ, and Jeremy and Rebecca together did not disappoint. They spent the next hour explaining that we all have sinned against God and that He is faithful and would forgive even Daniel if he would acknowledge his sin and ask to be forgiven. They also explained in detail how they were able to forgive him and that he needed to forgive everyone who had hurt him in his life. They finally told him that Jesus died "even for you," and that if he would accept that free gift God had provided for him, he would be saved from the punishment that was due him. Daniel did that and then he did one more thing. He told both his children that he knew he had treated them horribly and asked each of them, "Can you forgive me?"

"So...what do you think?" the Narrator asked. "Can it happen that quickly? Is it possible for a man like Daniel Townsend to just roll over and give it up like that? Well...yes, it most certainly is possible. It must be genuine to count, of course, but only God knows that for sure.

I have told this story on other occasions, and I know how intense it is. There are so many characters and so many scenarios attached to this in-depth tale that it may not be easy to track completely the one time you hear it. However, the main thrust of this over-the-top emotional tale *is* easy to grasp. That being, of course, the huge topic on *forgiveness and unforgiveness*. But…the real punchline in this saga comes into play with me telling you about one other person whom I have not yet included anywhere in my story.

The real *heartbeat* of this entire tale has less to do with any one of the characters in my story than it has to do with…*that one other person*. Much more, in fact, than Mac and Annie who had to wait seventeen years for their happily ever after. Or about our unbelievably rude, inconsiderate, unforgiving Mrs. Sanford, who did die a bitter feeling like she had never been loved, death. More also than Rebecca's mother who was forced out of her home, for no fault of her own, or even Rebecca, who at an early age was so hurt that she seriously thought she may want to commit suicide. Or Jeremy's mother who became an alcoholic, and who also died a horrible unloved death. Or even about Daniel Townsend, that evil man who was responsible for so much destruction, although in the end met and accepted the truth about the Maker of the rain. The real heartbeat of this narrative does not even have, as a headliner, the outcome of our poor Jeremy who almost died. Or the powerful ending of him being transformed and reuniting with Pat and Randy.

You see, when I started speaking here tonight, I gave you a chance to choose which of my stories you would like me to tell you about, and honestly, that was a short list. There are so many more stories that I could have told you. Most likely, each of you can come up with some stories of your own. But in all those stories…yours or mine, the ending *should* be and like this one *will be*, talking about *that one other person*. The Narrator waited yet again for effect, but then he said…That one other person is…*YOU!*

I chose this story to tell you for a reason. It is to help you see *afresh* that the impossible always was and always will be possible with God. Forgiveness is *the key*, though, to see that happen. Forgiving yourself, and forgiving anyone who has ever wounded you, or you think has wounded you, opens your door to experience God's possibilities on so many levels. It is also important for you to forgive all your "*Why do they do that*" issues, like government misconduct or an unfair legal system. That is not to say you shouldn't do something about any of them, but it does mean that you lay down all your condemnation, your malice, and unforgiveness for them. This story tells of so many scenarios where the wounded party had every right for revenge and who would feel justified in not giving the offender any form of forgiveness, believing that the perpetrator was deserving of punishment. We need to remember, though, that all of us are deserving of as much punishment for our sin. We will not have to face that punishment, though, because of what Jesus did for each one of us on the cross. But whether *they* deserve forgiveness, ask for it, or even acknowledge their need for it, it is *critical* for you and for me to forgive them no matter what. To simply be content to give up my rights or my need for a pound of flesh, and let God deal with that wrongdoer in your life."

The Narrator had seemingly finished but stood still and silent for a moment. Suddenly, a very broad smile kind of bounced onto his face. He raised both his hands, gesturing his surprise as he just stared down into the audience and then waved at someone. He stepped up almost to the very edge of the stage and began to speak again. "When I was asked to come here and speak, they did not give you my name. I like to be known only as the Narrator or some like to just call me the storyteller. I have been doing this for some time now, and I have carried that title happily with no one really knowing who I was." He paused again thinking, "Until tonight," he said. "Until tonight, I have enjoyed that anonymity. Tonight, however, I *will* share my name with you because tonight is special. I just noticed that sitting right there in the third row, and, no, I did not know that they would be here—my sister Rebecca and my Pastor Sam, and my name is…," and he smiled that now familiar smile, "Jeremy Townsend." A thunderous long-lasting applause was inescapable. When they had finished, Jeremy told them, "Certainly, let's give God all the glory, but without these two precious souls, I would never have learned the difference between what the world calls forgiveness and what God calls forgiveness." With that, he turned to walk off the stage. A second applause rang out, but Jeremy just lifted his right arm, pointing one of his fingers to the heavens.

"How on earth can you top that?" one of the women in attendance said. She was standing right behind Rebecca, who heard her and turned to offer an answer.

"Well," Rebecca said, "It's simple, just take all that you have just heard from Jeremy's story and put it into practice in your own life, and see what God will do with you."

THE END...?

Not until you can tell a story of your own about how *you* have overcome that devastating disease of unforgiveness!

ABOUT THE AUTHOR

JERRY THOMAS IS A STORYTELLER. He has been writing or telling his stories from an early age. He also was an avid reader. To him, sitting down with a good book would be the ultimate relax. His favorite read always was a novel, thus the novelist was born. *Father Forgive* is not his first novel, but like everything he has written in these last many years, they always reflect his faith in the Bible. His endless desire to project that faith is where we see this novelist show up on the bookshelf.

His earlier years were not so pretty, though, but like what so often happens, once one gives his life to live for Christ, God uses that born-again life for his glory. Today Jerry doesn't only understand what God's grace is all about, but he writes about it. He is happily married living in the same town he was born in and never ceases to raise his hand if asked to tell a story.